One Beach, Two Babes, and The Squid

One Beach, Two Babes, and The Squid

A Thriller

BUCK BUCHANAN

KEYLIGHT
BOOKS
AN IMPRINT
OF TURNER
PUBLISHING

Keylight Books

an imprint of Turner Publishing Company

Nashville, Tennessee

www.turnerpublishing.com

One Beach, Two Babes, and The Squid

Copyright © 2025 by Buck Buchanan. All rights reserved.

This book or any part thereof may not be reproduced or transmitted in any form or by any means, electronic or mechanical, including photocopying, recording, or by any information storage and retrieval system, without permission in writing from the publisher.

This is a work of fiction. All the characters and events portrayed in this book are either products of the author's imagination or are used fictitiously.

Cover design by Remy Chwae

Book design by William Ruoto

Library of Congress Cataloging-in-Publication Data
Names: Buchanan, Buck, 1942- author.
Title: One beach, two babes, and the squid / by Buck Buchanan.
Description: Nashville, Tennessee: Keylight Books, 2025. | Audience term: Adults
Identifiers: LCCN 2024024200 (print) | LCCN 2024024201 (ebook) | ISBN 9781684426751 (paperback) | ISBN 9781684427802 (hardcover) | ISBN 9781684427819 (epub)
Subjects: LCGFT: Thrillers (Fiction) | Novels.
Classification: LCC PS3602.U2425 O54 2025 (print) | LCC PS3602. U2425 (ebook) | DDC 813/.6—dc23/eng/20241108
LC record available at https://lccn.loc.gov/2024024200
LC ebook record available at https://lccn.loc.gov/2024024201

Printed in the United States of America

CONTENT GUIDANCE: This novel contains scenarios involving human trafficking, implied sexual abuse of underage girls, and mild profanity.

CHAPTER ONE

The Face Rang a Bell

HER

My bikini was drenched even though I hadn't dipped so much as a toe into the Gulf of Mexico.

Hot! Hot! Hot! The refrain from the band spilled over the beach. The Sunday afternoon Island Party was in full swing at the Buccaneer Baywater Resort on Crooked Foot Key. Shade from a giant umbrella didn't prevent my frozen margarita from becoming a misnomer in mere minutes. April fifteenth—income tax day. How hot would it be by August? Global warming or unseasonable weather? Who cared? I craved a refreshing drink, not sticky glop.

I turned to my BFF and real estate business partner studying her makeup in a low chair under the other half of the umbrella. A total waste of time since she was a natural beauty. Her name was another matter. Beulah Mudd. Someone in her history had nicknamed her Mississippi in honor of her birth state and a reference to an antique song. She was happy to be called Missy.

Demonstrating her ability to read my mind, she spoke to me in her soft Southern accent that guys loved—like she needed another weapon. "You're hankering to go to the Pirate's Booty on the veranda, get under the fans, and lap up puffs of air conditioning when the waitresses go in and out."

So annoying when she does that.

She stepped out into the sun and stretched—which I was sure skyrocketed the heart rate of every male within eyeshot who didn't use a service dog to cross the street. We were both about five-foot-seven and frequented the gym religiously to keep the margaritas from going to our hips. One difference was that if we switched bikini tops, she might get arrested for indecent exposure.

The sunlight glinted off her golden hair. Another difference: My hair was a little darker, sort of an ash—definitely not dishwater—blonde. Tightwad condo developer Ralph Miller hung the tag of Gold Dust Twins on us, allegedly because of our appearance. I suspected that selling a dozen units in his less-than-desirable buildings in three days was the real reason.

He also hung Florida Freddi on me. Fredricka Barnes is my real name, but I've gone by Freddi since I was old enough to come up with a creative spelling. Ralph felt "Florida" in front of my name made Missy and me sound like a professional wrestling tag team. That was okay with us. We considered ourselves pretty tough broads when it came to real estate sales.

We were having a pre-birthday celebration drink since Missy was days away from thirty, a few months before I faced the same fate. We tried not to shudder about that milestone.

She pointed down the beach. "I declare that face rings a bell. Didn't we sell him unit one-oh-three last week?"

I pushed my sunglasses down to the tip of my nose. Jules Armand sat by himself between two empty chairs. Black wavy hair cut by a hundred-dollar barber, nearly six feet tall, wiry build, and a toothy smile. The whole time we were showing him the condo I felt like he was waiting to sell us a bridge with a used car on it.

"He's a little on the slick side," she said, "but way above average."

Was her thirtieth weighing that heavily? I didn't think so. It was for my benefit. She thought I'd never find Mister Right staying at home in my jammies watching cop and classic TV shows. Not that she had anybody serious in her life either.

"Let's surround him and see what he does," Missy said.

Not Missy's first bad idea. Nor would it be her last. Bad ideas were her hobby. I said, "Have you forgotten Ralph saying Armand complained that we intimidated him using high-pressure unethical tactics during the sales pitch and that he wants his deposit back?"

Missy continued to stare in his direction. "How can that be? What's he going to do? Report us to the Real Estate Commission?"

"That's what he threatened if he doesn't get his money back."

"All the more reason to go over there. Once he talks to us socially he'll sure enough realize we couldn't possibly have intimidated him."

I squinched my eyes shut as I tried to grasp that logic since Missy in a bikini was maximum intimidation in itself. By the time I opened them, she had covered half the distance to his chair, striding purposefully with her beach bag on her shoulder. I couldn't let her approach him alone. No telling what she might say.

The beach chair resisted my initial effort to lever my sunscreened body out of it. I pushed harder, dumping my drink in the process. Right into my lap. Yikes, colder than I thought. I lurched forward. My foot caught in my towel and sent me sprawling face first. I stood and glanced down. A sand and margarita mix coated my legs. I looked like I was fit to be fried.

I didn't hear what Missy said but "Stay away from me! Stay away from me!" reached my ears.

Jules Armand walked rapidly, beer in hand, yelling over his shoulder at Missy, who was five steps behind but keeping pace. He leapt up the three wooden stairs separating the beach from the veranda. All the stools at the bar were occupied as were the tables around it.

Armand stumbled through the tables and crashed against the bar, spraying beer everywhere. His forehead banged against the big brass gong the bartender rang when a patron left a tip.

Two thoughts raced through my mind. Maybe I wasn't the clumsiest person on the beach and Missy was right—his face did ring a bell.

"Stay away from me," Armand yelled, "or you and your partner are going to have a lot more trouble than you have now." He staggered to the steps leading to the parking lot, rubbing the red welt above his eyes.

Missy sputtered for a second as she followed him, and then screeched, "Don't do anything you'll regret, jerk! We'll get you, and payback is hell."

Great. Missy just threatened him.

For both of us.

In front of fifty witnesses.

CHAPTER TWO

Whaziznamε

HIM

I had everything a guy on vacation could need—bikinied babes, great beach, excellent rum—except I wasn't on vacation. I leaned against the crowded bar with a perfect view of my target. Then the jerk plows up to the bar, bangs his head on the bartender's tip gong, and dumps lukewarm beer all over me.

Why? Because he was getting away from a blonde the average guy would eyeball with his tongue hanging out. Get away, hell. Stop and let her catch you. Of course, I knew he wasn't the average guy or even the average jerk. He was my target. He threw some kind of a half-assed threat at her. Then she threw one at him. Definitely not a lover's spat. A business problem?

A dishwater blonde thundered onto the porch, skidded on the spilled beer, and slammed into me. My sunglasses hit the floor. We were mashed together for a moment while she regained her balance.

"Sorry," she said—hardly glancing at me—as she continued after the other blonde.

"My pleasure," I said to her backside. And it was. The feel of her nearly naked body against my chest—exposed by my unbuttoned beach shirt—and my bare legs made me wish I had on a Speedo. How much longer could I swear off women?

The grief my ex-wife caused me—caught last year *in flagrante delicto* with the clichéd tennis instructor by *his* wife—kicked in and bolstered my resolve. But that was a helluva piece of womanhood right there—as was the other blonde. Not that it mattered. Involvement with Boris Nabokov would have them on my radar screen even if they looked like sumo wrestlers in drag. They engaged in animated conversation on the sand at the edge of the paved parking lot.

I stooped to pick up my shades. The frame had broken in two between the lenses. What was that song about cheap sunglasses? I set the pieces on the bar and turned until their voices started to come through my earbuds.

My high-tech snooping device was a ten-dollar gadget that allowed a semi-deaf TV watcher to turn the volume low enough to avoid a divorce or a neighborhood uprising. The receiver rested in the pocket of my shirt and had to be aimed directly at the target. I rotated my torso until my back was against the bar.

The dishwater blonde was talking. "...hell do you think you're doing, Missy?"

Missy put her hands on her hips and said with a charming Southern drawl, "I was downright sociable. He got hostile and jumped ugly. That started me on a deal's a deal. No backing out."

I hoped they'd say more about the deal. Women like these were perfect for a Boris operation.

The dishwater blonde slapped Missy on the arm. "Pull yourself together. The only thing you're going to accomplish by talking to him about anything is cause more problems for us. We'll have to take care of him another way."

Missy rubbed her arm. "You don't have to thump on me, Freddi. That hurt. Save it for him if he doesn't do the right thing."

"A love tap isn't going to change his mind."

"You're right. We might have to come up with something drastic to get things straightened out or get rid of him."

That sounded serious. Could Boris be in harm's way from whatever he did to these women? They looked dangerous only in a luscious-woman way, not in a bury-him-in-the-flower-garden way. Or was my judgment being clouded by that brief body-to-body collision?

Missy glanced in my direction then focused on me. "Hey, what's with that guy staring at us?"

The bartender banged a glass on the bar. I looked over my shoulder at him. He said, "Sorry about your glasses. Here's a drink on the house to ease your pain."

"Not your fault but thanks. You have anything I can use for a temporary fix till I can get another pair?"

"I'll see what I can find."

I returned my attention to the blondes. I had missed some of their conversation.

Missy's thumb was pointed in my direction. "...can't miss him. The one leaning against the bar, facing our way."

"I ran into him trying to catch up to you. My guess is he's staring because of that or he noticed your natural assets—or both."

"Whazizname?"

"How would I know? I literally ran into him. I didn't stop to get his autograph."

"Heavens to Betsy, you should have. He looks really good from here, and you couldn't have stopped me from straightening out Jules Armand."

Jules Armand? So that was the name Boris was using here. New scheme, new name. The only name he never used was his real one.

"He does seem to be paying an inordinate amount of attention to us. Let's go up there so I can apologize and see who he is."

I wasn't about to introduce myself as Rick Dante to Boris Nabokov's associates. I'd stay with my cover name.

Behind me, the bartender said, "This is the best I can do. Got it out of our first aid kit."

I turned around as he laid a roll of adhesive tape on the bar. "Thanks. It'll work."

The tape was sticky, but it only took seconds to wrap a few turns around the broken nosepiece and make the glasses wearable again. I reached into my pocket and shut off the eavesdropper as I felt a light tap on my shoulder.

I put the sunglasses on so my eyes would be harder to read and turned to face two gorgeous creatures.

Or gorgeous criminals?

CHAPTER THREE

Blue Bayou

HER

I was curious about the guy, so the last thing I wanted was to laugh in his face. But when he turned around with the crooked taped glasses and earbuds, a small giggle slipped out. Last man standing in a dweeb-a-thon?

Missy did an even worse job. Her choked-back guffaw sounded like a muted horse snort.

Once I got past the glasses, Whazizname wasn't dweebish at all. Tall with lean muscles—and he didn't act like a dweeb. He was cool. Too cool.

He smiled and removed the goggly-woggly glasses. "They didn't look like this prior to an encounter with a dishwater blonde." He set them on the bar and removed mine from my face. "Maybe I can borrow yours until the mobile sunglass repairman arrives."

I was ticked that he snatched my glasses. I was ticked that he called me a dishwater blonde. I was ticked that he wasn't ticked. When his super-dark eyes zapped a beam into mine and caused a tingle in my bikini bottom...that *really* ticked me off.

He slowly eyed me from top to bottom and back again. "You might want to consider a lower-grit sunscreen." He turned his head toward Missy, eyed her the same way, and put his hand on her shoulder. "Like your friend here. Very smooth."

Missy stared at him with her mouth slightly open.

"I'm an *ash* blonde," I said with more than a touch of acid in my voice.

He smiled. "Of course."

Should I *accidentally* stomp on his foot? Then the eye thing again. Same tingle, ticking me off even more. My blood pressure threatened to Vesuvius my eardrums. I didn't dare clench my fists for fear of breaking a nail.

We stared at each other. There was a serious hardness and intensity in his eyes. I wasn't going to blink. He smiled throughout the stare down then slipped his taped glasses onto my face and said, "Hmmm, they look a little dorky."

"Think how dorky I'd look if I had earbuds stuck in the sides of my head."

"Earbuds? Oh yeah, earbuds. I'm not a big fan of reggae so I had some music playing to drown it out. Blues. Classic blues. John Lee Hooker, *King of the Boogie*. You know. *Boom Boom*. That kind of stuff."

That was a lot of reaction I didn't expect. Too much of an explanation. Something about the earbuds had him discombobulated. I decided to push it. "So, you can't hear me?"

"Of course I can hear you. I'm talking to you, aren't I?"

"How?"

"I turned the music off to ask the bartender a question."

I didn't respond. Let him run with it.

And he did. "I was going to ask him if he knew the gorgeous woman who bumped into me."

Damn, this guy was good. Almost deflected my attention from his overreaction to the earbuds. "Are you considering a lawsuit if the mobile sunglass repairman declares these a total loss?"

He laughed and removed his wrecked sunglasses from my face. "No, I want to thank you."

"Thank me? I don't..." The memory of a lot of our flesh pressing together—combined with his penetrating stare zapping me again—generated heat in my face and took my voice away.

"Sorry, didn't mean to embarrass you."

Suuure, he didn't. I didn't know how it happened but this guy was in *my* seat—the driver's seat. He was too much in too many ways and I didn't even know his name.

He stuck out his hand. "My name's Tom."

So annoying. I shook his hand. Strong, dry, and warm with an electric tingle to go with my other tingle. "Mine's Freddi. And this is Missy."

To his credit, when he shook her hand he looked at her face. She smiled but didn't say a word, which was as rare as a favorite lipstick shade not being discontinued. She hadn't uttered a word since he touched her shoulder.

"It's a pleasure to meet both of you ladies. This is my first day here, so I don't know anybody or anything about the area. I have to make a business call right now, but could I buy you dinner later in return for teaching me about the town and surrounds? Restaurant of your choice, no restrictions."

I thought about it.

New in town. Good—might want to buy a condo.

Too smooth. Bad—highjacked the driver's seat.

Well-mannered. Good—talked to Missy's face.

Annoying. Bad—dishwater blonde, indeed. If I had a daisy, I could have played a modified version of *He Loves Me, He Loves Me Not*. But before I could get to the tingles and earbuds petals, the decision was out of my hands.

The queen of bad ideas—after her self-imposed silence—had to pipe up at that moment. "We'd be delighted to teach you. Nobody knows the area like we do. The Royal Squid at seven?"

He choked on his drink then said in a strangled voice, "Sorry, went down the wrong way. If you recommend the place, fine with me. Where is it?"

"On the beach about a half-mile north. Dress is casual but the food is not. I'll make a reservation for us."

He gave us an exaggerated head nod that was close to a bow. "I'll be counting the minutes."

Had I seen that in a movie somewhere?

Tom threw down a twenty, waved at the bartender, and weaved his way through the crowd.

I turned to Missy. "What are you *thinking*? We don't know him."

She looked around and lowered her voice making it hard to hear over the crowd noise. "I'm thinking...delicious meal with... reminds me of Tom Selleck...reruns...original *Magnum, P.I.* from back...early eighties. I'm also...because you were all pissy about him calling...dishwater blonde your mutual...Blue Bayou."

"Blue Bayou? What are you talking about?"

"I said your mutual attraction blew by you."

If only she knew about the bikini tingle. "Actually it didn't. But he's so annoying—"

She rolled her eyes. "Hush now. Trust me. Give this one a second look."

Missy liked her world simple, so I didn't mention my worries about the earbuds. Plus, the way he set up the dinner date and rushed off didn't seem right. Plus...well, just plus.

Was he here because of Sabrina's Showstoppers?

That couldn't be. My two worlds were completely separate. I'd taken steps to ensure it. But still....

There were reasons to take a second look at Tom Whazizname, but not the ones Missy was thinking.

CHAPTER FOUR

The Squid

HIM

As I hustled to my vehicle, Freddi and Missy still had my attention. Too much of my attention. I tripped on a curb, barely catching myself in time to prevent the skin on my knees from fusing with the pavement.

Focus, Rick. Focus on business, not those babes. Damn. Focus, *Tom*. Make the name you gave them second nature.

I jumped into the gray Ford SUV leased by one of my boss's companies—and about as unobtrusive as you can get in today's world. I opened the console, grabbed the cell phone that I used for tracking, fired up the GPS monitoring app, and sped out of the parking lot to catch up with Boris.

The GPS tracking device under his bumper showed only the location of the Borismobile—a black top-of-the-line Lexus leased by a Cayman Islands corporation. I needed to know what would happen once he parked, including who he was meeting. His scams involved getting victims to participate in illegal activity. When Boris ripped them off, the victims couldn't go to the police to complain about being a victim in a crime they were committing.

Time to call my boss. I choked when Missy suggested the Royal Squid for dinner. Too appropriate. I worked for Roy Alan Squire, owner of Squire Detectives, frequently referred to as SquiD.

The company nickname carried over to Roy himself as The Squid, a moniker engendered by his physical being. He resembled a four-tentacled squid with his short bulky torso, disproportionately long skinny arms and legs, and an elongated—some say cone-shaped—bald head. His long legs didn't make him tall, just helped him get close to five-foot-five in elevator shoes.

The name Roy Alan Squire easily became Royal Squid—especially if you incorporated his nickname—not that *he* ever used that detested appellation. But he had a sense of humor—albeit abrasive as hell like his personality. His voice and delivery were Danny DeVito–like, and he made most of the caustic characters played by that actor look like Mister Congeniality. The Squid might have given that name to the restaurant as an inside joke on himself—if he owned it.

An incredible coincidence or a secret investment? He had many. I just didn't know what they were. Nobody did. If he wanted something hidden, it was hidden. On the upside, he had more information at his fingertips than Siri. The difference was Siri didn't hand out rations of grief with the answers.

My Tracker Phone showed Boris heading up Gulfway Drive. I wasn't too far behind. He could go straight to the north end of the island and even continue through several state preserve islets until the road dead-ended miles ahead. Or he could turn off and go to I-275 and head toward Saint Pete and Tampa. If he didn't stay on Crooked Foot, would I learn more about what he was up to locally by tailing him or by keeping my date? The Squid's orders were to follow him.

I called the poster boy for micromanagement, a trait of his I usually ignored. Before the first ring finished, he answered in his usual charming manner. "What?"

He was a pain in the ass but—in an inexplicable way—nearly likeable. "I'm on Boris. He's headed north off the island. I can hang in or get with two of his female associates. I'm supposed to meet them at a restaurant called the Royal Squid. Mean anything to you?"

No pause, no hesitation. "Might have heard of it."

My gambit yielded nothing. He could be the owner or have seen a review on the internet. I didn't expect him to give anything away. A good guy never to play poker with. He said, "How do they compare to Natasha?"

Natasha was The Squid's name for Tanya Yeshenko. He couldn't help himself once he learned Boris's real name. Boris and Natasha, cartoon spies, perfect names for real Russian criminals. Natasha was a major player in several of Boris's latest schemes. "Why do you care?"

"I uncovered more of Boris's capers since I sent you up there. Now we're over a dozen. No matter what the scam, he vectors a woman at the target, a woman like Natasha, almost carbon copies except for hair color—pretty, classy, nice body, but understated so the mark doesn't get scared off by a blatant honey trap."

"Understated doesn't exactly fit Freddi and Missy."

"I have pix of four female accomplices. After a couple of scams—poof. Back to Russia? Fish food? Who knows? Natasha's been around the longest. Maybe he dumped her too. But he's never used more than one woman at a time. You say two women, my eyebrows go up. Maybe they have some kind of connection to the new mark, whoever it is. I think these two would have scared off X."

X was what The Squid and I called our client. My guess was everybody who knew him did the same. Full name—Xavier Xeven Xanos. His parents should have been arrested for child abuse.

"Has X come up with anything else?"

"I just talked to him again. He maintains he was lucky to find out Boris's location and doesn't even know what alias he's using, let alone who his victim is."

"So X marks the spot and that's it."

The Squid snorted into the phone. "Your wisecracks vary between terrible and god-awful. But that sums it up."

"At least we know his alias, thanks to the flap with Freddi and Missy. So what's it going to be? Stay with Boris or follow up with the babes?"

"Keep your date with his women. I'll track Boris's signal. If anything happens that needs you on the scene, I'll text and you get your ass in gear."

The Squid had the knack of making a win feel like a loss. I'd be eating at a good restaurant instead of watching Boris and hoping for the chance to grab a convenience store plastic-wrapped sandwich. "Sounds like a plan—a good plan."

"Yeah, yeah, yeah. Shocking you'd rather have dinner with two beautiful women than be on surveillance. Just remember they're crooks, nobody to take home."

"We're not a hundred percent sure they're crooks."

"You're already making excuses for taking them home."

"I'm hurt. I'm the ultimate professional."

"Yeah, yeah, yeah. You wouldn't be the first ultimate professional to let the wrong part of his anatomy do the thinking. Especially an ultimate professional who hasn't had a woman in his life lately. That makes the ultimate professional more likely to forget to be professional ultimately." He clicked off.

I turned my car around with X on my mind. My problem was I wouldn't trust him with a burnt match. Something didn't ring true about him knowing Boris was at the Crooked Foot Sands. Why would he think Boris was in this sleepy spot?

X was the victim of a Boris bait-and-switch scam in Boca Raton. Boris contacted X about stolen diamonds, gave him a sample of genuine diamonds to examine, and delivered phonies in the end. Instead of being a meek sucker, X wanted revenge.

Our job was to catch Boris with his hand in the cookie jar. I was happy to nail a con man to the wall, but it would be a lot easier if I knew what Boris was up to and who he was up to it with. He ran different scams from gems to fine art, tailored to the victim.

I knew one thing—if Boris was breathing, he was scamming. I stuck a tracker on the Borismobile as soon as I arrived in Crooked Foot on Saturday but hadn't come up with anything until the dustup with the two babes at the Pirate's Booty.

The dashboard clock showed I had plenty of time to go to my motel, run on the beach, and swim in the Gulf before I cleaned up and dressed for the evening.

Then on to the challenge to my ultimate professionalism. Which wouldn't be a challenge at all.

Some unexpected heat flared between Freddi and me during our brief encounter, but that would be the end of it.

In addition to being—at a minimum—an associate of Boris, she had the makings of an extraordinary pain in the ass.

CHAPTER FIVE

Tea for Three

HER

I didn't want to be late for our business date with Tom so I picked up Missy at her town house in time to arrive at the Royal Squid a few minutes before seven. I waved at the head parking valet, pulled into one of his spots near the entrance, and raised the electric top and windows. I never gambled on anything bad happening to my pride and joy such as a surprise shower blowing in from the Gulf or a moron carelessly flipping a cigarette butt.

The valet grinned as I handed him a five. "Thank you very much. As always, you ladies are beautiful tonight, even more beautiful than your car."

My car was a Toreador Red—crimson to me and most people—1960 Chrysler 300F convertible in primo condition including the white top and interior. I kept it garaged, using it only for special occasions and important real estate deals.

Going to the Royal Squid was a special occasion—always. Wanting to blow Tom's socks off had nothing to do with it.

At the hostess station Tom's voice came from behind us. "What a night. Two gorgeous ladies and an incredible car."

We stopped. He bent forward far enough to avoid Missy's hard-to-avoid assets and gave her a cheek-to-cheek greeting.

Missy was right. Tom did bear a resemblance to a young Tom Selleck without a mustache, only even more handsome. He didn't bend far enough forward to avoid my lesser assets when he hugged me cheek-to-cheek.

That tingle again—doubled. He smelled great. Shower soap and the scent of his skin. Make that a triple tingle.

What was I doing? This guy wasn't to be trusted. All I had to do was figure out why.

The hostess led us to our waterside table. Ever the gentleman, Tom held two chairs for us.

We sat with him in between us. I would have preferred sitting across from him instead of being in knee-bumping range. As I feared, our knees bumped. He placed his hand on mine. "Tell me about that car."

I quickly slid my hand out from under his. I needed both of my hands to tell the story. Honest. "Four years after my 300F rolled out of the factory, my grandfather bought it from the widow of his next-door neighbor with less than a hundred miles on it. Six months later my grandfather died in Vietnam. My dad never knew his father and couldn't bring himself to drive it. He preserved it for me until I graduated from college."

Tom put his hand on mine again. I felt a tear forming even though I'd told the story many times before. He squeezed my hand gently. "Tough story but a fantastic car. Fastest, best-handling car in its day. Let's drink to it." He released my hand. "And here's the man who can help with that."

My favorite waiter stood next to our table. He smiled at Missy and me. "Ladies, nice to see you again. Sir, you're a lucky man to be in this fine company. Something to drink?"

Tom nodded. "Couldn't agree more about the company. We'll probably have wine with dinner but I'm too thirsty for that now. Freddi and Missy, will you join me in an Arnold Palmer?"

Missy pursed her lips. "I might could if I knew what the heck it is."

"Half iced tea and half lemonade, but I'm going to have it spiked with a shot of rum. Very refreshing."

Missy nodded. "I'll give it a try."

He raised his eyebrows at me and I nodded too. "Great." He held up three fingers.

The waiter nodded. "Got it. Tea for three."

With all the nodding going on we could have been at a bobblehead trade show.

Then it struck me. He'd done it again. Moved right in and took over—effortlessly. I damn sure wasn't going to let him select my wine for me. This wasn't going well. I blabbed on and on about my car and hadn't even learned his last name yet.

"Ladies, I apologize. I haven't introduced myself properly. My last name is McCall." He handed us business cards. "Some people call me Mac but I prefer Tom. I'm in private investments."

Just like Missy, he knew what was on my mind. Annoying with her. Beyond annoying with him. And private investments! Talk about dubious. The only occupation in Florida shakier was import-export.

"I'm Missy Mudd and Freddi is Freddi Barnes. We work together in real estate. Bikini Realty."

He didn't react to Missy's name any more than he did to her boobs. A cool customer. Or maybe he wasn't surprised. Did he research us and already know Missy's unusual last name? What was up with Mister Earbuds?

"Two beautiful women—in that car—pitching real estate? The potential buyer doesn't stand a chance." He turned to me. "The crimson color is perfect for blondes—particularly *ash* blondes."

Smooth. Way too smooth. And that crack about the buyer not standing a chance? Had he heard about the Jules Armand complaint? That was stupid. My distrust had to stem from my other business—Sabrina's Showstoppers. A business guaranteed to induce paranoia. But paranoia or not, something about him wasn't genuine.

"A hundred-point car like yours is easily worth a half mil," he said. "Yours isn't near a hundred points but it's probably worth a couple hundred K. A lot of money to put on the street with all the crazy drivers in Florida."

Now he was insulting my car. "Are you saying it's less than the best?"

"A beautiful car but only perfection earns a hundred points. Like a beautiful woman who upon closer inspection has flaws that move her down from a ten to a nine to an eight to a seven—even lower—when the whole package is taken into consideration. Never going to bring top dollar at the Barrett-Jackson auto auction."

Okay, he was using my car to needle me. Just a little boy pulling my pigtails? I didn't think so. He was going somewhere with this. I wasn't going to fall for it. "You know a lot about classic cars."

He shrugged. "Not that much. In high school I had a part-time job at a body shop that specialized in them."

Our waiter arrived with menus and the spiked Arnold Palmers. I took a sip. Tasty and refreshing as Tom promised. I was hoping it would be awful to give me an opportunity to knock him off his stride.

He lifted his glass. "A toast to the only guy I've ever seen run from two beautiful babes in bikinis."

Missy raised her glass. "Why would we want to toast that jerk?"

"Without him dumping his beer, Freddi wouldn't have slid into me and we wouldn't be here having dinner together."

He raised his eyebrows at me. I raised my glass. Missy said, "To the jerk trying to weasel out of a deal." We all clinked.

"What kind of a deal?" Tom said.

The expression on Missy's face telegraphed she was about to go on a rant. "That lyin'—"

I kicked her shin. She gave me a dagger look but after a one-beat pause kept it as neutral as possible—for her.

"That no-good snake wants to back out of a signed-and-sealed real estate transaction. My mama would've taken a switch to me if I'd ever pulled such shenanigans. Your word is your word."

"People shouldn't try to worm out of done deals," Tom said. "This guy really has you riled up."

I prepared to kick her again if she brought up Armand's complaint about us to the developer.

She kept it simple and spared her shin. "He's naturally irritating. He probably irritated the doctor who delivered him, and I reckon he'll irritate the devil when he goes to hell."

Tom laughed. "Now *that's* irritating." He opened his menu. "Recommendations?"

I was certain he hoped Missy would spill more information—but was it about Armand or us or all three? Or my other business? He managed to act like dinner was the only thing on his mind.

"Red Snapper Française," Missy said.

I chimed in. "It has to be the best on the Gulf Coast—if not the world."

He snapped his menu shut. "That settles it. Would you ladies be amenable to champagne with your meal? I noticed Veuve Clicquot on the wine list. One of my favorites."

Missy clasped her hands together. "Mine too."

The most expensive bottle in this beachside restaurant. I said, "*Mais oui,*" in my best French accent—which wasn't that good. Then I realized he had selected my wine for me in spite of my resolve that he wouldn't.

The next two hours were spent enjoying several courses of fine food and champagne. We exchanged business cards and personal histories—including all of us being unattached and divorced without children—and discussed real estate opportunities in the area.

We made arrangements to get together tomorrow at three to show him potential investments.

The empty champagne bottle was inverted in the ice bucket. The espresso cups were drained. Tom was signing the credit card slip. He was great company. Maybe I was being overly suspicious.

A soft ding came from his cell phone. Obviously a text. He glanced at the screen. "Damn. Sorry, ladies, I have to run. This was a terrific evening."

He gave us a seated cheek brush and quickstepped out. I didn't have to resist another of his full-body hugs. Or an offer for a nightcap and some dancing somewhere. Slow dancing.

I took another look at his business card. In addition to his cell number the only information on it was *Thomas J. McCall, Private Investments.* His tires squealed on the street as he drove away in a gray Ford SUV.

How much of an emergency can a private investment be at nine thirty Sunday night? Enough for an unattached guy to rush off when he's hanging out with two women he called gorgeous?

I reflected on the information we shared. Missy and I did most of the sharing. The only significant thing we knew about him was his marital and fatherhood status. If any of that was true.

Was Tom McCall even his name? Twice during dinner I called him Tom to draw his attention and both times he was slow to react.

And what about him needling me and then dropping it? A failed ploy? To get me to reveal what?

Something was not right about Thomas J. McCall.

He won today's round.

Tomorrow's would be mine.

CHAPTER SIX

Tenderloin Tips

HIM

The Squid's text said to drive toward Tampa International and call him. I charged out of the lot with a light tire squeal and headed to I-275—pissed. I wasn't ready to call him yet. I wanted to calm myself. Had he sent the message to ensure my professionalism?

Electricity between Freddi and me be damned. She was part of whatever Boris was up to. Period. But she was something. As smart and smooth as she was good-looking. My attempt to knock her off balance in the hope she'd reveal something when I brought up Boris was a total failure. She brushed it off and even made sure Missy didn't spill what was on her mind.

The feel of her body against mine at the Pirate's Booty was permanently etched in my psyche. Under other circumstances she would have already shattered my resolve to swear off women. Instead I added *especially Freddi* to it.

I called The Squid. Wait until he saw the tab for tonight's dinner. He answered instantly and cryptically. "Tenderloin."

"No. Red Snapper Française."

"Huh?"

"Served with angel hair pasta. Fabulous. Highly recommend it if you ever eat at the Royal Squid."

"I'm telling you where to go in Tampa, not asking for a restaurant review."

"Tenderloin?"

"Strip clubs, massage parlors, and other sex-related places are concentrated there. That's where Boris went. Near the western edge of it. Not far from the airport. The tip of the Tenderloin."

I turned on my Tracker Phone. "I'm bringing up the GPS now. I'm not familiar with Tampa. It has a Tenderloin? Like San Francisco?"

"I use the term for that kind of an area in any city. The action isn't as concentrated as San Francisco, but there's plenty of it. Boris parked on a back street near—according to Google Maps—a strip joint and a motel with parking lots. Maybe he didn't want to expose his car to a parking lot security camera."

"Or he went someplace on the back street."

"Near as I can tell from the map it's light industrial stuff. That's why I want you to check it out. He's been there so long it might be significant."

"Orrrrrr he could be shacked up in the motel."

"If so, you could be in for a long night. The Ibis Inn is one of those hotel/motel setups. Three stories with a main lobby entrance. Sixty rooms that open onto interior halls. All parking is in front. Who he's with and why that location could mean something."

"Why did you mention the strip club?"

"The organization that owns it and a half dozen others stretching to the eastern tip of the Tenderloin is run by the Russian mob. This one—the Panty Free Zone—is close to the bottom of their barrel."

Only The Squid could come up with that info that fast.

"Impressed?" His snicker sounded like a steel chain caught in a power saw. "I'll let you in on a little secret. When I learned Boris was in Crooked Foot Key I thought *What the hell?* Unlikely he could pull off one of his typical scams in that burg and slip away unnoticed. So I researched the general area for the Russian mob. I started with the Tampa Tenderloin. *Voila*."

Voila, my ass. Typical of The Squid. Playing it so close to the vest that it made my job tougher. "So you knew about this?"

"I've been working on it. I didn't know Boris was connected to anybody in Tampa. And still don't—but this is too much of a coincidence. You know how I feel about those. Top Russian dog is Nicolai Hutchko. Also involved in trafficking women—as expected with a Russian mobster running strip clubs. Goes by Nick Hutchins. Blond and blue. Good-looking guy. Reminds me of the actor who played the Russian boxer in one of the Rocky movies."

"I'm not planning on asking him for a date."

"Okay. Okay. About your height, six one or so, but it ends there. Two-twenty-five or more. He's got you by a good thirty pounds and he's a mixed martial arts guy."

"Everybody's a mixed martial arts guy. Armed?"

The Squid snorted. "He's Russian mob. I'll text you a few pictures—none are great. I'm still working on his green-card photo. I have shots of some of his crew. The outlaws in the Clint Eastwood spaghetti Westerns look angelic in comparison."

Uh oh. The references to old movies told me The Squid was uncomfortable with the situation. The only pastime he had was movies—classic or just plain old and not so classic. The more he referenced them, the more worried he was.

"The word I get is he runs his *gentlemen's* clubs by the book—a loose book including lap dances and private rooms in violation of laws never enforced. He uses the clubs to funnel select customers to other places to utilize the charms of trafficked females—some underage...very underage."

My stomach flipped faster than pancakes on a short-order

griddle. I lost my law enforcement job by busting a politically connected sexploitation ring involving young girls after I was warned off.

I found a sick fourteen-year-old Black girl on the street. She told me about her abduction, forced heroin addiction, and prostitution. I took her to a shelter. The next morning she was gone, and so was my case. Three months later her body was found in a dumpster. My attempt at a media exposé fizzled. The only things that changed were the location of the operation and my employment status.

Silence filled the line for a few seconds. The Squid said, "Are you packing?"

"You know I never do, Roy."

"Then don't get too close. Whatever scam Boris and the two broads are running is one thing, but Nick and his crew are another. He's suave and congenial on the outside but a vicious bastard to the core."

The Squid letting his worry show? Next, the sun will rise in the west.

"Back off if you get the slightest whiff of danger," he said. "No shame in coming back to fight another day. What did you learn at your dinner with Boris's new accomplices?"

"It's not clear if they're his allies or enemies." I told him their names and business. "If you can come up with anything, text it to me.

"If? *If?*" he sputtered and clicked off.

I rolled on in the clear, moonless night, thinking about the top-dog Russian and whether I'd have to go head-to-head with him. I didn't think so. There was almost always a better option. Although considering what he was into, head-to-head didn't seem all that bad.

Rick and Nick.

Sounded like a cartoon.

But I didn't see the humor in it.

CHAPTER SEVEN

Double Agent

HER

Missy and I left via the beach boardwalk rather than going out through the restaurant. She said, "Goodness gracious, Tom's a great guy. I swear the sparks really fly between you two. Both kinds. The good sparks make all kinds of sense. The attraction was obvious right off the bat at the Pirate's Booty. But the friction? I don't get it. If a stud like that tuned into me, I'd do backflips."

She was right. As a real estate agent, I had no reason to be leery of Tom. My other life as Sabrina was a different story. It made me leery of a lot of things, but it also gave me a rush and a satisfaction that no real estate deal—no matter how large—could.

We got in my car and I lowered the top and windows before we pulled out of the lot. Lightning flashed far out over the Gulf. Even if it came this way, I'd have my 300F tucked away in the garage before a drop of rain could touch it.

"I'm downright sorry he had to skedaddle," Missy said. "I wasn't ready for this evening to end."

"Private investments frequently become emergencies on Sunday nights."

"There you go being tough on him again. He didn't say it was an emergency."

"He didn't say it but he read a text then ran off. Emergency?

Hmmm? He also didn't say it had anything to do with private investments. It could have been the wifey telling him to get his ass back to wherever with a bottle of milk for the baby."

The dash lights emphasized the astonishment on Missy's face. Evidently she bought what he was selling. Another sign of just how smooth he was. She was super skeptical about men. "You don't reckon he's lying about being married, do you?"

I shrugged. "I'm making the point that we don't know anything about him other than he professes to be in private investments and is staying at the Beachsider. We did most of the talking tonight and didn't give him a chance to contradict himself if he's lying."

"Truthfully," she said, "I didn't notice. I was enjoying the evening and his company."

"I have to admit I was too." Damn, he was good.

"You don't suppose your work as Sabrina is making you paranoid about him, do you?"

Missy did it again. Picked the thought right out of my mind. "It's a possibility."

She shook her head. "I wish you'd get out of that darn business. It's not like you make a ton of money fooling with it. You say it's not dangerous—hah...how can that be? Look at the sleazebags you deal with."

"I also deal with nice people—my dancers and models who need my help. And we work with some undesirable people in our real estate business—like Ralph Miller."

"He's on the sleazy side alright, but not the kind of sleaze that would hurt you—physically, that is."

"Missy, you worry too much. Sabrina can handle whatever comes up."

We pulled into her townhouse complex and stopped in

front of her unit. She opened the passenger door. The courtesy lights came on, clearly illuminating a mischievous smile on her face. "When we meet Tom tomorrow, maybe you'll get a chance to pump him for information."

It was an old line used between us many times but we laughed anyway. Sometimes old jokes between good friends are the funniest. She said, "See you at Grams' at eight."

As I watched her waving in the rearview mirror, Sabrina's cell phone—which I dubbed Cellphony—beeped the tone announcing a text message. My place was only a few minutes away. I pushed my Chrysler and made it in two.

My rental house was a small two-bedroom cottage—which was all I needed and then some. The feature that caused me to pay the overpriced rent was a detached two-car garage. I raised the door, pulled my 300F into its spot, checked the text, and groaned.

Brandi—my biggest headache.

My night wasn't over.

I raised the top and the windows. No dust for this interior. I got out, carefully closed the door, and stepped over to my other car—a non-remarkable eight-year-old gray Chevy sedan. Blah-looking but born with a powerful engine. Emblems announcing that fact were gone and the suspension beefed up. Kids driving daddy's hot car wouldn't have a chance off the line or come close to keeping up on a curve.

The Chevy was my everyday car and—with a quick alteration—my Sabrina car. I opened the door and plugged Cellphony into the hot port in the console between the front seats to bring it up to a full charge.

Cellphony was a prepaid phone given to me years ago by one of Sabrina's Showstoppers that I helped out with her childcare until she got her finances straightened out. Her ex-boyfriend bought it shortly before he became a guest of the state for ten years. I used prepaid cards purchased with cash to keep the account current, resulting in a phone untraceable to me.

The Chevy had its legitimate license plate on it. I quickly swapped it for Tagphony—an old plate I found in a parking lot and outfitted with a homemade expiration sticker. Since I was the rightful owner of the car, if the police ever stopped me I'd be the victim of a tag theft and swap—which criminals sometimes did to prevent their stolen cars from being identified during routine tag checks.

I used Tagphony and Cellphony to conceal Sabrina's true identity.

The last step. I went into the house and remade myself, first removing my makeup and inserting brown-tinted contacts into my eyes. I put on a loose-fitting man-styled black shirt, baggy black pants, matching flat shoes, brunette wig, and black-rimmed glasses. Plain Jane. All business. Not worth hitting on. Last item, a black shoulder-strap purse nicely accessorized with pepper spray and stun gun.

Real estate agent in Crooked Foot Key by day. Exotic dancer agent in Tampa by night.

CHAPTER EIGHT

Bond, Jamie Bond

HIM

At ten thirty, an hour after I left luscious Freddi and phoned The Squid, I arrived at the back street where my Tracker Phone pinpointed Boris's car. I parked a quarter of a block behind him in a spot that also gave me a view of the entrances to the Panty Free Zone and the Ibis Inn.

Distant lightning backlit approaching clouds. I didn't need a squall to roll in and make learning what Boris was doing even tougher. I eased out of my rental and looked around. Not a soul in sight. I strode to the Borismobile like a man in a hurry to get to his car. I hoped it was unlocked so I could get in and search it. If not, I'd have to creep it from the outside with my mini flashlight. I didn't know what I was looking for, but a peek never hurt.

Until now.

Something slammed into my spine between my shoulder blades. A short person with a squeaky voice said, "Don't move, punk. This is a .44 Magnum, the most powerful handgun in the world."

A Clint Eastwood reference for the second time in an hour? Almost a line from his *Dirty Harry* movie. I had a fleeting thought of The Squid messing with me but that didn't make sense. There were a lot of people—short, tall, middle of them all—hooked on classic movies. No matter, this guy made amateurish mistakes.

He told me it was a revolver and was touching me with it. I knew exactly what and where the weapon was.

I spun, batted the gun to the side with my forearm, snatched it with both hands squeezing the cylinder so it couldn't turn, then bent his wrist back and twisted. Like magic, the most powerful handgun in the world was in *my* hand pointing at my assailant. I took two steps back. I didn't want the idiot to lunge, thinking he had a chance to recover the gun.

Enough illumination from the streetlights came through the overgrown trees lining the sidewalk for me to see he was vibrating, lower lip protruding, on the verge of tears. "Give me that. It's mine."

I had to give him credit for not stamping his foot or threatening to hold his breath. He wore a dark suit and tie. Small, maybe five-foot-four and 115 pounds. Not that I discounted him because of size. One of the most dangerous men I ever ran into—a sixty-year-old remnant of the terrorist Irish Republican Army—was about the same size. Palpable fanatism, veined forehead, and tightly muscled frame screamed *beware.*

This guy—not so much. I said, "You don't seem to understand that as long as I'm pointing it at you, it's my gun."

He went into a TV Kung Fu stance. "I don't fear guns. I'll take you with my bare hands before you can pull the trigger."

What a piece of work. "Didn't we just go through this in reverse?"

He dropped the stance. His shoulders slumped. "I had to do something. Go ahead and kill me. The world won't be missing much." His voice quavered.

Was I going to have to play shrink and pull him off a metaphoric ledge? "Why would I kill you?"

He peered at me through Woody Allen–style black-framed

squarish glasses—favored by intellectuals and nerds throughout the universe. "You're not one of them?"

I didn't have time to drag this out. Boris could show up at any minute. "One of who?"

"The people holding the girls."

That got my attention. I opened the cylinder, removed the cartridges, and handed him the gun. "I'm a private investigator. Let's get away from this car." I jerked my thumb toward my rental. "We can talk in mine."

He glanced at my car and his eyes widened like he hadn't seen it there. "Private investigator? I thought you were the guy that drives this car. I saw him park here and walk to the strip club two nights ago. When I saw the car again and you about to open the door..."

Two nights ago would have been a day and a half before I put the tracker on the Borismobile. "If you accost everybody that goes into a strip club, you're a busy guy."

He pulled his suit coat open and put the Magnum—which had at least a ten-inch barrel—into a shoulder holster that almost reached his belt. He pointed to a building on the other side of the street with a gated side lot. "I can help. Park over there. We won't have to sit in your car. I can redirect security cameras to wherever you want. We can monitor from inside the building."

Help? We?

I hesitated then said, "Sounds like a plan," and stuck out my hand. "Tom McCall."

He shook my hand while he ran his other one over thinning light brown hair. In his squeaky voice he said, "Bond."

"Huh?"

"Bond. Jamie Bond."

CHAPTER NINE

Uncle Tony

HER

I texted Brandi I was on my way.

Most of my work as Sabrina was done during daylight hours. Phone negotiations. Meetings with new club owners and new dancers and models. Dance training sessions. I probably averaged ten hours a week on the Showstoppers including travel time. But problems almost always occurred at night and required Sabrina's in-person attention.

Brandi was absolutely stunning, but like the rest of the dancers I represented, she did not want to be touched. No lap dances. No table dances. No private room dances. She was almost psychotic about the touching. According to her text, she locked herself in a private room at the Panty Free Zone, where she was dancing tonight.

My dancers were college students, housewives, office workers, and so on. All were opposed to participating in any activity bordering on prostitution. They were okay with nude exhibitionism. Period. My girls could set those rules because they were so good-looking and such good dancers that they could pack in the customers by performing on the stage untouched.

Eight minutes after I arrived home as Freddi, Sabrina backed the Chevy out of the garage and drove toward I-275. My dad taught me to drive when I got my license but my stockcar-racing uncle taught me how to take a car to its limits.

Traffic was light, but I didn't dare speed and attract the attention of a radar gun. Getting to the Panty Free Zone would take at least an hour. Too long. I had to talk to the man in charge. His number was in my directory on Cellphony.

I hoped to deal with him by phone. He went by Nick Hutchins, and his English was nearly accent-free, but I was sure his real name was Russian. About forty-five, tall and muscular with carefully coiffed hair—blond, slightly wavy, combed straight back just over the tops of his ears—and impeccably dressed whether in a suit or sport shirt and slacks. Classy for someone in his business but all too slick and studied.

He obviously considered himself an irresistible ladies' man. He was always a gentleman in our dealings, but too often his eyes were on my body, probing my loose-fitting clothing. Plus his flirtatious—on the level—kidding. Sabrina was a challenge to him.

My instincts told me a dark, dangerous, and slimy person lurked beneath that façade.

Part of the rush provided by that side of my life.

When I pulled onto the interstate, I called his cell. He answered in a deep seductive voice. "Ah Sabrina, are you calling because you miss me or could it be connected to your dancer at the Zone?"

"What do you think, Nick? Your bouncers didn't do their job. They let a customer get to her and grab her ass. She freaked and is hiding in one of the private rooms."

"You're some kind of woman, Sabrina. As tough and smart as you are beautiful and desirable. You're already negotiating because you know having that room out of service is costing me money. I'm on my way there now. We'll be able to finish our negotiations in person."

Damn. "Okay, Nick. Don't let anybody go near her. You know she's...delicate. I'll straighten it out."

"For you, my lovely, anything. Of course, business is business and money is money."

"We'll talk, Nick. I should be there around eleven."

I was going from a great dinner with Missy and Tom McCall to a mess with Brandi and Nick Hutchins.

Talk about an evening running downhill. Downhill? How about falling off a cliff?

Enough of Tom McCall.

Brandi needed me.

As I settled in for the drive, Tony Catalina—the second cousin of my college roommate Angela—popped into my mind. He always did when I drove to Tampa to solve a Sabrina problem. How could that not happen? I got into this business because of him. The thought of Uncle Tony—as Angela called him—made me smile. He was fun to be around with his quick wit, big grin, and hearty laugh.

The son of Angela's great-uncle, he grew up with her dad—more like brothers than cousins. When she was twelve her dad died and Tony stepped in as the father figure in her life, including putting her through college. He owned a popular restaurant and lounge named the Jumbo Shrimp.

He took us to dinner at least once a week—a blessing for a student on a shoestring budget—but never at his place. He claimed he had the best food in the area but part of our education was learning our way around the city. The maître d's, managers, and owners gave him special attention wherever we went. Somewhere along the way I started calling him Uncle Tony.

A wide-bodied guy with thick hands and arms that could do damage in a bear hug if he weren't so gentle with us. His wonderful wife Maria made his eyes light up even after all the years they'd been married. Unfortunately these two people—born to be parents—were childless.

A wall of brake lights flashed ahead of me.

Damn! Traffic had to cooperate for me to get to the Panty Free Zone by eleven.

CHAPTER TEN

Video Game

HIM

Jamie Bond? What was I getting into?

Sometimes you take stupid chances—like grabbing a loaded gun from somebody holding it against your back. I took my second stupid chance in less than a minute. Maybe it would work out too. I had Boris to worry about and now these girls. Were they the Russians' trafficked girls The Squid mentioned?

"I'll go to the office and open the gate," Bond, Jamie Bond, said.

He walked toward the building, and I trotted to my car. By the time I drove to the lot—which was long but only two vehicles deep—the motorized gate was rolling open. About half the slots were filled with work vehicles festooned with *Term Limits Pest Control – One and Done.* I parked in the darkest corner with a van between me and the street.

Jamie opened a door on the side of the building as the gate rolled closed. He locked the door behind us and said, "Security is down this hall."

He stopped at the third door on the left and swung it open. A dozen monitors sitting on a curved console spilled light into a dim room. His manner of speaking changed, almost like a salesman trying to close a deal, voice not so squeaky and shaky. "All cameras are digitally recorded twenty-four seven and the recordings kept thirty days with double backup, here and in the cloud."

"Impressive—not to mention amazing—for a pest control company."

"This isn't a great area. The boss wants the best possible evidence to fully prosecute anyone breaking in or vandalizing. The alarm system is state-of-the-art."

"Are you the security chief?"

He shook his head. "I'm the accountant." His voice reverted to squeaky and hesitant. "I'm familiar with the equipment because the boss has me research all major purchases prior to him negotiating."

I could understand the boss wanting Jamie to research but not negotiate. "So why are you here at this hour on a Sunday night?"

"The boss doesn't care when I work as long as I get the job done. I did some part-time work for a couple of other businesses Thursday and Friday and wanted to catch up here before the Monday morning staff meeting."

Wondering if he'd get the James Bond reference I said, "Saving up for an Aston Martin?"

He gave me a whipped puppy dog look. "My mother is in a nursing home. It's pretty expensive."

Ouch. Not the first time my quick mouth caused a faux pas. "Sorry."

He shrugged.

Time to get on with the surveillance. Before I could ask about directing the cameras toward my targets, Jamie said, "You must have an exciting life as a private eye."

"Usually sort of boring except when I don't want it to be—like when someone slams me in the back with a .44 Magnum."

His face turned red. "I...I...I'm sorry. I..."

"Why are you carrying that cannon?"

"I don't want to shoot anybody. A .44 Magnum should scare—"

"Don't ever pull a gun—any kind of gun—unless you're ready to shoot. If you're not, the gun becomes a liability."

"What kind of gun do you carry?"

"I don't."

His mouth dropped open. "You're a private eye and you can't shoot?"

"I didn't say that. I used to be a cop. I'm an excellent shot. I'd carry if I were a butcher, baker, or candlestick maker. But in this line of work, I could get caught up in a situation where a gun might complicate things. Better to talk my way out of tight spots."

He looked disappointed in me. "I watch all the detective and spy movies and read all the novels. Everybody has at least one gun."

"Jamie, how about we get the surveillance set up and then you tell me what's going on around here."

The camera system was sweet. He already had a camera aimed at the strip club, which had the front half of the Borismobile in the foreground. I had him zoom in that camera on the club entrance and another one on the motel entrance then rotate two more cameras to cover their parking lots as much as possible. Finally, one for the Borismobile. He redirected their feeds to the five monitors closest to my chair.

He handed me a remote control. "If you see something of interest and want a still photo, point this at that monitor and click. The frame will be copied to a flash drive, time and date stamped." He rolled a chair next to mine.

I needed him. This guy was doing a lot more with the cameras than his boss intended. With a slight shudder, I gave him his cartridges. He reloaded his cannon.

"Okay, Jamie, what's happening around here? You think girls are being held captive? Wait. Let me watch this."

A woman with a large rolled-up black umbrella and a choppy stride was in view on the monitor displaying the front door of the Panty Free Zone. Dark hair, slim build, loose-fitting black clothing, eyeglasses, flat shoes, shoulder-strap purse. Not a stripper. Almost something familiar about her. Had I seen her on the tapes The Squid acquired from X—Boris's last victim and now our client? Could it be Natasha? Even with the zoomed camera, the image wasn't large.

Sometimes trafficked girls confined as prostitutes had what they called housemothers.

Wardens would be a more accurate term.

Could this be one?

I clicked the remote to send a frame to the flash drive.

The time on the monitor showed eleven minutes after eleven.

The woman and the umbrella entered the Panty Free Zone.

CHAPTER ELEVEN

Russian Around

HER

My Chevy's dashboard clock showed eleven-ten as I parked in the lot at the Panty Free Zone. The fabulously interesting sight of a motorist changing a tire in the breakdown lane of I-275 had clogged the roadway with rubbernecking drivers.

I talked to Brandi three times along the way. She was under control. We agreed she'd stay in the private room until I settled the situation with Nick.

The storm over the Gulf appeared to have stalled. Maybe I wouldn't get drenched. I took the black golf umbrella I used for escorting prospects on rainy days anyway. It was a decent weapon in a pinch—a pinch that might cause me to bop a drunk.

I rushed to the entrance using a shorter stride than my normal gait, all part of being Sabrina. The bouncer gave me a mock bow as I approached him. "Miss Sabrina, Nick said you should go to his office and knock."

"Thank you." I turned up the corners of my mouth slightly. The ice queen.

I stepped into a room with a bright stage and dim lighting everywhere else. The smell of booze, too much humanity, perfume, aftershave, and desperation was overpowering. I navigated around nearly nude waitresses and through tables that had to be in violation of fire code maximum capacity.

Pounding music came from a DJ stand in the corner. The edge of the stage was piled two deep with patrons stuffing bills into the garter of the otherwise totally nude dancer. The classic stripper song "Foxy Lady" by Jimi Hendrix ended. She picked up the pieces of her costume and blew a kiss to the crowd as she walked off.

Several customers chanted, "Brandi! Brandi!"

Proverbial music to my ears. It strengthened my position with Nick. I hostilely squinted at the men crammed at the tables I slid between. Nobody pinched or groped. I patted my umbrella. Nick's office door was barely ajar but enough for me to hear him say, "...back office and stay with him." Then he said something in what sounded like Russian.

I waited ten seconds so Nick wouldn't think I overheard anything then knocked.

His voice came through the door. "If that's the lovely Sabrina, please enter. If it's a solicitor, I gave at the office."

Besides fancying himself a ladies' man, he thought he was a comedian.

I pushed the door and stepped in.

He rose from his chair, stepped around his desk, and gripped my hand with both of his. "Ah, my good fortune. It *is* the lovely Sabrina." He raised my hand and kissed the back of it.

I gave him a small smile. "My goodness, Nick. You are even more gallant than usual tonight."

He returned to his desk and motioned me to a guest chair. "You bring out the best in me."

I dropped the smile. "Or you're trying to soften me up."

He spread his hands. "How can you think such a thing? You know, Sabrina, these girls of yours are more trouble than they're worth, especially this Brandi."

I rolled my eyes. "Puh-lease, Nick. It's Sunday night and this joint is packed to the rafters. Usually you wouldn't be one-third full. Brandi's the difference, and you and I both know it. If your security guys had escorted her off the stage like they're supposed to—instead of allowing her to get groped—I'd be home in my jammies watching a mystery on BBC."

"I don't know which is worse. You wasting your beautiful self in jammies watching TV or Brandi holed up in one of my private rooms. The difference is you in jammies doesn't cost me. Brandi tying up the room does. And I have to think of my customers. I advertised four shows for her tonight."

I waved my hand dismissively. "Let's speed this up. Forget about the private room, which may or may not have seen action. She did two shows. I'll see if I can get her to do one more. She keeps all her tips from that show—no splitting. She gets full payment for tonight from you. I get two hundred bucks cash for my time and effort."

No emotion crossed Nick's face. Had I overplayed or underplayed my hand? I figured two hundred bucks was what he would expect from Sabrina.

He finally reacted. "A good deal for you and Brandi, my dear, but as for me? What do I get?"

"My goodwill for one thing. The reason you get priority on my girls is I consider you a man of honor—not common in this business. You know how Brandi is and you know your security caused the problem. For another thing, you'll have happy customers. They're out there chanting for Brandi now. If after her next show you announce she got sick and had to leave but drinks will be half-price, you'll sell a lot of drinks and the replacement dancer will get a lot of tips. Everybody wins."

He lowered his head for a second as if in thought, then said, "You are a smart woman, Sabrina. Why don't you come to work for me? I need a manager for my best club."

"I'm flattered. I honestly am. But I'm happy with my little business and I'm not tied down like a club manager."

"True, but someday somebody might take exception to your demands."

"Why? Everybody makes money because my girls bring in a crowd. You pay my corporation which pays the girls. Their names stay out of public sight. You have a legitimate expense to write off. The IRS is happy. Everybody is happy.

"Still, as you said, not everybody is honorable and some people are dumb enough to kill the goose that lays the golden eggs."

"Very sweet of you to worry, but I'm okay."

"Here's my counteroffer. Everything is good except only one hundred for you and I'll throw in dinner at the best restaurant in town."

"I'll settle for the hundred, but you know what they say about mixing business with pleasure."

He shook his head and barked a laugh. "Brandi's in the second room."

I stood. "She might want me to wait for her."

"Unfortunately, I have business to take care of or I would love to have the pleasure of your company here. There's a small security office past the private rooms by the back door where you can wait. Use that door when you leave with her."

"Thanks, Nick. I'll make sure none of your customers see us sneaking out."

I walked to the hall with the private rooms, nodded at the bouncer standing at the entrance, and went into the second one.

Brandi wearing her gauzy ballroom dancing costume jumped up and hugged me. "I'm so sorry to cause you trouble. I can't help freaking out when someone gropes me. And this guy grabbed my naked ass and touched the side of my cha-cha. I completely lost it."

"Don't get yourself worked up again. We have a good deal. This will be your last dance for the night. We'll slip out the back door after you get into street clothes. Is this what you're going to wear for your performance?"

"I have to go to the dressing room and change. I'm doing my *Swan Lake* routine."

"I'll be in the security office by the back door."

The bouncer waved me into the office which held a small desk and two chairs.

I sat and thought about Brandi's *Swan Lake* routine in which ballet met pole dancing, but mostly ballet. That was the secret to the success of Sabrina's Showstoppers. My dancers were real dancers—jazz, ballet, ballroom, urban, and whatever—which they combined with a minimum of stripper moves. Naked women who could actually dance struck a chord with the strip club crowd.

My dancers brought me other dancers. Women who were dancers first, in need of money second, and exhibitionists third. In their minds, they were dancers, not strippers. And definitely not available for anything but performing on stage. Periodically I rented a dance studio where they could practice and teach each other new moves—clothed of course. Usually, I worked out with them.

The Jules Armand problem came to mind. Missy and I would have to address that with condo developer Ralph Miller tomorrow. Miller was on my Uh Oh List, which contained the least trustworthy people to ever inhabit the planet including Nick, Ponzi scheme king Bernie Madoff, and Jack the Ripper.

It would be at least twenty minutes before Brandi finished her act, got dressed, and packed her costumes.

I yawned.

The late-night rushin' around—or was it the Russian around—had worn me out.

CHAPTER TWELVE

Heavy Traffic

HIM

Bond—Jamie Bond—and I watched nothing significant happen on the monitors. A few guys entered and a few left the Panty Free Zone. A couple with three shuffling preteens went into the Ibis Inn. We had time to talk.

"Jamie, tell me about the girls."

He put his face in his hands and spoke through his fingers. "I should have done more. I'll never forgive myself. I've been timid my whole life, but because of the girls, I'm going to overcome it. I went through firearms training right after that night. I'm starting at a Brazilian jujitsu gym next week, and I've been taking an online self-confidence course. None of it's helping. I'm a disaster."

Damn. I *was* going to have to pull him off a metaphoric ledge. "Don't fall apart on me. Facing personal demons like you're doing takes bravery. I need you. The girls need you. Accosting me tonight wasn't the act of a timid person. It was brave—not smart, but brave. If we work on this together, I'll teach you the smart part of it, which will be easy because obviously you are smart."

He lifted his face from his hands. "Brave…really? Work together as private eyes? This is like a dream."

Maybe a nightmare. "I mean work on this specific situation you still haven't told me about. There are a lot of state hoops you have to jump through to get a PI ticket. Now what about the girls?"

He pointed over his shoulder. "The building next to us was a garage, a big garage, room for at least a dozen cars inside and a bunch more in the lot. We used to have them maintain our fleet. They did mechanical, bodywork, even restorations, everything but paint. They had a shop down the street do their painting."

This was going to be a long story. "The girls are mechanics?"

He shook his head. "The owner died last year. A few days later I saw a black sedan parked in front and the customer door standing open. I walked over to see if I could talk to somebody about continuing to service our fleet. Three big guys talking in Russian came out of the building."

"You speak Russian?"

"Not exactly."

"What does that mean?"

"I've seen enough spy movies to recognize it."

I mentally wrung my face.

"I assumed the slick one was the boss and spoke to him. He said they were converting it into offices, which didn't make sense. It's a metal building with a big overhead door suited for a garage. Or maybe another industrial use. Very suspicious. And Russians doing it. I know a lot about the KGB, FSB, SMERSH, and Russian Mafia."

SMERSH? This was painfully slow. "So the girls were spies, characters in early double-oh-seven movies, and criminals?"

Jamie got my drift. "Okay, I'll speed it up."

He told me about watching the remodeling, including the open delivery of studs and wallboard and the surreptitious delivery of beds. Jamie's boss said to forget about it. It probably was a brothel, but they'd get caught without Jamie getting involved and inspiring them to torch the extermination business for revenge. A small cheap sign announcing *Gasparilla Business Suites* was mounted on the wall but no For Rent signs.

After the remodeling was complete, the Russians in the black sedan showed up again. Bond's description of the boss matched The Squid's description of Nicolai Hutchko. After they checked out the building, Jamie followed them to a strip club several miles away. His research showed it and six others—including the Panty Free Zone—were owned by the same corporation.

Whenever he had the opportunity, Jamie aimed a security camera at the Panty Free Zone and one at the building next door. Because of the angle and poor nighttime lighting, he couldn't capture much at Gasparilla Business Suites. The pattern of activity suggested not only was it a brothel with the johns being delivered by limo, but also the girls were living there. His conclusion was trafficked girls forced into prostitution. He saw two women who could have been housemothers bringing in groceries, but neither of them were the woman we photographed going into the Panty Free Zone.

He finally got to the incident that changed his life. "A week ago at dusk I returned the cameras to their normal security views and stepped out front for a final check before leaving. A white van left their lot and started my way. Two girls jumped out of the side door while it was moving. It screeched to a stop. A stocky woman and a huge guy jumped out, ran them down, and dragged them back. I did nothing. Nothing. Didn't even get the tag number. I stayed hidden in the shadows. There's been no activity over there since." He bowed his head.

"So you thought you missed your chance to do anything. When I showed up tonight you mistook me for the guy you'd already seen sneaking over to the Panty Free Zone and made your move. Your last chance to find the girls. Except it was me instead of the driver of the car."

"You look alike from the back, although I now think he's a little smaller."

This shaky guy had valuable info. "You have another shot. I'm sure my case is going to lead to that operation. We'll free those girls."

He squared his shoulders. "Really?"

"Or die trying."

"Look," he said, pointing to the Panty Free Zone monitor.

I swung my head around. A man near the end of the strip club building was dashing across the street toward us and then went off camera. Less than a minute later, he came back into view beside the Borismobile. He pulled his cell phone off his belt. The clock showed two minutes after midnight. "Damn, that's Boris. I wish we could hear him."

Jamie pressed a button. "No problem."

Street sounds accompanied the picture. Problem solved.

Boris spoke into the phone in Russian. Problem not solved. Jamie said, "It's being recorded. You can get it translated."

I got a better look at Boris's face as he lit a cigarette. It was a worried face with blotchy cheeks like he'd been slapped around—or was I imagining that? He leaned against his car and continued his phone conversation.

On the Panty Free Zone monitor, movement in the alley next to the strip club caught my eye.

CHAPTER THIRTEEN

Frying Pan

HER

Something startled me and my eyes snapped open.

Brandi stood in front of me dressed in street clothes, packed, and ready to go.

I checked the time on my cell phone. Midnight.

With Brandi behind me, I went to the back door and eased it open. The outside light above the door wasn't on. I stuck my umbrella out. Nobody grabbed it. We stepped into darkness.

To the left, more darkness. To the right, garish neon on the front of the building to light up a stealthy departure. I took Brandi's hand and tugged her toward flashing pink and purple colors.

We passed another door. It had to be an exit from Nick's back office. Loud Russian words came through. Nick's voice? Then what sounded like three hard slaps followed by Nick speaking English. "If you're lying, next time I close my fist and that's just the beginning."

I sped up. I just wanted to get Brandi to her car and get home to my jammies. I heard the door open behind us and pulled her behind a dumpster. We crouched and tried not to breathe.

Footsteps went by. I sneaked a peek as two men—one very large—reached the street. One ran across. The large one said something in Russian that sounded menacing before he turned around. It was one of Nick's bouncers.

We stayed hidden for two minutes after I heard him go back into the building. I whispered, "Let's go." We walked at a casual pace to the street, turned, and went past the front of the building, then into the parking lot.

Behind us someone spoke in a deep male voice. "Hey, that's Brandi. Where the hell's she going after we came all the way down here to see her?"

Uh oh. Out of the frying pan...

My umbrella wasn't going to be enough to settle this.

CHAPTER FOURTEEN

Slipping Away

HIM

The Panty Free Zone monitor showed the dark-haired woman coming from around the back of the club accompanied by what I guessed was a stripper in street clothes. "Look at this, Jamie. I need to follow them but if I drive out of this lot, my target will panic."

Jamie clapped his hands. "There's another gate at the far end of our lot. He might not notice if we go out that way and drive away from him."

We again, but I had no other option. "Let's do it, but you have to promise to do exactly as I say."

"No problem, boss."

No problem other than putting my fate in the hands of this guy.

Jamie disabled the motion-activated lights before we stepped into the parking lot. We quietly walked to my car. Boris's Russian words carried through the still night air, occasionally drowned out by traffic on the street in front of the club. Jamie used a remote to open the gate and close it behind us. I wheeled out of the lot and looked in the rearview. Boris was still engrossed in conversation.

I turned left at the cross street and a short block later another left onto the street that would take us past the club. I looked ahead and saw a commotion in the parking lot. The women were having a confrontation with a couple of guys next to a pickup truck.

CHAPTER FIFTEEN

Pop Goes the Weasel

HER

I knew Brandi and I had a problem as soon as I heard that voice full of alcohol-fueled testosterone. I turned to face them.

They both looked like the voice sounded. Scruffy big-bellied guys—like linebackers gone to seed—standing by a white pickup truck. Each weighed more than Brandi and I combined.

I couldn't guess which one mouthed the words and didn't give a damn. The first one to get too close would win the prize. I slipped my hand into my shoulder bag and said, "Sorry, guys. She's sick, but they have a great dancer taking her place and half-price drinks. Enjoy the show."

The one with a face like a weasel pushed his ball cap back, grinned, and said, "I think she's going to dance for us right now. And you too, bitch."

He stepped forward and claimed his prize minus a blue ribbon. I drove my umbrella into his gut then jammed my stun gun against his throat. He wavered. I kept the electricity flowing into his neck until he dropped to the ground. The other guy bent over to help him.

Brandi and I ran to my car and peeled out of the parking lot before his buddy could get the prizewinner off the ground.

CHAPTER SIXTEEN

Balancing Act

HIM

Jamie also saw the confrontation. "Did she poke him with her umbrella then zap him?"

"She knows what she's doing. She rode him to the ground with her stun gun against his throat. It's not a powerful zap like with Taser barbs imbedded in his body. He's already trying to get up."

The women ran to a gray Chevy sedan. The stripper jumped into the passenger side. The Zapper got behind the wheel and screeched out of the lot. The guy standing got into the driver's side of the pickup while the Zappee managed to haul himself through the other door. His feet flapped in the air as the pickup took off.

"They're going after those women," Jamie shrieked. "I can't let that happen again."

He was breaking down. I glanced at him. Eyes so wide open the whites showed all around the irises.

"Calm yourself," I said. "The Zapper might be a house-mother for the trafficked girls and could lead us to them. The guys chasing them look like drunks with bad intentions. We have to stop the drunks without getting burned by the women."

CHAPTER SEVENTEEN

A Right Turn Gone Wrong

HER

Brandi screeched, "They're coming after us!"

I looked back. The pickup was moving with the passenger door not completely shut. I could either outrun them, which might attract the police—leading to a legal mess involving police reports revealing my name—or try to give them the slip. I took my first right hoping they wouldn't see me turn.

The street was quiet so I pushed it but not enough to draw attention.

A cat ran in front of me. I braked hard, missing the critter by a few feet.

I checked the mirror.

My ploy didn't work.

The pickup was entering the intersection.

But with an SUV passing it.

What the hell?

CHAPTER EIGHTEEN

Whack-A-Pole

HIM

"There she is!" Jamie screamed like I couldn't see her turning right a half-block ahead.

Her left taillight was dimmer than the right. I caught up to the truck. If I could get in front of it, straddle both lanes, and slow down, the driver might abandon the chase when he saw he was stymied.

The pickup braked to make the turn. I swung wide around it, accelerated, and dove into the turn, skidding slightly. I felt air rushing in from the passenger's side. Jamie was lowering the window. As I pulled even with the truck, he stuck his revolver out the window—gripping it with both hands—and cocked it. The driver's face turned into a fright mask and he slammed on the brakes.

"Jamie, nooooo!"

I tried to control the skid with one hand and grab Jamie with the other. Sweat stung my eyes. We bounced over a pothole and the most powerful handgun in the world went off with an eardrum-disintegrating blast. The bullet smashed into a steel light pole in a shower of sparks. The light went out.

The recoil knocked Jamie backward across the center console onto me. His arm jammed against the steering wheel sharpening our skid into a one-eighty. I hit the gas and straightened the wheels.

We stabilized but were now headed back the way we came from— straight at the pickup.

No problem.

The pickup was making its own U-turn to get away from us.

CHAPTER NINETEEN

Special Effects

HER

A movie scene unfolded in my rearview mirror. The SUV dove into the turn to cut the truck off. Then a boom and sparks. The streetlight went out. Both vehicles ended up facing the way they came. I wished the screen credits would scroll so I could see who the players were.

I realized I had a death grip on the steering wheel. This was no way to drive. Forget about the movie in the mirror. I didn't know what happened, but it was time to go. I relaxed my grip, stomped it, and at the second street powered through a left turn.

One block later I drifted a right turn onto the main drag in front of a city bus so smoothly the driver didn't even blow his horn. Thank you, Uncle Dale.

Saucer-eyed Brandi uttered her first words since I zapped the jerk. "Slow down! Please, please, please!"

"Don't worry. I was taught by the best."

CHAPTER TWENTY

Prey or Pray

HIM

To the guys in the pickup, it probably looked like I was chasing them. If it hadn't been for Jamie being knocked into me, I would have been headed away from them. Being shot at with a handheld artillery piece must have made them feel like prey with no time to pray.

The Zappee in the passenger seat struggled to get a gun out the window. I hit the brakes, bouncing Jamie off the dashboard. The pickup reached the intersection and made a hard right, rolling the Zappee back into the cab. His arms flailed. A flash illuminated the interior and the roof bulged. If he had Jamie's gun, the truck would have a new sunroof.

In my rearview mirror the Zapper's car made a left turn two blocks behind me. Impossible to pull a U-ey and catch up without being obvious. *If* I could catch her. How did she get that far away so fast?

With my ears ringing and my brain clanging, I had to get us out of there before we were covered up in police.

I semi-stopped at the intersection then shot straight through—earning a few irate honks. More sweat burned into my eyes. Maybe we got away with it. We weren't within range of a traffic signal cam. Nobody was around to make a cell phone video of Jamie playing whack-a-pole. The steel pole should have destroyed the bullet, eliminating any chance of a ballistics match.

Was I whistling past the graveyard?

CHAPTER TWENTY-ONE

She Doesn't Cha-cha

HER

I squeezed Brandi's shoulder. "We're safe now."

She was shaking. "Once again, I'm so sorry to cause you problems, but when that guy almost grabbed my cha-cha..." She shook even harder.

"It's over. Push it out of your mind. Time to go home. Where's your car?"

All my dancers followed the same procedure. Park in the lot of an all-night grocery or big box store and take a cab or ride service to the club. Reverse the procedure when their gigs were over.

As I drove to her car—checking the mirrors every few seconds—I explained the deal Nick agreed to. She began to cry softly. "I wondered why Reggie didn't count my tips."

Reggie? Oh yeah, the head bouncer with the heavy accent whose name was no more Reggie than mine was Sabrina.

"Every dollar counts right now." Brandi's voice caught. "I couldn't do this without you. My little girl..."

I pulled into the sparsely filled lot, took the space next to her car, and patted her hand. "Keeping you safe and anonymous is why I'm here."

She leaned over and gave me a hard hug. "We all appreciate it. You're our rock." She dragged her bag out of my car into hers.

I waited until she drove away.

Nobody followed her out of the lot.

I smiled as I thought about the jerk twitching after I zapped him.

Life was good on the edge.

I headed to I-275.

CHAPTER TWENTY-TWO

Kills on Both Ends

HIM

I glanced at Jamie. His face was ghost white. We were going too fast. I braked hard, released, and without a screech made the left turn toward Term Limits Pest Control. The Borismobile was gone. He couldn't escape the GPS tracker. I'd locate him later. Now I needed the video of his phone call.

Jamie still had the cannon in his hand, staring at it like it was an object from outer space. The ringing in my ears was subsiding. I said, "Put that damn thing away and get us into the building."

He put it in his shoulder holster and looked at me, zombie-like. "I had no idea."

"You didn't know that thing kills on both ends."

He slowly shook his head. "I never fired it. When I took the course for my permit, I only had to shoot once, and I used a twenty-two." He opened the gate with his remote. I parked next to the building since I didn't have to worry about Boris seeing me.

As we worked our way to the control room, he said, "I was just trying to scare them."

"You definitely succeeded. Especially when that thing went off. What did I tell you about pulling a gun? And what made you think cocking a revolver in a bouncing car was a good idea?"

He hung his head. "Does this mean you won't let me work with you?"

The guy was pathetic, but trying to overcome personal demons and save the trafficked girls earned him a lot of points with me.

Also I was sure he had a lot of information he hadn't revealed yet.

I knew the answer to his question. Yes, I'd work with him.

But I didn't know the answer to *my* question.

Would he get both of us killed?

CHAPTER TWENTY-THREE

In the Beginning

HER

After Brandi drove safely away, my smile stayed with me for blocks. I had negotiated a good deal with the Russian and handled the dirtbags in the parking lot. Playing Sabrina and dealing with people like Nick and the pickup jerks had its moments. Most importantly, helping Brandi was gratifying—which is what really kept me in the business.

Missy's words about me getting out of Sabrina's Showstoppers—for probably the hundredth time—were taking some of the glow off the moment. My grin faded.

My wig was hot and the glasses annoying so I took them off as I pulled onto the interstate. I thought about the Sabrina part of my life.

One night while I was still in college, Uncle Tony and my roommate Angela and I had dinner at possibly the finest white-tablecloth restaurant in town. He turned to me and said, "You're killing yourself with part-time jobs. Think about this. Every Wednesday I have a fashion show in the lounge during happy hour—which includes lingerie, swimwear, and sexy clubbing clothes. You can make more money modeling for a few hours than you're making working twenty hours for chump change."

The astonished look on my face caused a hurt look on his. "Hey, you should know I wouldn't offer you anything that wasn't legit. The lingerie isn't any more revealing than the bikinis you and Angela wore the time Maria and I took you to the beach."

"Uncle Tony, I wasn't doubting you. You're the best. I was surprised—that's all. I've never thought about anything like this."

He toyed with his drink like he was thinking over his answer. "You'd be doing me a favor because the company that provides the clothes and the models let a hooker do it a week ago. I told those bastards—pardon my French—I'd provide my own models. I need a beautiful girl I can trust. Good deal for you. Good deal for me."

I wasn't sold. I didn't want to let him down but... "Being nearly naked at the beach in the midst of a lot of other nearly naked women is not the same as being the center of attention in a bar full of drunk men."

"Not just men. Happy hour is about fifty-fifty men and women. You might even meet Mister Right. We have a classy clientele—businessmen, stockbrokers, teachers, doctors, yuppies, buppies, and guppies—you get the picture. And I guarantee nobody will lay a hand on you. I personally oversee the show."

"Would anybody have to know who I am? Could I use another name?"

"Use any name you like. I'll be paying your wages and I'll have the clothing company funnel your commissions through me. The only check with your real name on it will come from my company."

"Did you say commissions?"

He drained his drink. When his glass hit the table, a waiter set a fresh one in front of him. "Here's how it works. I pay you three—make that four—times minimum wage. You get twenty percent of anything you sell. If the customer wants the actual garment you're wearing, you double the price and you get fifty percent."

"Why would anyone want what I'm wearing?"

He stared at me. "Who's studying psychology? You or me?"

My face heated up. Uncle Tony was a father figure to me, and who wanted to talk about sex with her father? I could help Uncle Tony, make money for college, and challenge myself. I smiled. "My happy-hour name is Sabrina."

He grinned his infectious grin and kissed my cheek.

Angela broke her silence with an almost-pout on her face. "Why didn't you ask me? I'm not pretty enough?"

His grin dropped a few watts. "You're gorgeous but Freddi needs money for college. You don't. If you want me to stop covering your expenses, I'll make you the same offer."

She screwed up her face like she was thinking hard about it. We all laughed.

It was a good gig. I never got groped, but a lot of guys bumped into me in the crowded room. Lingerie sales to men—as presents *for* their women—and to women—as presents *to* their men—were about equal except for the things I wore. Those were purchased only by men. Clubbing clothes only by women.

My first week, the other model was provided by the clothing company. By the second week Uncle Tony found his own model to work with me. A very sweet girl named Chloe who had a bit of a deer-in-the-headlights look about her. We went to a Starbucks after our gig. She needed college money as I did but was more skittish about the modeling.

The following week, near the end of happy hour I noticed Chloe wasn't in the lounge. Uncle Tony came to me. "Chloe's been in my office for about ten minutes, nearly hysterical. Would you see if you can do something with her?"

She was still crying when I went into Uncle Tony's office. She downloaded about being bumped once too often, the lingerie modeling, being desperate for money, not making many sales, and on and on. I consoled her, focusing only on getting her emotions under control. Eventually she calmed down enough for us to leave.

We went to Starbucks again. Chloe's time was consumed with classes, studying, a part-time job that paid little but was related to her major, and caring for her mother recently injured in a car accident. The infusion of money from the once-a-week gig at the Jumbo Shrimp was a necessity.

I worked with her to focus on selling clothes—ignoring the revealing nature of some of the articles—to achieve her objectives of getting her degree and helping her mother. She decided to give it another try. The next week she was a different person and sold more than her first two weeks combined.

Uncle Tony pulled me aside that evening. "Listen Freddi." He looked around. "Excuse me—Sabrina. I don't know how you did it, but Chloe's doing great, which is good for her and for me. Could be there's a niche for you here, taking care of these girls. Maybe start an agency where you provide models...and dancers too. You can always throw my name around. If anybody gives you trouble, it won't just be my name. I'll talk to them. You and my Angela are very close. That makes you family to me. Nothing's more important than family."

I was touched.

He patted my shoulder and smiled. "This calls for a big hug, but the boss hugging a model wouldn't look good."

The foundation for Sabrina's Showstoppers was laid. Over the years I helped dozens of girls who didn't have another quick path for a resolution to financial problems. I couldn't give up that gratification. Or the rush of operating in a somewhat dangerous environment.

Regardless of Missy's concern, Uncle Tony had set me on a good path. Sabrina wasn't going away.

Headlights approaching rapidly in my rearview mirror caught my attention. I checked my speed. I was only five over the limit, not enough to attract the attention of a trooper.

The vehicle swung into the fast lane and sped past me. It was a gray Ford SUV that made me think of Tom. Could it be him? Was he following Sabrina? That didn't make sense. How would he know about Sabrina or care? But why was he sticking to Missy and me? She'd say it was just our good luck. The tingles made me want to agree with her. But...

Tomorrow was the day. During our real estate investment tour I'd be pumping him for information—not in a Missy joking way.

Something wasn't quite right about the guy.

Unfortunately.

CHAPTER TWENTY-FOUR

Heart of the Hunter

HIM

Jamie and I sat at the security console. He copied Boris's conversation onto a flash drive, handed it to me, and said, "What's next, partner?"

Partner Jamie? Scary.

Partner Jamie with a .44 Magnum? Terrifying.

I forced the thought into the back of my mind. "Go through the videos of the Gasparilla Business Suites and the Panty Free Zone and compile anything significant onto a flash drive."

A crooked smile crossed his face. "Done. Except for the past two weeks. The system purges after thirty days. I didn't know if the videos would ever be useful, but I didn't want to lose them. The coverage isn't continuous. They were taped only when I was here *and* had the opportunity to redirect the cameras."

I suppressed a smile. Jamie was doing it on the sly, possibly risking his job. He wasn't as timid as he thought.

"If you want to review the videos here," Jamie said, "we'll have the place to ourselves after seven."

Not a bad idea. If I saw something to be checked out, I'd be here to do it. From Jamie's point of view, that kept him in the game.

I stood. "Let me out. I'll call you tomorrow and set a time. With luck I'll have Boris's conversation translated by then."

When I got to my car, I turned on the Tracker Phone, which

I didn't tell Jamie about. No need for him to know at this point. Boris was southbound on I-275. Headed for Crooked Foot Key and his motel? I hoped so. *My* motel was sounding good. I drove toward the interstate.

Instead of pulling up Boris's GPS driving history, I called The Squid—without compunction. As far as I knew he never slept.

Mister Charm answered on the first ring. "About damn time you called. Boris is on the move."

"I know. Did he go anywhere before he got on 275?"

He snorted. "My operative on surveillance is asking *me*? Me—who has a million things to do—what's going on with *his* surveillance? Boris went straight to the interstate."

"Trying to catch up to him now. I need a Russian conversation interpreted by tomorrow night. Any chance you can pull that off?"

"I speak Russian."

Should have known. "I'll send it to you after I finish up here. I hope not too much later since it's after midnight and I might turn into a pumpkin at any second. The rest is complicated."

He snorted again.

I told him everything that happened from the time I located the Borismobile across the street from Term Limits Pest Control.

The Squid didn't speak. I could almost hear his wheels spinning.

The highway was close to deserted. I was rapidly catching up to a dark car with the left taillight slightly dimmer than the right. Could it be? "Hang on, Roy. I want to see who's in the car in front of me."

I swung into the left lane and passed a dark gray Chevy, but not the right gray Chevy. Only a driver. No passenger. And from what I could see of the driver through the heavily tinted windows, it was a female, but her hair wasn't nearly as dark as the Zapper's. No way could I be that lucky. I sped past. "Sorry. False alarm. Where were we?"

"Where were we? We were nowhere. Are nowhere. We know nothing about Boris's new scheme—other than he's operating out of Crooked Foot Key with two bimbos you identified. And now we're knee-deep in human trafficking. And you're working on that with a loose cannon who carries a cannon. Speaking of those bimbos, I'm sending you their info. All pretty basic stuff. Nothing criminal."

He was right about Jamie, but Freddi and Missy weren't bimbos, and we didn't know one hundred percent they were a criminal part of Boris's operation. I couldn't make those points without risking a digression into one of his professionalism tirades so I said, "I have to do something about the trafficking."

"We're on the same page. Do all you can...at arm's length. Then put it in the hands of the police without getting enmeshed and alerting Boris to our investigation—the investigation for which we're being paid, I might add."

"One other thing we've accomplished is linking Boris to Nicolai Hutchko."

"But," The Squid said, "that's not going to help us figure out Boris's scam. The link is simple. Nicolai is the top Russian dog. Boris has to give him a piece of whatever he earns."

"Maybe Boris's phone call will explain it."

"Along with the surveillance you're on—as we speak."

The Squid didn't sleep so he expected nobody else to. I said, "If he goes to his motel, I'm calling it a night and setting the alert on my Tracker Phone to signal me if the Borismobile moves."

"Can you get an eyeball on him?"

"I'm gaining, but I won't catch him before he gets to his

room if that's where he's going."

"He might be going someplace else. Some people work late. Don't forget to send me the phone call video."

He clicked off before I could respond to that dig—double dig. One of his specialties. He was a pain in the ass but he backed his people.

I might get to see just how strongly if Jamie's whack-a-pole became a police matter.

My thoughts went to Freddi and Missy. In spite of my reservations about their association with Boris, I was looking forward to my real estate tour. And that damn Freddi—if only she weren't part of whatever Boris was doing and not quite so much a pain in the ass....

I mentally shifted gears. Thinking about her wasn't a good thing when I should be focused on driving.

Clouds thickened and the night got darker as I hauled ass to close the gap with Boris.

Nailing Boris in his current scam was my assignment.

Nothing personal.

Trafficked girls were another matter.

A matter of my heart.

I was hunting Boris.

And now Nick.

CHAPTER TWENTY-FIVE

Unhappy Hour

HER

Missy's call woke me. "Freddi, are you alright? You're never late."

The word *alright* dragged out even longer than usual in her sultry drawl. She was worried. Music was playing on my clock radio, but it hadn't awakened me. Ten after eight. Holy slug-a-bed. We were supposed to meet at eight to strategize the day.

"Sorry, Missy. Bad night. Didn't fall asleep until after two. I'll be there in a flash."

"Now don't you hurry yourself. You'll want to look your absolute best since we're seeing Tom this afternoon. I need to pick up a few things at the drugstore. I'll do that and see you at the office at nine or thereabouts."

I decided not to respond to her Tom comment. She wasn't going to let it go. She was on a mission to find Mister Right for me.

We had a busy day ahead. Two possible buyers at the condo office at ten. Chamber of Commerce membership committee meeting at noon. The Tom tour sometime this afternoon. A potential house buyer at our office at five. And the Jules Armand problem—exacerbated by Missy yesterday—had to be resolved.

On the non–real estate front, I needed to check with Brandi to make sure she recovered from last night's trauma; arrange for a dance studio session for my girls next week; and call my newest dancer, Desiree, to rein her in. She was showing signs of wanting to go beyond the no-touch policy. If she did, I'd cut her loose. The only way I could protect my dancers and models was for all of Sabrina's Showstoppers to follow the same rules.

I rolled out of bed, got the Keurig going with super high-test, and jumped in the shower. The warm water washing the shampoo out of my hair and the soap off my body melded with my thoughts of Tom. Damn. What was wrong with me? I turned the water to cold and jolted myself into reality.

My second cup was almost cold when I finished my makeup. I didn't wear much, but I took extra pains to ensure it was perfect and *looked* like I wasn't wearing much.

I put on my favorite black bra and panty set and gave my hair one last fluff with the hair dryer. Black knee-length skirt, medium black heels, matching purse complete with pepper spray but not the stun gun, crimson scoop-neck top to coordinate with my Chrysler, and a lightweight cream blazer to counter the icicle-forming air conditioning in our office—controlled by our native Finnish landlord.

A quick assessment in the full-length mirror. Professional and not bad for someone rapidly approaching that don't-want-to-say-it-out-loud age. I walked to the garage and got into the 300F. I didn't know why I was glad Tom wasn't going to see my Chevy, but I was. I left the top up and turned on the air conditioner. Calm, cool, and collected. The mode for the day—I hoped.

That hope was dashed before I got out of the driveway. My cell phone rang. Uncle Tony. A call from him before nine couldn't be good news. He worked late and slept late. "Good morning, Freddi. Heard anything from Sabrina lately? She needs to come up to the Jumbo Shrimp at happy hour today."

"Sounds ominous. Problems with the models?"

"Not at all. They're sweethearts like all the girls she sends me. Might be problems elsewhere. Sabrina and I should get together."

"I talked to her yesterday and I'll be seeing her later. She's busy. It could be closer to the tail end of happy hour."

"No problem. That's better. Say around seven."

"I'll let her know."

He clicked off. Uncle Tony didn't like the phone, and he insisted when we speak about business we maintain the Sabrina facade.

I was already concerned about Tom being for real and now this. Probably nothing. Relax and compartmentalize. Missy and I had serious prospects to pitch at ten.

Uncle Tony's request knocked out any possibility of us having a drink with Tom after Missy and I finished with our five o'clock appointment. I was hoping after a drink or three he might slip up.

I thought about Missy's joke last night and smiled. Drinks would have to work because I wasn't going to pump him for information—regardless of the tingles.

Instead of happy hour with Missy and Tom, it would be unhappy hour with Sabrina's problems.

CHAPTER TWENTY-SIX

Mistaken Identity

HIM

I vaulted out of bed. GPS alert. The Borismobile was on the move. Damn. Almost nine o'clock.

Getting ready took no time. Last night I flopped on the bed in my clothes in case I had to roll. I was wearing the black polo shirt and khakis I had on when I ate dinner with Freddi and Missy and when Jamie Bond stuck his .44 Magnum in my back.

Bladder relief. Gargle of mouthwash. Splash of cold water on my face. Wet fingers through my hair. I was out the door. Boris was staying at the Crooked Foot Sands, a couple of buildings down the beach from my room at the Beachsider.

The Borismobile had already stopped moving by the time I started. The GPS took me to a small municipal lot two blocks inland and a block south, next to a little breakfast and lunch place called Grams' Coffee Spot.

His windows were too dark for me to be sure he wasn't inside his car. However, no sign of heat coming from his exhaust pipes showed his engine was off. Sitting in a closed vehicle without air conditioning in the Florida sun? If so, he'd soon be a crispy critter and this case would be closed.

I found a semi-hidden shady spot on a side street with a partial view of the driver's door and the front door to the restaurant. I had an even better view of the two-story U-shaped Nook Motel.

Parking and exposed stairways in the interior of the U, neatly maintained with white fencing and nature's barbwire—bougainvillea, magenta in this case—on the perimeter.

Where was he and who was he with? Given his propensity for avoiding motel cameras, he might be at the Nook. He might be at Grams'. I was fairly certain he wasn't at the kitchen shop or antique store in between. He could have walked somewhere else. I lowered the windows, killed the engine, and settled in—wishing I had a cup from Grams'.

I texted The Squid to let him know I had an eyeball on the Borismobile and to learn if he'd made any progress on the translation. He replied that the audio was poor and he was still working on it.

That took a good ninety seconds.

I hated surveillance.

People came and went but none of them Boris. Just as I was despairing that I was going to sit here for hours with nothing to show for it, Boris stepped out of Grams' with a woman. I peered through my mini binoculars and confirmed my initial thought.

The woman was Tanya Yeshenko, Boris's accomplice in several scams. Natasha—as The Squid called her. In the past Boris worked only with one woman and was always successful. Was he now working with three?

They didn't go to the Borismobile. They walked to the motel and went up the stairs on the far side of the U to the fourth room—number *Fourteen* on the door.

I broke off my surveillance, stowed my binoculars, and drove toward the Beachsider, anticipating a shower and toothbrushing. I called The Squid and told him about Natasha. He was surprised also.

"So what are you doing now?" he said. "Sitting on them?"

"I'm going to my hotel to clean up.

"What? You could be missing a chance—"

"I'm not missing anything. When they got to the room her arm was around his waist and his hand on her ass. He had a late night so I'm figuring he'll nap afterward. I have plenty of time. How's the translation going?"

"Slow. The quality sucks. The mike was stretched to its limits and background traffic noise intermittently overpowers the nearly inaudible conversation. I have an expert working on enhancing it. Boris talks about diamonds and real estate. Now that I know Natasha's in the picture, the diamonds make sense. She's done several precious stone scams with him."

"And the real estate part?"

"It's giving Boris problems, maybe with Nicolai Hutchko and the broads you're working on. I can't find where he's ever done a real estate scam before and I can see why. No quick in and out. Too many paper trails. But now? Is he pulling two scams at once? After the technical enhancement, I'll have a native Russian speaker listen to the tape."

"I'm pulling into my hotel lot. I'll give you an update after my real estate tour this afternoon."

A fast shower and a cold rinse revived me. Dark gray cargo pants to hold all the gear I was taking—including my eavesdropper and a mini digital recorder—with a two-pocketed navy short-sleeved shirt. Clothes that were a little harder to see if I had to sneak around Tampa tonight but not make me look like a cat burglar.

My appetite was roaring. I knew the perfect place to eat, a place where I might get lucky and learn something. I bypassed the municipal lot where the Borismobile was still parked and went to my previous surveillance spot. I walked across the street to Grams' Coffee Spot.

The kitchen was in the rear with a long counter in front of it, booths lining the side walls, and chrome-framed tables and chairs with red vinyl seats in the middle. The only customers were a senior couple in a booth, reading the newspaper and drinking coffee. I sat on one of the backless red vinyl swivel stools at the counter.

An attractive, sturdy, fiftyish woman with short blonde hair and dark roots headed toward me with a coffee pot in her hand and a warm smile on her face. "Coffee, honey?"

"Before I die right here."

She flipped over the mug sitting on the advertisement-covered paper mat in front of me and poured. "Cream and sugar?"

I shook my head. "Just black unless you want to stick your finger in to sweeten it a bit."

She giggled. "That's an old one."

"I'll bet you never get tired of hearing it."

"You have that right, darlin'. Now that I'm old enough to drive, I appreciate it even more."

I laughed. "You obviously aren't Grams."

"Lordy no, I'm Madge. I'm a paralegal, not a cook."

I made a show of sniffing the air. "Best-smelling law firm ever."

She giggled again. "I should have said a paralegal on the side. I took over when my granny couldn't handle it anymore. I have to ride herd on the cooks to make sure they stick to her recipes and techniques." She looked behind her at the guy working on the other side of the kitchen partition.

"What do you recommend?"

She glanced at the wall clock above the end of the counter. "At this time of day...our incredible seafood omelet." She pointed at it on my mat. "You might notice it's the most expensive thing on the menu, sugar. I have to admit that does prejudice me a tad, but if it isn't the best omelet you ever had, it's on me."

I had to laugh again. "I'm sure it will be fabulous."

She scribbled on a ticket, turned, reached over the service counter, and handed it to the cook.

I read the ads on the mat while the omelet was cooking. I felt her studying me. In just a few minutes, she slid a plate covered with an omelet bulging with seafood in front of me and said, "I was serious about my guarantee."

My first bite told me she had nothing to worry about. She was right. It was the best ever. When I finished I said, "I owe thanks to the people who recommended your restaurant."

"Locals?" She dropped my bill on the counter.

I got off my stool. "They're staying at the Nook where I am. I think they're Russian."

"They friends of yours, sugar?"

I looked at the total, added a fat fifty percent tip hoping the information would keep flowing, and put the money on the mat. "I met them in the lobby."

She looked around. Apparently satisfied the couple in the booth weren't listening, she said in a low voice, "Stay away from them. They're bad news."

I didn't have to fake the shocked look on my face. "In what way?"

"They're crooks. They have a sucker on the line in some kind of a diamond deal."

"How do you know that?"

"I heard them talking about it. They thought they were safe by speaking Russian."

"And they weren't?"

"I speak Russian."

Who didn't? "You mean beyond *nyet*, *babushka*, and *Sputnik*?"

She reached across and patted my cheek. "You are such a kidder. Naval Intelligence for six years intercepting those bastards."

"A name? Did your Russian speakers say a name?"

She smiled and came around the counter. "You're very, very smooth but you just gave yourself away. The name they said was Ralph Miller. Mentioned his wife Rita too. And a Russian named Nicolai. I couldn't tell if Ralph's the sucker or in on the deal with them. So I'm keeping my mouth shut. I don't want some damn Russian doing something to my sweet granny or her restaurant to get even with me."

"Who's Ralph Miller?"

Her smile became a grin. "I knew when you came in, you weren't an ordinary customer. He's a local developer. I did the prenup for him and Rita. His third wife. Or is it his fourth? You're after those Russians, aren't you?"

"Why would you think that?"

"Do you know you look like that private eye Magnum from the TV show? The old original TV show. A diamond fraud is something he'd investigate."

"We're not in Hawaii, Toto."

Madge put her hands on the sides of my head, pulled me to her, and gave me one hell of a kiss. She released me then gave me a quick peck. "I've been wanting to do that since I was in high school, and if I still looked like I did then, we'd be on the floor."

As I spun away from Madge, two couples entering the diner stood there with astonishment pasted on their faces.

I nodded to them on my way out and said, "Mistaken identity."

CHAPTER TWENTY-SEVEN

Hell Toupee

HER

Missy and I left the noon Chamber of Commerce committee meeting on a high. It had mercifully lasted only forty minutes, but that wasn't the reason for the high. Our ten o'clock appointments had resulted in two condo sales. When we called the developer—sleazy tightwad Ralph Miller—and told him, he was ecstatic to the point of promising to take us to dinner. I could hardly wait. We made a two o'clock appointment with him to discuss Jules Armand.

We decided to celebrate with one of the delicious seafood omelets at Grams' Coffee Spot. We'd split one of those and the mixed greens salad.

The always cheerful Madge was even more cheerful than usual. After expressing her concern and receiving reassurance about my health—the result of my not showing up for coffee with Missy this morning—she took our order. She walked away whistling tunelessly.

Missy shook her head. "I'll bet you two to one, Madge got laid last night. Or this morning. Or both."

I was drinking water and it spewed out of my nose. Missy got me again.

As I was blotting my blouse she said, "I swear I don't know how you can be such a great dancer and be so klutzy. But it's urgent that we come up with a strategy to handle Miller the Pillar this afternoon."

Missy's nickname for Ralph stemmed from his being anything but a pillar of the community. Some of his projects were so substandard we wouldn't sell units in them.

The condos we concentrated on were built by CFK Development. The construction was good but the location too far from the water to be an easy sell. That developer went under. Ralph bought the corporation.

"What baffles me," Missy said, "is why did Jules Armand go to Ralph instead of us if he had a problem with the sale?"

I dropped my damp napkin on the table. "We need to finesse that out of Ralph this afternoon. It might have some bearing on Armand's complaint about us. Should I text Tom and confirm we'll pick him up at the Beachsider at three? Surely we'll be done with Ralph by then."

She put her hands together prayer-fashion. "Lordy, I hope so. A little Ralph goes a long way."

I texted Tom and he replied with a grin emoji.

Grams' was busy but fast enough that we finished lunch and parked at Ralph's office—a converted cottage on the main drag—with five minutes to spare. Before we entered, Missy looked to the heavens. "Please let his toupee be on straight so I don't have to bite the inside of my lip."

The receptionist desk was unattended. His wife Rita handled those responsibilities when the mood struck her. Rumor had it that Rita took over the job when she figured out Ralph and the former receptionist were playing house—or more accurately—cottage. She would know because that's how she became the third—or fourth—Mrs. Ralph Miller.

His voice boomed from the bedroom—now his office.

"Freddi? Missy? Are my Gold Dust Twins here?"

Missy and I rolled our eyes simultaneously.

He stepped out with a practiced smile on his face and his arms spread wide. No matter how much he was worth, he was a control freak and came across like a cheap chiseler. Hawaiian shirt and white slacks—his idea of a tropical tycoon look. A thin but paunchy build and barely an inch taller than his proclaimed Gold Dust Twins. Fortunately for Missy's lip, his black toupee was fairly straight.

In spite of his appearance, he considered himself a ladies' man. My second in two days. At least Nick the Russian had a physical reason for the delusion.

He gathered us into a group hug.

Rita bolted through the front door along with a blast of hot air. Was it the heat wave or had she upgraded to a rocket-powered broom?

She slammed the door. "Are we having a throwback hippie love-in?"

Rita had the ability to overcome my pacifist nature. She was not only annoying, but also gave blondes a bad name. If a picture of her wasn't in a dictionary under *gold digger*, it was because she ripped it out to autograph it for a moonstruck admirer. Two inches taller than her husband, contrived windblown hair, shapely full body—a few pounds shy of Rubenesque—made even fuller surgically, and dramatic makeup. Like some other people in the room she was pushing thirty, which made her young enough to be Ralph's daughter.

Ralph dropped our hugs and rushed over to hug her. "Darling, you're just in time to congratulate Freddi and Missy."

"For draping themselves all over my husband?" she said while glaring at Missy's assets.

Ralph ho-hoed. "Rita, you kill me." He rolled his hand in our direction. "They sold two condos this morning!"

"How? With intimidation? Like Jules Armand?"

My jaw wanted to drop open but I wouldn't let it. Why did Rita know anything about Jules Armand? I never saw her take an interest in Ralph's business other than firing the receptionist—which actually was taking an interest in Ralph's monkey business. The Jules Armand mess was getting weirder.

I needed to knock them out of their comfort zones. "Rita, what's your connection to Armand? He's a good-looking guy. Part of your past life?"

Her natural haughtiness left her face. "I'm not...I mean...I mean Jules is a friend of a friend who referred us to him for a business deal."

Ralph shot eye darts at Rita.

Missy stink-eyed him.

"You sure enough didn't tell us," Missy said, "there was a personal connection. Maybe that has something to do with him thinking he can back out."

"Wait a minute," Rita said. "We didn't know you sold him the unit until he came to us. He responded to your internet ad. After you coerced him into buying the condo, he decided he wanted out and called the building owner, CFK Development. When he used the number on the sign in front of the building, the call forwarded here. He was surprised to find out he was talking to me but after a minute lodged his complaint."

Ralph shot more eye darts at Rita then turned to Missy. "If he ducks out of the deal, I'll pay your commission."

Hell just froze over. Tightwad Ralph giving away money. I said, "Seems like an unlikely coincidence that we're having a problem with a guy who's in separate business negotiations with you. And how about our reputations? This guy is threatening to file a complaint against us."

"In small towns, coincidences are a way of life," Rita said. "Once Armand has his money back and the contract shredded, the problem will disappear."

Again my jaw wanted to travel south. I glanced at Missy. She appeared to be hiding her own amazement. Rita not only was the contact with Armand but also sounded like she was in control.

If eye darts were real, Rita would have looked like the board in a British pub tournament. She made a production of looking at her watch. "I forgot. I have a hair appointment." She rushed out.

Ralph patted us on the shoulders and donned his best I-want-to-sell-you-some-swampland smile. "Don't worry about a thing, ladies. Your money will be in your bank account before you know it."

Sure. And the check is in the mail. But I didn't care about the money nearly as much as I cared about being caught up in something we didn't understand and Missy and I being the fall gals.

He ushered—if not pushed—us to the door. "Keep up the great work. We're going to make even more money together." He closed the door behind us.

We walked toward my car. I stopped by Ralph's 1979 Corvette.

Missy touched my arm. "Oh my, what in the world was that all about? Ralph and Rita are in cahoots with Armand on some kind of business deal. But Rita is the connection to Armand, not Ralph. Before we can pull on that ball of yarn, Rita escapes and Ralph hustles us out."

"Armand didn't contact us about canceling the contract because he called CFK Development to complain and found himself talking to Rita. That's when he decided he wanted out of the deal. Why wouldn't he want to buy a condo from Ralph?"

She shrugged and turned her palms up.

"There's something rotten in the state of Ralph as Shakespeare would have written had he known the Millers."

Missy struck her exaggerated thinking pose with her eyes to the sky and her forefinger tapping her lips. "Heavens, do you suppose Rita is shtupping Armand?"

"Only if she gets the chance. Which could make whatever is going on even worse. He doesn't like us and neither does she."

"She doesn't cotton to any female who has outgrown her training bra."

"Maybe she's insecure because she's part of Ralph's midlife crisis, which could turn another direction on a whim. Fortunately for her, his male menopausal whims tend toward cheapness, not quality."

I smacked the fender of his car. "Look at this thing. Like a lot of guys his age, he buys a Corvette. But does he get the latest mid-engine version? No. Does he get a classic from the fifties or sixties? No. He gets the worst model ever made—which means least expensive. It needs paint so he goes to a cut-rate shop. The finish is now bumpier than an alligator's butt."

Missy nodded. "And that ridiculous toupee. He could get himself a transplant or hair weave or something that doesn't slide around like *Disney on Ice*."

"So if he's too cheap to spend money on his midlife crisis, why is he willing to give us our commission on Armand's deal if it falls through?"

Missy shrugged. "It's a puzzlement."

"One that I hope doesn't come back to bite us."

CHAPTER TWENTY-EIGHT

History Lesson

HIM

I slid into my car, smiling about Madge's surprising—to say the least—kiss. What a character. Somewhere a fiftyish guy was smiling about her also—with a lot of great memories, probably still making them.

Calling The Squid was my first order of business. I could do that while keeping an eye on the Nook and the Borismobile. My phone rang before I closed my door completely. The Squid beat me to the punch. "Sorry if I woke you," he said.

"No problem. We needed to get up anyway."

"We?"

"Freddi, Missy, and Natasha. I decided this was the best way to keep an eye on them."

"Har-de-har-har. I told you nobody likes a smartass."

I started my engine and closed the windows. Even in the shade it had gotten too hot to sit in an unair-conditioned car. "Translated the call yet?"

"My tech guy is having equipment problems. He might be able to do it this afternoon."

"How good is your Russian?"

"Better than conversational but not expert. I'm going to find someone I can trust."

"I have one." I told him about Madge and what happened in Grams'—omitting the kiss.

"She sounds loose-lipped to me."

That was one way to put it but not in his context. "She's gregarious but must be able to keep secrets if she was in intelligence for years. She only opened up to me because of my superior interviewing skills." I smiled and gave a silent tribute to *Magnum, P.I.*—eighties version.

"Going back to last night," he said, "now that we know Natasha is around, is there any chance she could be the Zapper?"

"I thought about it. About the same size and dark hair but the walk and carriage are different. Also it doesn't seem likely she'd be driving an old Chevy. And it doesn't compute. The Zapper might be a housemother. Natasha does scams with Boris, not human trafficking."

"I'll research this developer Ralph Miller and get back to you. It might be a little while. I have some other things hanging fire."

"Text me any info you dig up on Nick's other clubs. While I eyeball the Borismobile and motel, I'll locate his clubs on Google Maps. Might be useful tonight."

The Squid clicked off and left me with surveillance. At least I had Google Maps research for relief. It wasn't difficult to research and observe simultaneously. Neither exactly demanding nor exhilarating.

The lunchtime rush started at Grams'. Madge was doing a good business.

The door to Natasha's room stayed closed.

At ten to one, a crimson Chrysler 300F pulled into the municipal lot and parked six spaces from the Borismobile. Freddi and Missy strutted into Grams'.

A new history lesson. All roads lead to Grams' Coffee Spot.

My mind was blown. It wouldn't make sense for them to meet Boris—Jules Armand to them—at Grams'. I witnessed the falling out with Boris, including a threat. And they weren't trying to sneak up on him in that car. If Boris and Natasha were working a diamond scam separate from a real estate scam, Boris wouldn't want them to see Natasha.

A coincidence—which The Squid and all cops say they don't believe in but know exist. Boris wants a nice place to stash Natasha that's secure, low-key, and not far from his room on the beach. The Nook fills the bill. Grams' is the closest restaurant so they go there for breakfast. It's a locals' place, and Freddi and Missy are locals. They happen to go there for lunch. End of story.

I got a text from Freddi confirming they'd pick me up at the Beachsider at three. I sent her a grinning emoji hoping that Boris didn't do anything that would force me to cancel.

No sign of Boris yet when Freddi and Missy left Grams'. I decided to follow them. They drove to Gulfway Drive, went a couple of blocks, and turned into the driveway of a small house converted to an office. I drove past it. The small sign over the front door was lettered Miller Development, Inc.

I did a mental double take, my smug conclusion about coincidence knocked right out of my head. Everything was back in play, including the trafficked girls. Boris could be using Freddi and Missy to acquire locations for Nick's Tampa brothels—with or without them knowing the purpose. The diamond scam with Ralph Miller could involve them also with Boris holding Natasha in the wings for another aspect of the operation.

I massaged the back of my neck. I couldn't eliminate anything at this point. Maybe The Squid's tech guy would come through this afternoon. With no other leads to follow, I returned to my surveillance spot and watched the Borismobile and Natasha's motel room door not move for thirty minutes.

My options for immediate leads were down to what I could squeeze out of Freddi and Missy during my real estate investment tour. I headed for the Beachsider. I didn't want to be late and not have them in the best mood possible. A tip straight out of *Sneaky Interrogations for Dummies.*

I went up to my room and brushed my teeth. Then I went to the lobby to wait. Five minutes later Freddi texted me that they were in front. Early. A good sign.

Time to joust with two beautiful now-I-was-almost-certain criminals.

CHAPTER TWENTY-NINE

Amateur Tail

HER

I texted Tom that we were waiting in front of his hotel. Ten seconds later the glass entrance door opened and he stepped out. Prompt. A good sign.

But no matter how handsome, how well-mannered, how entertaining, how charming, and no matter how many tingles in my favorite black panties, I would control the situation today. There was a lot about this guy I needed to know—especially after Uncle Tony's cryptic call.

Missy swiveled her seat and got out of the car. Tom gave her a cheek-to-cheek kiss. "You look terrific, Missy. I forgot these cars had swivel seats. Don't know why all cars don't have them. Makes it so much easier for women in skirts."

She made a move to flop the seat forward and get in the back. He put his hand on her shoulder. "Absolutely not. We'd be defeating the purpose of the swivel seat. I'll get back there. You might have to slide your seat up a little to give me some leg room."

The perfect gentleman. Considerate of a woman's comfort and modesty. So smooth. The first tingle. Damn.

Missy smiled at him in a way that made me think if he wasn't Mister Right for me, she might try to convince him she was Miss Right for him.

Before he settled into the seat behind Missy, he leaned forward and awkwardly gave me a cheek-to-cheek kiss. "You look great too and, um, that's a fabulous scent, Freddi."

"I don't wear perfume, Tom." I was irritated with myself for sounding haughty.

He gave a lighter-than-a-feather brush to the side of my neck with the back of his fingers, so light I might have imagined it. He said, "I wasn't talking about perfume."

I turned toward him intending to make a retaliatory quip until we stared into each other's eyes and that spark...that spark... and that tingle again.

He broke eye contact and quickly pushed himself deep into his seat. "Ladies, I don't how you do it. Work all day in this wilting heat and look as fresh as if you just stepped out of the shower."

Stepping out of the shower. With Tom. Another tingle. I glanced at Missy and thought she might be having similar images. Three tingles and we hadn't left the parking lot. Time to get moving. I pushed the drive button and eased toward the street. The power of the engine rumbled around us.

"These push-button transmissions," Tom said, "were the best automatics in their day. Is there any chance you'd let me drive this—even just around the block—if I bribed you and Missy with another meal at the Royal Squid?"

"You were awfully mean to my pride and joy last night."

He laughed. "I hope it didn't come across that way. I was only trying to point out the vagaries of the classic and restored car market. It fluctuates wildly with the economy and evaluations of the show judges. This is a fabulous ride."

"Since you put it that way, it can be arranged. You can even drive it on the beach road where there are a few challenging curves and almost no traffic after ten on weekdays."

Why did that fall out of my mouth? I didn't want to be anywhere with him after ten. And I didn't let *anyone* drive my 300F.

I was going to get on top of this. Keep it vague, one of those let's-get-together-soon plans that never happen.

"How about tomorrow night?" he said. "The Royal Squid menu said they're closed on Mondays. That means they'll be happy to see us on Tuesday."

Missy's face broke into a big smile. "I swear, that couldn't be more perfect. We don't have anything going on."

I loved Missy. She was the sister I never had. But occasionally I wanted to throttle her. Like now.

Three tingles, a spark, and a dinner and driving commitment before we even got to the street. Damn. Damn. Damn.

I stepped on it, the tires squealing in protest. I glanced in my rearview mirror to make sure I hadn't attracted the attention of any nearby police. A white Nissan compact driven by a dark-haired woman jerked away from the curb and fell in two cars behind me. Very similar to a car and driver I had noticed when we left Ralph's office.

Tom leaned forward far enough that his head was between Missy's and mine. "Last night you mentioned you sold a lot of condos. Are you house realtors for a developer?"

"Not hardly," Missy said sharply. "That would make Ralph happy so he could save on commissions, but we have our own office and business. That's why we have real estate investments to show you. That's not to say the condos aren't good investments if you're interested in rental property at a reasonable price with steady appreciation potential."

"Show me everything. My clients have a variety of needs."

"We won't have time for anything but Crooked Foot Key," I said. "There are opportunities on other keys and on the mainland, but we have another appointment at five."

"Then let's start with whatever's closest. Tomorrow's another day, Scarlett."

Missy turned in her seat to smile at him. "Your timing is right on again. So far we're clear after two o'clock.

He did it again. With a cheesy quote from *Gone with the Wind*, he insinuated himself into our tomorrow afternoon—on top of dinner tomorrow night.

"The condos are nearby," I said.

I drove to Gulfway Drive and turned south. The white Nissan hung two cars behind me. That didn't mean much. I was on the main drag. But had we picked up a tail as they say on the cop shows?

Missy pointed to Ralph's cottage office. "That's the developer who owns the condos."

"Miller Development. Is he big-time around here?"

"A big frog in a small pond is what he is—with more warts than there are lima beans in a pot of my mama's Brunswick stew," Missy said as she pointed to the next intersection. "The second building down that street is where our office is."

Time to determine the Nissan's intentions. Without signal or warning, I took a sharp left in front of a city bus, throwing Missy against the passenger door.

She yelped. "Hey!"

"Sorry, I thought you wanted me to turn and there was traffic behind the bus."

The white Nissan turned behind me after the bus and a car went by. We did have a tail. An amateur tail for me to be able to spot her so quickly.

Missy rubbed her shoulder. "Be it ever so humble, our little office is on the right."

I glanced at Tom in the mirror expecting to see him facing our Bikini Realty sign. Instead he was looking out the rear window.

He snapped around as we passed our office.

I was impressed. From checking out the Nissan to feigning interest in our office in a millisecond.

Did he know the woman following us?

Was she following him?

Or me?

CHAPTER THIRTY

The Boardroom

HIM

From where I sat in the backseat of Freddi's car, I had a partial view of the rear and side-view mirrors. I wasn't checking for a tail but the sudden maneuver of a white compact car pulling out behind us caught my attention.

The car, color, and light factory window tinting indicated it could be a rental. Most Floridians have a darker tint added. The driver looked a lot like Natasha. I wasn't positive because she kept a car between us.

Freddi's tail-shaking move in front of the bus made it obvious she knew she was being followed. I took a quick peek out the back window. Now with no car between us I was able to confirm it was Natasha. She must have left her hotel room when I wasn't watching. Why was she following Freddi and Missy? Because of them threatening Boris?

If Natasha photographed me getting into Freddi's car, Boris soon would know my face, making the investigation of him that much tougher.

When we arrived at the condo building, I realized Freddi took a longer route than necessary. Extra turns to verify the tail? Why was she tail conscious?

The four-story building sat beside a small shady park. Freddi pulled her car into the parking garage that took up the ground level. As I worked my way out of the backseat, I looked toward the street but didn't see the white Nissan. Maybe Natasha determined where we were going and backed off.

Freddi watched me looking around then said, "We have a number of units available here."

"Take me to the best one first."

Missy looked at Freddi. "I guess we could show him Armand's since that deal is going away."

We took the elevator to the top floor and went to a corner condo overlooking the park. Freddi said, "This is the best in the building. It was sold but the buyer is backing out."

"Oh, the guy running from you at the Pirate's Booty. Why did he change his mind? This is perfect if you're looking for a non-waterfront condo."

Freddi shook her head. "Who knows? That's ancient history."

"He's a jerk," Missy chimed in.

The look on Freddi's face told me to stay away from that subject.

We went from there to the least desirable in the building before moving on to other Crooked Foot properties. A defunct motel on the beach near the south end of the island seemed like something The Squid might be interested in. Numerous times during our tour I spotted Natasha. She might have talents but surveillance wasn't one of them.

At a quarter to five we arrived at the Beachsider, leaving them time to get to their five o'clock. I said, "I'd love to try to convince you to meet me for a drink after your appointment so we could discuss these properties—particularly the old motel—but I have an appointment myself in a couple of hours."

A cheek-to-cheek to both of them from the back seat.

"Thanks for showing me around. Looking forward to tomorrow." I slid out and waved as they drove off. Natasha wasn't far behind them.

I ran through the parking lot to my car, hoping Freddi and Missy's five o'clock was at their office. I broke several traffic laws, but I got there in time to see the Chrysler drive away from Bikini Realty with the client in it. More importantly I was right behind Natasha when she pulled out to follow them.

On the way back to my hotel, I called The Squid.

His usual "What?" greeting blared in my ear.

"Natasha's tailing Freddi and Missy."

"*What?*"

"It is what it is. I didn't say it makes sense. But I got her tag number."

"What?"

I gave it to him and said, "I think it's a rental. Can you do anything with it?"

He snorted and hung up.

Three what's and a snort. Another scintillating conversation with The Squid.

I checked the Tracker Phone. The Borismobile was still parked in the municipal lot. Had Natasha dropped him someplace? No way to tell. That meant I had an hour to kill before leaving to meet Jamie Bond.

The hotel bar—the Boardroom—beckoned. If I learned anything from the bartender, the beer would go on my expense account. If not, I'd pay for it. Either way I'd have a cold draft.

The bartender and waitress wore bright blue shirts printed with images of surfboards, paddleboards, sailboards, and boogie boards. I walked to the far end of the nearly deserted bar. The lanky thirtyish surfer-dude bartender was in front of me by the time I planted my butt on a barstool.

He watched me eyeballing the draft beer handles and said, "Can't beat the Cigar City Lager. Brewed in Tampa. Perfect for a hot day like this and..." He pointed to a sign with the happy hour specials, which included Cigar City drafts.

"Sold."

"Good choice, guy," he said with a grin.

He set it in front of me, and we shot the breeze about the area. His name was Chad.

I wanted to build rapport to pick up local info, but he was making it too easy.

Almost like he was working *me*.

CHAPTER THIRTY-ONE

Desiree

HER

Missy and I finished one of our best days ever. Our five o'clock appointment resulted in the sale of a three-bedroom fixer-upper a block from the beach to a local contractor who wanted to renovate it, not knock it down. The kind of sale we felt good about. We shook hands with him and set an appointment for ten in the morning to do the paperwork.

I dropped Missy at her car by our office and drove home with the Nissan not far behind me. Damn. I didn't want her to see the Chevy with Tagphony on it. Uncle Tony stressed he wanted to see Sabrina, so I couldn't go in the Chrysler or as myself. I had to look like Sabrina.

When I began modeling at the Jumbo Shrimp, I went by the name Sabrina but looked like me. Once I started my business I decided to use a disguise along with my alias to deal with club and bar owners as well as models and dancers. Models from my pre-disguise days were long gone. So everyone who knew Sabrina today knew her as my disguised self. I intended to keep it that way.

The solution was to drive the 300F to the shopping mall located a half-mile from the Jumbo Shrimp, park, and traipse inside. There I'd do a Superman costume change in a phone booth—or a ladies' room since phone booths left the planet with the space shuttle. I'd walk into the mall as Freddi and leave by a different entrance as Sabrina. My tail could watch my car while I Ubered to Uncle Tony.

I arrived at my house, left the 300F in the driveway, and hurried in. I inserted my tinted contacts and stuffed my brunette wig and black-rimmed glasses into one of my larger purses along with flat shoes and a gray blouse that would cover my scoop-neck crimson top. I locked up, got in my Chrysler, and headed for Tampa.

About halfway up I-275 I used my untraceable Cellphony to arrange for an Uber pickup at the mall. I checked my mirror. The white Nissan was two cars back like a well-trained dog heeling on a leash. Who was she?

The feeling that Tom McCall knew something about her wouldn't go away. Missy and I would be with him tomorrow afternoon and evening. If I couldn't drag something out of him in that amount of time, I should shred my psychology degree.

I spent the rest of the drive fretting about Uncle Tony wanting to see Sabrina.

Everything at the mall went as planned, and my Uber ride dropped Sabrina in her wig, glasses, and gray blouse at the Jumbo Shrimp at five minutes to seven. Uncle Tony was waiting at the hostess stand and escorted me to his office.

He closed the door behind us and gave me one of his gentle bear hugs. "Freddi. So great to see you."

I gave him another hug. This burly man with a big grin always made me feel special. "You warm my heart, Uncle Tony, but your call worried me all day."

He sat at his desk. "Sorry, but that's how I am about phones. Things you say can be misconstrued when words aren't attached to expressions and gestures. In my case, you know how I kid around. If you don't see me rolling my eyes or whatever when I make a crack, you might think I'm serious. And because my last name is Catalina I have to worry about phones even more. Some of my family have made unwise decisions that cast a shadow on all of us. Have you talked to Angela lately?"

I sat in the contoured chair across from him. That was Uncle Tony. Family before anything else. He wanted to be sure my college roommate and I were still good. "We haven't talked for a couple of days but today alone she sent me four photos of baby Lisa. That's kid number three. Surely Angela's figured out what causes it by now."

Uncle Tony roared like that was a new joke. "It's time you settle down and start making babies yourself. My one regret is Maria and I couldn't... Sorry. We need to get down to business. You have a dancer named Desiree working at the Naked Truth?"

"She hasn't been with me long. Beautiful, great dancer. But might want to go beyond the no-touch policy, which surprises me. I told her not while she's with me."

"I thought she might be yours. All her tips went into a bucket instead of a garter."

My eyebrows shot up. "You were at the Naked Truth?"

He laughed while shaking his head. "The bar action is slow here on Sunday nights. It's a dud night for tips. Ray—a distant cousin—works it for me. He thinks he's John Travolta when he was skinny, dancing around in that white suit in the movie, ah...ah..."

"*Saturday Night Fever.*"

"Yeah, That's it. Ray likes pouring drinks on Sunday nights because sometimes lonely ladies show up and don't have anybody to talk to but the bartender. He takes it from there. You get the picture. He'd probably pay *me* to cover the Sunday night shift. I'm telling you this so you understand Ray's *really* into the ladies. If Ray tells you this woman is this woman then it is this woman."

"Okay, but what does that—"

"Ray calls me this morning. Says he didn't want to bother me last night because it wasn't that big a deal. Just a little unusual. Says a woman comes into the bar around eight asking for me. He tells her I never work on Sunday but he'll give a message to me. She says her name is Jasmine and it's about modeling at happy hour but she'd come back when I was here."

"So she left?"

"Not without Ray doing his damnedest to get her to stay. He says she's gorgeous and he knows she has a great body because he's already seen her naked."

Now it was starting to make sense. "Desiree?"

"Ray was with some friends at a bachelor party at the Naked Truth on Wednesday night. Desiree was the featured dancer. He's positive Jasmine is Desiree."

CHAPTER THIRTY-TWO

Valley of Un-love

HIM

I was trying to figure what was up with Chad when he said, "I'm the relief bartender at the Royal Squid on Sundays. You're the dude with the knockout babes that drive that knockout car?"

"You know them?"

"Only from afar. Missy and Freddi. I'm surprised your skin isn't peeling."

I laughed. "Yeah, they're pretty hot." I swigged my beer. "Make that very hot. They showed me some properties this afternoon."

"They have a good rep even though some of their sales are for Ralph Miller."

He did everything but spit after he said Miller's name.

"Not a straight shooter?" I asked. "I'm considering a significant real estate project in which Ralph Miller is a player."

He looked around before answering. "I'm not saying this just because he's a bad tipper. Don't get near anything he builds. He also picks up properties when a builder goes belly up. Some of that's okay. But what he builds..."

I sensed there was more so I stayed silent to give it a chance to come out.

He looked around again. "Have you met his wife Rita?"

"I haven't even met *him*."

"He's bad. She's worse. She's my age—about twenty years younger than Ralph. She's taller than he is, maybe five-nine, and has this dark blonde hair blown out like she was riding a motorcycle without a helmet. A great body but not a lightweight." He thought for a second. "Like a Norse goddess."

"Sounds like you know her well."

"Better than I want to. In case you haven't figured out why she's married to that middle-aged dweeb..." He rubbed his thumb against his fingers in the universal sign for money. "And I guarantee she's the one who wears the pants."

The waitress called his name.

"Got to get to work. Be careful of Ralph and Rita."

The place was filling up fast. I had questions—including how he knew Rita so well—but he wasn't going to be able to answer them anytime soon. I already had more than a beer's worth of information. Unfortunately, it didn't bring me any closer to determining whether Ralph was a victim or conspirator. An unethical guy with a younger gold-digging wife could play either role.

I drained my beer, pulled a five and a twenty from my pocket, and waved them at Chad. He hustled over. I said, "Thanks for looking out for me."

He grinned. "Anytime you need to know about the local scene...I'm around most of the time. Besides part-time bartending, a buddy and I have the beach concession here—umbrellas, chairs, beach balls, that kind of stuff. Great way to meet the tourist chicks." He winked and saluted me with the money.

Chad's vivid description of Rita was on my mind as I stepped outside. Twenty feet away walking toward me was a woman who matched that description perfectly. She eyed me like a chocoholic eyes fudge. She passed without smiling and went into the Boardroom. Looking for Chad? Ralph Miller had his hands full with that one.

I went to my room and removed the beer from my teeth and my bladder. It was time to head for Tampa in case rush hour stragglers were clogging the road. On the way I checked the Tracker Phone again. The Borismobile was on I-275. At six-fifteen the Borismobile parked near Term Limits Pest Control. I called Jamie. He told me he was on it, had the cameras focused on the right places, just videoed Boris going into the Ibis Inn, and reconfirmed I could come in after seven.

The traffic gods smiled on me, and I arrived in the Tenderloin at six-thirty, thirty minutes before I could get with Jamie. Thirty minutes I could use to check out the other clubs.

I started at Tangy, the farthest club from Term Limits Pest Control. It was in an industrial area like all of Nick's joints. Zoning restrictions? Easier to protect from prying eyes? The building—which had to have been built for another purpose—was a utilitarian concrete block structure with mortar lines showing. Now it was plum-colored with *Tangy* in pink neon script on the side facing the road.

I circled the area a few times looking for buildings that could be used to house and exploit trafficked girls. Nick had converted a garage near the Panty Free Zone. Why? Who knew? Maybe he saw an advantage in doing business that way. There were several possible properties nearby but nothing that screamed out at me.

After Tangy, I did the same at Naked Truth, Barely Here, and the Valley of Love and learned nothing. I decided to skip the remaining two because it had become obvious the best way to do this was online through property records and building permits. Also I'd seen a lifetime's worth of pink neon.

Seven o'clock. Late enough that I could go to Term Limits and start reviewing Jamie's videos. I stopped at the traffic signal on the side street beside the Valley of Love. Two black SUVs roared out of the parking lot. One screeched to a stop on my rear bumper. The other slid sideways in front of me. I suspected they didn't want my car to move.

A shaved-headed guy in an unbuttoned black sport coat got out of the car in front of me. It took him a while. He was about the size of Rhode Island with a face more appropriate for the Valley of Un-love.

He had a Glock stuck in his belt in the front of his pants. Not only sartorially verboten but could cause serious damage in the area a guy wants least to damage. He lumbered over.

I lowered my window. "Sorry, I always buy my Girl Scout cookies from the neighbor's kid."

Sometimes I just can't help myself.

His face—and bald head—turned tomato red.

I refrained from advising him a person of his size should avoid undue excitement.

"Out of the car, funny man."

CHAPTER THIRTY-THREE

Connections

HER

What was up with Desiree? Was she playing games with Uncle Tony or me or both?

"Uncle Tony, all my girls know what jobs are available. Desiree knows Sabrina's Showstoppers provides the models here. They also know they can either model or dance. Not both. And if they model then change to dancing they can't go back to modeling. Establishments that have fashion shows don't want to be associated with strip joints."

"You've always done it the right way, Freddi. What do you know about Desiree, outside of your background check? Did you do your usual interrogation—excuse me, I mean interviewing."

"Of course. I did my standard three-interview set over ten days. You can joke about it, but I've exposed hookers and serious head cases through the process and rejected them."

He smiled. "Just teasing. If you didn't run such a tight ship, I couldn't back you."

I shook my head. "Sorry. I'm on edge. Most of my girls are nice women with relationship, money, or personal problems. Some I've gotten into various rehab programs. Desiree is different. I couldn't identify any real issues. She wanted to dance and not be touched, spurred on by a past experience."

"Local girl?"

"Orlando. This is her story according to her—emphasis on *her* after this Jasmine bit. She started gymnastics and dance very young and had Olympic dreams, but her parents couldn't finance that. She won all the local competitions but never attracted a sponsor. Then she had the misfortune of normal female maturity."

"As in boobs?"

"And a growth spurt that knocked her out of serious gymnastics. After high school she earned starvation wages dancing at local theme parks and attractions. She was studying radiology nursing at a local college when a guy she trusted as a friend nearly raped her. That turned her against men and into stripping, the best revenge—men would desire her but never touch her."

Uncle Tony rocked back in his desk chair. "How did she end up here?"

"The birds and the bees. She needed a man, dropped her guard, and let one in. He turned out to be a jerk. She wanted a new start, so she came to Tampa where she could support herself in strip clubs and continue her radiology studies. Again, this is according to her. As always I ran a background on her. She checked out. She's never been arrested or had legal problems."

"Text her file to me. Use this number." He wrote on a piece of notepaper and handed it to me. "I'll see what my sources can come up with. Now, what's bothering you?"

I put the number in an inside zippered pocket in my purse. "The reason I'm on edge—a woman's been following me all day. I don't have any idea why. I came up here in my Chrysler, changed in the mall, and Ubered over here."

He sat immobile, eyes closed, hands on his belly like Buddha. After ten seconds he opened his eyes. "I'll take you to the mall. When you leave I'll get the tag number of the car that follows you out and we'll go from there."

"It looks like a rental."

"No problem. I have connections who can help with that."

I rubbed my temples. "This woman can't be connected to Desiree. That would mean she knows Freddi and Sabrina are the same person and wouldn't need to follow me."

"Let's find out who she is and who Desiree is before we drive ourselves crazy speculating. I mentioned unwise decisions of some of my family members. Sometimes these have caused *certain* agencies to erroneously pay undue attention to me. And I probably add to the problem when I let *certain* people think—when it's advantageous—I'm speaking for my entire family. Like when *certain* Russians and other club owners start to get annoyed with Sabrina."

I was shocked. "I had no idea I was causing you problems. I can shut my business down. It's not like I make much money from it."

"What about your girls? A lot of people would see them as throwaways. You help them—and their kids. It's the social worker in you. You do your part. I'll do mine. I can take the heat. Now let's get out of here."

Uncle Tony drove me to the mall. He and I talked about Angela's children most of the way. I told him where the 300F was parked, got out, and went in the entrance I used as an exit an hour earlier. In the ladies' room, I changed back into Freddi and walked to my car without looking around.

The white Nissan followed me out of the lot and stayed one or two cars behind me as I worked my way to the I-275 ramp. Just before I got there, red and blue lights flashed behind me as a police car pulled the Nissan over.

Those were some connections Uncle Tony had.

CHAPTER THIRTY-FOUR

The Incredible Bulk

HIM

My car was boxed in. A giant with a Glock pistol in his belt was ordering me out of my car. I must have been in worse spots, but offhand I couldn't think of one.

"I said get out of the car. Now."

The color of his face and bald head brightened to sunset in a polluted sky. Could I come up with a line that would make his head explode?

Know thine enemy. A bald out-of-shape Incredible Hulk? No, not green. *The Tomato That Ate Cleveland*? Didn't really fit. I settled for the Incredible Bulk.

I eased my door open. He used his mass to prevent me from swinging it far enough to exit easily. I sort of slithered sideways, stumbling a little when I was completely out of my car. He reacted by grabbing my left shoulder with his massive right paw, probably planning to slam me against my car.

Unfortunately for the Bulk, like so many plans of mice and men, his went awry. His move allowed my right hand to reach the Glock unwisely stuck in the front of his pants. I grabbed it and pushed my finger against the trigger guard, pressing the barrel into him. "If you even breathe, you'll never have another intimate moment. There's nothing you can do to stop me from pulling the trigger."

His face darkened to the crimson color of Freddi's car but his head still didn't explode. "I'm going to help you save face with your men. They can't see my hand on your gun. Wave them off. Tell them you know me. If one of them shoots me, my dying twitch will relieve you of worrying about finding a date for Saturday night."

He didn't move but I could see he wasn't convinced.

"Think about this. After I eliminate your private parts, I'm going to take out your men. I don't like to brag but I'm a really good combat shooter. I was the best in the Special Forces on the range—and even better on live targets."

He took his hand off my shoulder and said something in what sounded like Russian. When the driver of the car in front of us replied, the Bulk turned his hand down and flipped it in a get-out-of-here gesture. Both SUVs backed up and drove into the club lot. I refrained from breathing a sigh of relief, thankful my Special Forces gambit worked.

I yanked the Glock from his belt and stepped behind the door of my car. No point in giving the Bulk a clear move on me. I said, "I'm a guy driving down the street and you show up. Why?"

"Don't insult me. I'm not stupid. A *guy* couldn't do what you just did. A *guy* wouldn't be casing our clubs."

He was careless with his weapon like Jamie Bond. The resemblance ended there. Not just because of a foot and a half in height and a couple hundred pounds. His English was unaccented and he used slang and sarcasm. No ordinary Russian. No ordinary man.

I got behind the wheel but left the door ajar and the window down.

We locked eyes without speaking. His stare had a defeated quality instead of the defiant if-you-make-the-wrong-move-your-ass-is-mine I expected from a guy like this.

"What happened to you?"

He jerked his head up. "What do you mean?"

"You were somebody. Now look at you. Fifty pounds overweight. Sloppy with a firearm. Never would have happened at your peak. I think you were once an honorable soldier. Life has changed—badly."

"You think you're Doctor Phil? And you can talk because you have my gun?"

"I'm guessing I'm talking to a man who doesn't like his life right now. I'm a financial advisor checking out the areas around strip clubs. I have a client who wants to open an adult superstore and thinks a building near a club is a smart idea. I think the whole thing is stupid, but I'm the advisor and he's the client."

"You expect me to swallow this?"

I shrugged. "What's your name? A name I can call you. I don't care if it's real."

He stared at me for several seconds. "Misha. A name my grandmother used."

"Misha, you can be the man you once were. I'm leaving you my number. When you want to purge what's dragging you down..."

I removed the magazine from his Glock, ejected the round from the chamber, locked it open, and stuck my business card in it. "I'm putting your gun and magazine on the ground and leaving. If you think of the building I'm looking for, call me. It will be our secret, and I guarantee you'll be safe."

He nodded almost imperceptibly. Otherwise he didn't move as I slammed the door, squealed a quick right into a small gap in honking traffic, and got the hell out of there. Misha knew what building I wanted, and I had no doubt his association with the operation was destroying him.

Maybe he'd regain his self-respect and call me. A long shot but I had nothing to lose. Thanks to The Squid and his elaborate security, Misha couldn't trace me through my phone number or tag. Just like nobody would be able to find Misha if The Squid hid him.

Checking for a tail before going to Term Limits Pest Control seemed prudent. I drove toward I-275 intending to go under it then double back. I was two blocks from the entrance ramp when I spotted Freddi's impossible-to-miss 300F ahead of me. Was she here on a real estate deal?

Red and blue lights flashed ahead of me as a police cruiser and a white car pulled to the side of the street. I passed by slowly. It was a Nissan. With Natasha driving.

Maybe there was even more to the Bikini Realty gals than I suspected.

I sped up and closed on the Chrysler before it went up the ramp. Just a driver. No passenger. It wasn't Bikini Realty. Just Freddi, no Missy. I went straight underneath the highway for several blocks. No sign of a tail. I turned right to begin to work my way to Term Limits.

Natasha's traffic stop and my encounter with Misha battled for my immediate attention.

Boris and Nick entered the fray.

Thoughts of Freddi knocked the Russians out of my mind like the Bolsheviks knocked the tsar out of the palace.

Freddi.

Our close encounter of the nicest kind at the Pirate's Booty.

I yanked my focus to driving and weaved my way through traffic.

Jamie's tape awaited.

CHAPTER THIRTY-FIVE

Turnabout

HER

My 300F rumbled up the I-275 ramp as I considered what just happened. Uncle Tony had to be responsible for the Nissan being pulled over. I always knew Uncle Tony had a lot of business connections. After what he told me about his family tonight, I felt he had derivative connections of other types. But how could he have caused that traffic stop so quickly through someone else's contacts?

I shook my head. It didn't matter. I needed to take advantage of the situation. Now my tail would be at least fifteen minutes behind me. She'd probably check to see if I went home. Then the hunter would become the hunted. I'd do a better job because I watched a lot of cop and spy shows. I knew all the techniques.

I had another advantage. My Chevy, which originally belonged to Uncle Dale—the stock-car racer who taught me how to really drive—had a special feature. A flip-down panel under the dash had switches that could disable either headlight and one or both taillights, brake lights, and parking lights to provide different profiles. He called them ticket avoiders for fast drivers. In other words, aids for escaping the police. I'd never used them, but they could be useful tonight.

Darkness had fallen on my old Crooked Foot home—hummed to the tune of *My Old Kentucky Home*—when I pulled into my driveway. Lights were on in the living room and kitchen thanks to timers. I drove the 300F into the garage and closed the door. I put Tagphony on my Chevy and hustled into the house with my oversized purse.

I swapped my skirt and heels for slim black slacks and black tennis shoes and removed my crimson top. I dug into my purse for my gray blouse, wig, and glasses. I packed a smallish purse with my wallet, cell phone, and usual lady things. I filled another purse with my stun gun, pepper spray, blinding tactical flashlight, ear-piercing whistle, and Cellphony. I was Sabrina again with a touch of Mrs. Peel of *The Avengers* thrown in.

After a quick bathroom break—in case I was stuck in my car a long time—I set timers in a sequence lasting one hour. It would appear I was in the kitchen, then watching TV in the living room, followed by getting ready for bed in the bathroom, and watching TV in the bedroom for a few minutes before turning out the lights. I drove my Chevy to a vacant house that had a good view of the wooded area I was certain she'd use to watch my house. The only difference between a real spy and me was a tan trench coat with a turned-up collar.

She showed up five minutes later and parked in the wooded area. I was trying to think of a famous female spy to favorably compare myself to when Cellphony rang. Uncle Tony said, "The woman following you is Tammy Yates. Mean anything to you?"

"No. But I'm watching her right now as she's watching my house."

"You're not in that car that can be seen from Alabama, are you?"

I laughed. "I'm in my Chevy with the phony tag on it."

"She claims to be from Atlanta but her accent is more like she's from the Georgia near Russia. She's here to take in the attractions and enjoy the nightlife. Here's the most interesting part—she gave her local address as the Ibis Inn."

"The motel next to the Panty Free Zone?"

"The same."

I thought for a few seconds. "So it's likely she's connected to Nick, but she can't be following me at his direction. If Nick knew the Sabrina secret, our whole dynamic would be different."

"Maybe she's not following you because of Sabrina but a different reason we don't understand. But that reason has to be connected to Nick somehow. Things are happening that involve you and me—starting with your dancer Desiree or Jasmine or whoever the hell she is."

"I'll send you her file in the morning. When you think the time is right I'll have a heart-to-heart with her. Meanwhile, maybe I'll learn something about Tammy Yates tonight."

"Be careful. I mean very careful. The scent of Russia is in the air."

Uncle Tony's emphatic warning caused me to remove my stun gun from my secret agent purse and put it in my console for easier access. There was that rush. Selling real estate was never like this.

At ten-thirty—fifteen minutes after the timer extinguished my bedroom light—Tammy Yates drove out of her hiding place. I kept my headlights off until she got to Gulfway Drive. I fell in behind her with one headlight on. When she reached I-275 I flipped the switch and followed her up the ramp with both headlights lit and three cars between us.

It was likely she was going to the Ibis Inn, her stated local address. The thought of driving to Tampa again deflated my rush. Was it worthwhile to follow her just to watch her go into a motel for the night?

The Outsider with Darren McGavin and *Harry O* with David Janssen—two of the best and most obscure sixties and seventies PI series ever—were on the retro channel tonight.

No matter how much I'd rather be in my jammies watching half-century-old TV shows, I forced myself to stay with her.

CHAPTER THIRTY-SIX

Polly Want a Hacker

HIM

At seven-thirty I turned onto the Term Limits Pest Control street. The Borismobile was parked in the same spot as last night. I called Jamie Bond and told him to open sesame. The wheels on the gate to the parking lot made their case for getting the grease.

Jamie let me in the building and we walked to the security room. Again I marveled at the extent of the system.

"Everything okay?" he said. "Thought you'd be here a half hour ago."

To avoid getting into a lot of detail I said, "Sorry, pal. Woman trouble." A true statement even though misleading.

He let out a quiet heh and squeaked, "I wish I had that kind of trouble—unless having no woman counts as trouble."

This was not a fun guy. He'd find a way to be depressing while giving away hundred-dollar bills. I said, "Right now the women we have to worry about are trafficked, and many of them aren't old enough to be called women."

That brought Jamie around to his clipped private eye mode. "Boris entered the Ibis Inn. Stayed long enough to have registered. Came out. Went into the alley behind the Panty Free Zone. No sign of him since."

I sat and stared at the screens without seeing them. Freddi and Missy, Boris and Natasha, Nick and Misha kaleidoscoped in my brain with guest appearances by *Magnum* aficionado Madge, bartender Chad, Rita entering the Boardroom, and a faceless image of Ralph Miller.

This wasn't getting me anywhere. I shook my head. The kaleidoscope swirled out of my mind like water down the drain—counterclockwise since I was in the northern hemisphere. Where in the hell was The Squid? I needed the information about Ralph and Rita, Natasha's tag number, and Boris's phone call.

"Jamie, let's look at your tape."

He clicked a button on a remote then handed it to me. "It's coming up on the large screen on the wall straight ahead. Same as with the console monitors—if you see something you want as a photo, click and it will save to a flash drive."

My phone gave an exasperated sigh, the tone dedicated to The Squid. "Sorry, Jamie. I have to take this."

He turned toward the door. "Yell when you're finished. My office is two down. I'll hear you."

The Squid opened with his best grunt, the one that sounded like a bullfrog being run over by a grocery cart.

"Any luck with Boris's audio?" I asked quickly before he grunted again and I pictured the critter's eyes bulging out.

"First, Natasha's car. A little birdy tells me it's rented to one Tammy Yates from Atlanta, G.A."

If a little birdy told him, it had to be a parrot whose owner was a database hacker. I said, "Same initials as her real name Tanya Yeshenko."

"Those internet lessons on investigations are really paying off for you," The Squid snapped. "As for Ralph Miller, besides basic DL and physical info, mostly lawsuits and legal stuff you'd expect from a developer cutting corners. I haven't found much on his wife Rita."

"I know a bartender who has the scoop on her. I'll talk to

him tomorrow."

"So this is going to cost me a fortune in beer. Stick with the happy hour specials. I'm not made of money, you know."

Comments like that always made me wonder if they were educated guesses or a transmitter had been planted in my head.

The Squid snorted. "Boris called Natasha—Tanya Yeshenko—who rented a car as Tammy Yates, a name with the same initials. Something only the keenest of internet-trained sleuths might notice and graciously educate me about the practice of using the same initials for the alias."

The Squid could be sensitive.

"Consider this a grovel," I said. "What the hell did Boris tell Natasha? The Twitter version please."

The Squid and Twitter versions were made for each other except snorts and grunts were difficult on Twitter.

"Boris wanted to look like a local guy for credibility working his scam. He bought a condo with an immediate occupancy agreement. When the scam was over he could walk away from the deal because he used an alias—an alias that did not have the same initials as his real name."

"Okay, okay. I'm sorry. You beat it to death already."

The Squid grunted. "Boris learned that the actual seller was the target of his scam. That meant the condo served no purpose. He decided to back out and save the deposit he'd lose when he skipped town."

"Did he say anything about the blowup with Freddi and Missy?"

"He was pissed they didn't tell him who was behind the corporation selling the condo."

"That's on Boris," I said. "He should have gotten that information out of them. Especially since the condo was part of his cover. The Bikini Realty babes had him off his game."

"Also Boris is worried that they might be connected to somebody and screw up the scam somehow. Most of that was unintelligible. Boris told Natasha to come to Crooked Foot immediately. He wants her to follow them to see what they're up to."

"So Freddi and Missy aren't involved with him."

"If he's telling the truth to Natasha. But he's suspicious of them. And there was something about diamonds. There are a lot of bad spots on the audio. Big chunks. I got about half of it. I'll text you the transcript."

I gave The Squid a rundown on my encounter with Misha.

"You hear that rattle?" he said. "That's me shaking my head. I know you want to rescue those girls. I do too. But you can't rescue anybody if you're dead. Taking chances like that, you need to be—"

"Packing." I finished his sentence for him. "What would have happened tonight? A shootout. Misha dead. Me being investigated. And our case blown. Now we have a chance—remote as it is—to get some help from Misha with the girls. If we don't, our investigation of Boris isn't blown and we're no worse off as far as finding the girls."

He exhaled loudly into the phone. "Quit risking your butt. I don't have time to find a replacement." He clicked off.

Warm and fuzzy.

"Jamie, let's get started," I said loudly enough to reach his office.

He trotted into the room and sat down. Since I had to have his help with them, I told him the Boris and Natasha story, but only what he needed to know.

He rolled the video and we spent more than two hours stopping, starting, backing up, rewatching, and making stills. Overall

I didn't see anything of instant help, but I had photos of the limo and white van servicing the brothel and of Nick and a number of his associates including Misha. I kept an eye on the live monitors as well. No Boris. Nothing of interest happening.

I didn't know if Nick was inside the Panty Free Zone. It was a reasonable assumption Boris was because he went into the alley leading to the back door. So it seemed likely Nick was there too. What could they be doing? Based on Boris's appearance last night I didn't think he and Nick were just hanging out.

At 10:20 p.m., Boris appeared on the strip-club monitor. He came out of the alley and trotted to the Borismobile. He didn't get in. He leaned against it, lit a cigarette, and puffed. And puffed. And puffed. He pulled out his cell, coughed, and said, "Tanya."

That was the last word I understood for sure. He was calling Natasha. He spoke in Russian for three minutes. A few words sort of sounded like "come here." A linguistic congruence or my imagination?

I scratched my head and copied the conversation to my flash drive.

He scratched his head and got in his car.

Jamie tapped my arm. "Let's go."

I shook my head. "I have a tracker on his car. Let's not chance him making us."

His eyelids opened wide. "A tracker? Like in the movies?"

"Not as effective as in the movies. If Boris checked in earlier, he'll probably be back to meet Tanya at the Ibis."

I followed him on my Tracker Phone. He went to a famous international restaurant—McDonald's. His car quit moving. Picking up or going inside to enjoy the ambience? Ambience was the answer. He must have really soaked it up because it was twenty-five minutes before the Borismobile was on the move again.

Another stop at a strip mall that had a liquor store. My guess—vodka. He returned and parked in the same spot across the street from Term Limits.

He got out and paced, then lit a cigarette. Those cancer sticks might be the end of him. But not his most likely cause of death if he was on the outs with Nick.

CHAPTER THIRTY-SEVEN

Revelations

HER

Déjà vu in reverse. I was following my tail up the interstate just as she had followed me five hours earlier. The difference—she didn't know it.

She took the exit for the Panty Free Zone but went past it into the Ibis Inn parking lot next door. I drove on to the next traffic light, made a U-turn, and thirty seconds later entered the Ibis lot from the other end.

I hoped to get a good look at her. Maybe a picture. She wasn't in sight. I spotted her car. She was still in it. I killed my headlights, backed into a space that offered me a view of her driver's door, and readied my phone camera.

Less than a minute later, Tammy Yates opened her door. I documented her exit with five quick pix. Movement caught my eye. A man was trotting across the street through a break in traffic.

He continued toward the Ibis but was intercepted by Tammy in the middle of the parking lot. The hug and kiss convinced me the guy wasn't her brother even though his hair was as dark as hers. They walked to the entrance with his arm around her shoulders and hers around his waist. As they walked into the brighter lights of the porte cochere, he turned his head toward her.

Jules Armand!

Holy didn't-see-that-coming, Batman!

Sorry, Darren McGavin and David Janssen, you're now a distant second. What was I thinking, considering you instead of following Tammy Yates?

Revelations.

Armand was having me followed. And him being up here next to the Panty Free Zone—the location of Nick's primary office—showed he was involved with Nick. I thought about last night when Brandi and I hid behind the dumpster. Armand had to be the guy who came out of the back door to Nick's office with the bouncer.

I called Uncle Tony on Cellphony. "Sabrina needs to see you."

"When?"

"Ten minutes."

"The restaurant's closed. The bar's only open till midnight. Tell her to come to the back door."

"She's on her way."

I drove directly to the Jumbo Shrimp, lost in thought about what I just witnessed could possibly mean.

Uncle Tony ushered me through the back door, gave me one of his gentle hugs, and led me to his office. "What's up, kiddo? Has to be important for you to be here like this."

I told him everything in chronological order—including things I'd told him already—about Jules Armand, the condo, his connection to Ralph and Rita, and his hooking up with Tammy Yates, the woman who followed me all day. I probably included the weather report and my horoscope as I downloaded. Not understanding the situation and not being in control didn't sit well with me.

Uncle Tony smiled beatifically and spread his hands. "You appear calm as always but I feel your anxiety. Don't fear the Russians—or anyone else you deal with. You know I have your back."

Of course I knew that, but hearing him say it soothed me. Uncle Tony was the person who should be doing counseling.

We discussed possibilities for a while then I threw in Tom McCall and everything about him—except for the tingles—including how we met, my suspicion of him, how he latched on to Missy and me, and his apparent interest in Armand.

Uncle Tony tilted his desk chair and stared at the ceiling for a few seconds. He rocked forward. "Your story could have been written by Agatha Christie. We might have unrelated things crossing paths here. Any chance this Tom McCall is an undercover cop?"

That shocked me. "A cop? I guess so. It would explain why I sense he isn't quite genuine. But why is he hanging around Missy and me? He wouldn't have met us if we hadn't gone up to him at the Pirate's Booty."

"Besides the obvious reasons any single guy would want to be around you and Missy, the answer is Jules Armand. Now we know he's connected to Nick and the Russians. If McCall's a cop investigating whatever Nick and Armand are doing and knows you have business with Armand..."

"So Tom thinks Missy and I are tied into whatever Armand is doing?"

"Maybe. Or after you fell into his lap—literally—at that bar, he thinks you have info about Armand that could help his investigation. Or he might be investigating whatever Armand is doing with Ralph and Rita Miller. You sell condos for the Millers."

"So he's investigating Missy and me?"

He shrugged. "A lot of pieces here. If you hadn't run into McCall, he might have found a way to meet you if he's interested in Armand. What's Armand doing with the Millers? Is it connected to what he's doing with Nick? Why did Armand have Tammy Yates follow you?"

"Tomorrow we're going to spend most of the afternoon and evening with Tom, so I'll have a lot of time to work on him."

"And let's not forget your dancer Desiree coming in here as Jasmine."

I glanced at the wall clock behind his desk. "Her last dance at the Naked Truth tonight starts in about fifteen minutes."

Uncle Tony gave me a questioning look.

I stood. "Sabrina needs to go over there and see what she can learn."

CHAPTER THIRTY-EIGHT

Babe Power

HIM

As I kept an eye on the monitors in the security room of Term Limits Pest Control, I read the transcript of last night's call from Boris to Natasha. I tried to flesh out what The Squid told me. It was difficult to piece the conversation together since the audio was only Boris's side of the conversation and a number of gaps noted as unintelligible.

Boris told Natasha he had a reservation for her at the Crooked Foot Nook and would call her in the morning. That explained how he and Natasha were already inside Grams' Coffee Spot this morning when I found his car in the municipal lot. He must have called or texted Natasha to meet him at Grams'.

He didn't have an easy time of it when he explained about the condo screwup and not finding out who was behind the corporation that owned it. Evidently Natasha thought he was trying to make a move on Freddi and Missy because several times he denied focusing on them instead of business.

Was Natasha checking out Bikini Realty on the internet while she and Boris spoke? I decided Natasha was on the right track. Freddi and Missy had overwhelmed Boris. Even a polished con man was susceptible to the high-wattage babe power those two generated.

My attention was diverted from the transcript when the ringtone of a phone came through the monitor trained on Boris. He whipped out his cell and slapped it against his ear.

On the monitor covering activity at the Ibis Inn, a white Nissan pulled into the parking lot. Natasha must have called him to announce her arrival. Another day, another motel. I wondered why he'd want one so close to Nick if Nick was on his ass.

A familiar gray Chevy passed the motel. It evidently U-turned out of the range of the camera because it then entered the lot through the other entrance. Boris walked across the street to the Inn. Natasha greeted him at the door. They went inside. The Chevy eased out of the lot.

"Jamie, open the gate. Call me if Boris comes out. I need to see who's in that Chevy."

The gate squealed open and I flew out of the lot. The Chevy was a block ahead of me doing the speed limit or I wouldn't have caught up. I read the tag number then dropped back. A woman was driving. It had to be the one who zapped the guy last night. A dozen blocks later the Zapper pulled into the Jumbo Shrimp Restaurant and Lounge.

The neon lights blinked out as she drove around to the back of the restaurant.

At a minute after midnight, I parked kitty-corner in the lot of a closed pizzeria.

This time I'd find out who the Zapper was.

Natasha was following Freddi.

The Zapper was following Natasha.

What did the Jumbo Shrimp have to do with anything?

I called The Squid.

Let's see what his little birdy could chirp about the Zapper's tag and the Jumbo Shrimp Restaurant and Lounge.

CHAPTER THIRTY-NINE

Naked Truth

HER

Uncle Tony walked me to the back door of the Jumbo Shrimp. I got in my car, took my stun gun out of the console, and returned it to my purse. Going to the Naked Truth wasn't necessarily dangerous. In fact it was Nick's classiest joint. But the incident with the two jerks in the Panty Free Zone parking lot was fresh in my mind. Plus having my stun gun and pepper spray handy was always comforting when I went to any club.

I checked my rearview mirror. I'd never been tail conscious before today other than when I was leaving one of the strip joints. No reason to be. My life as Sabrina was totally separate from my real life as Freddi. Now I wasn't so sure. Jules Armand and his woman had me looking over my shoulder—possibly forever.

The Naked Truth was less than a mile away in a commercial area instead of a light industrial area like most of Nick's clubs. The building housed a large restaurant before Nick took it over. He kept an emphasis on good food to maintain the illusion of a gentleman's club. The kitchen was open all day from lunch on through to the wee hours.

Perfect for my dancers. The clientele ate them up. Art to accompany a good meal or wind-down cocktail. I usually had three girls dancing there several hours a day—lunch, dinner, and late night. The place had to be Nick's largest grosser by far. I often wondered why he didn't have his main office there. Instead he had that cubbyhole at the Panty Free Zone.

The Naked Truth came up on my left, next to a small shopping plaza filled with stores closed for the night. An open Jack & Mack's convenience store was on the corner next to the plaza. I made a left turn, went halfway down the block, and checked my mirror. Nobody followed me.

I made a U-turn, parked at Jack & Mack's in the spot closest to the shopping plaza, and stepped over the foot-high concrete barrier separating them. My intention was to catch Desiree in the dressing room at the end of her act then take her out the back door to give her a lift. She'd have no time to think or call anyone before we talked.

Anybody watching her wouldn't see us together because of where I parked—fingers crossed. To have pulled that Jasmine stunt, she was either a flake or under some kind of heavy pressure. She got through my interviewing process. She wasn't a flake.

As I started across the L-shaped plaza parking lot, voices reached my ear. I stepped into the deep shadows under the overhang covering the walkway around the building. Two figures—dimly backlit by the neon of the Naked Truth—stood at the other end of the walkway. In the still night air their hushed conversation was channeled to me by the acoustics of the overhang as clearly as if I'd been standing next to them.

"I'm telling you for the last time, I can't help you if you don't quit dragging your feet," a male with a deep voice and slight New York accent said, waving his hand.

A female voice responded, "I'm doing everything you say, including that stupid idea of going to the restaurant last night."

It had to be Desiree. Who the hell was she talking to?

"It was stupid because of the way you handled it," Deep Voice said. "The only thing the tape proves is the bartender has the hots for you."

"How is it my fault?" She threw her hands in the air. "Tony wasn't there. I'm doing everything I can. You have to believe me." She lowered her hands and reached one toward Deep Voice.

He brushed it away and said, "Don't try to cozy up. This is strictly business. You knew he wouldn't be there. You're trying to drag this out without accomplishing anything, thinking I'll give up. That's not going to happen." He punched his finger at her like a woodpecker drilling for supper. "We've been through this before. Your problem isn't going away unless you produce. Got it?"

Desiree put her hands on her hips. "And we've been through *this* before. I'm not framing anybody. If Tony's a hitman like you say, that's one thing—but if he's a guy with bad relatives, that's another. See, I understand that. It's a lot like a boyfriend doing things you don't know about and leaving you to hold the bag. You don't have any respect for me because I'm *just* a stripper but contrary to what you think, I have principles. You got *that*?" Her voice grew louder and shriller as she spoke.

"Calm yourself. You know I'm not asking you to frame anyone. We want you to gather information. Period. Call me at ten tomorrow morning."

"It's time for my last show," she snapped, then turned and trotted toward the back door of the Naked Truth.

A dark blue Dodge Charger eased into the lot and stopped beside Deep Voice, who opened the passenger door. A female voice came from the interior. "Nice clear signal. Should be a good tape. Sounded like she was coming on to you."

"I don't think so." Deep Voice slid into the passenger's seat. "A stripper with scruples. I hate this case. Let's get the hell out of here." He slammed the door.

The Charger screeched out of the plaza.

I was stunned.

Uncle Tony a mob guy? A hitman? Uncle Tony?

Impossible. He broached the possibility of Tom being a cop and wasn't worried about it in the least.

I'd know a lot more when I talked to Desiree after her act.

The naked truth at the Naked Truth.

CHAPTER FORTY

Carlo the Blade

HIM

A few minutes after my latest scintillating conversation with The Squid, the Chevy left the Jumbo Shrimp. The Squid said he'd have the tag registration and info about the restaurant in a few minutes. I hoped he did. I needed to know who I was following and whether she might lead to a bad surprise. After Misha's trap earlier, I was in a cautious frame of mind.

Traffic was light so I had to stay back and hope I didn't catch a red light and lose her. Four blocks later I saw a Nick strip joint ahead on the left. That couldn't be a coincidence. The Zapper surprised me by passing the Naked Truth and turning left at the corner onto a side street. I slowed to give her time to do whatever she was going to do.

Thirty seconds later I passed the street she took and saw her halfway down the block making a U-turn. Checking for a tail. I'd have to be careful. I pulled into a parking space in front of an oversized SUV, killed my lights, and watched the side-view mirror.

The Chevy drove into the Jack & Mack's on the corner and parked in the end slot. The Zapper stepped out of her car and over a low wall into the shadows of a closed-for-the-night shopping center. At the far end of the darkened plaza a man and a woman engaged in an animated conversation that looked like an argument. The Zapper stayed hidden from them.

What the hell? While I was chewing on that I got a text from The Squid saying the Zapper's tag hadn't been registered for years and the last person that had it was deceased. Before I could digest that, the woman engaged in conversation spun away and headed for the side entrance of the Naked Truth.

As soon as she entered the strip club, a Dodge sedan charged—appropriately enough—into the lot. The man stepped out from under the overhang, got in the passenger's side, and slammed the door. After the Charger roared out of the lot, the Zapper came out of hiding and walked across the plaza parking lot to the front door of the Naked Truth.

I had a lot to think about but first I needed a better vantage point. I drove to the next corner, hung a right, then two more rights to put me on the side street that ran beside Jack & Mack's. I parked with a view of the Zapper's Chevy as well as the front and side doors of the strip club.

My head was swimming. What was that all about? The woman who went in the side door was probably a stripper.

The guy arguing with the stripper and the Dodge picking him up had all the earmarks of a police operation. A cop dealing with a woman would be careful about meeting with her alone. So the meet was probably recorded and the driver of the Dodge probably a female cop.

Probably after probably added up to one more probably. The stripper was probably an informant. But for what purpose? Were the police looking into Nick's human trafficking activities? Or another crime? Narcotics? And which police? City, county, state, federal, or a task force?

Then there was the Zapper. Natasha followed Freddi. At some point the Zapper started following Natasha. How did that happen? Why did the Zapper go to the Jumbo Shrimp immediately after she saw Boris and Natasha go into the Ibis Inn? And what about the Zapper's bad tag? Law enforcement agencies can get special tags for undercover work, but if she was a cop, she wasn't part of whatever just happened with the stripper.

My phone vibrated. A text from The Squid telling me to call when I could. I wasted no time.

A grunt when he picked up. Nonverbal communication or a remnant of our simian ancestry? I said, "Please tell me you can unscramble this mess."

"The mess is now equivalent to the inside of a screaming baby's diaper. The Jumbo Shrimp is owned by Anthony—Smiling Tony—Catalina, one of the nephews of Carlo Catalina."

"As in Carlo—the Blade—Catalina, boss of the Tampa crime family."

"It's not a simple hierarchy in Tampa. The Italian and Cuban mobsters have always coexisted there. The Russian mobsters who have moved in with human trafficking, international scams, and other crimes pay appropriate homage—meaning money—to keep the peace."

"So the Zapper could be a go-between. She deals with Nick and with Smiling Tony. But why would she be following Natasha then run to Tony right after she saw Natasha hook up with Boris?"

"Here's something else," The Squid said. "Tony might not be mobbed up, other than by blood."

"Whoa! You're telling me a nephew of Carlo the Blade isn't mobbed up?"

"Carlo is reputed to be a mobster who doesn't want his offspring in the life—except almost everybody related to him is in it."

"Other than Tony?"

"Loved by all. Chairman of the Board of the Tampa Restaurant and Tavern Association. In addition to promoting their member businesses, they support local food banks and children's hospitals. He's not only chairman but also their biggest contributor. Likable guy, as you'd expect from someone called Smiling Tony. Record is clean as a whistle. But..."

"But?"

"But a number of agencies suspect he's the elusive hitman for the Catalina criminal enterprise. A little birdy told me he's a corollary target of a task force formed a couple of months ago looking into the Russians."

The little birdy strikes again. I gave The Squid a full rundown on what I saw tonight.

Another grunt. "We're sliding further and further away from figuring out what Boris is up to."

"Something to do with the Millers but he's heavily involved with Nick right now. I don't see Nick being a part of Boris's new scam other than getting a piece of the profits. And I don't see Boris being a part of the trafficking since he runs scams in South Florida most of the time. The Bikini Realty babes are linked to Boris and the Millers. Maybe I'll learn something tomorrow when I'm with them."

"Yeah, I'll bet. And your bartender? Watch the expenses."

"I might have to buy a round for the house."

He clicked off.

I thought about running across the street and slapping a GPS tracker under the Zapper's bumper but decided the juice wasn't worth the squeeze. The Zapper could come out at any minute and security cameras might memorialize my actions. Because of where I was parked, I'd be able to follow her whether she went left or right.

Even without a tracker I'd have her.

The Zapper was in my sights.

I sat back and waited.

CHAPTER FORTY-ONE

Olympic Feet

HER

The garish neon of the Naked Truth helped light the way as I walked through the deserted plaza, stepped around some trimmed bushes, and reached the front door.

A muscle-bound Latino collecting admissions outside the entrance looked at me, the valet station, both ways up the street, then back at me. "Where the hell—"

Nick's righthand man—a huge human being—stepped through the door and intervened. "This is Sabrina. She's Desiree's manager. Let her in."

I smiled. Most of the times I'd seen him he was with the boss, which I hoped wasn't the case tonight. I said, "Nick's here?"

He shook his bald head. "He's at the Zone. He sent me over to close up. The manager had to go home sick—again, maybe for the last time."

Evidently the manager had a problem—most likely drugs—which might have been behind Nick offering me his job.

"Are you here to give Desiree a ride?"

"She's not expecting me."

He gave me a nod of approval. "Always good to surprise the employees. She's about to get on stage now. Want to wait for her in the dressing room?"

"I'll watch her dance then meet her there. Quality control."

Another nod of approval. "That's why Nick says you're the best." He motioned me inside and said to the scantily clad waitress standing next to him, "Whatever she wants is on the house."

I thanked him and patted his arm. I told the waitress Perrier in a bottle and gave her a ten-dollar tip when she brought the sweating bottle to my table at the back of the room. Possibly the only strip club in Florida where Perrier was served.

Desiree's routine was a derivative of Olympic rhythmic gymnastics using a wide red ribbon that had to be at least fifteen feet long. She started clothed in a gymnastics warmup suit as "New York, New York" thumped over the sound system. As she twirled and flipped and spun with the ribbon flowing around her, the warmup suit went away revealing the gymnastics outfit beneath it. Eventually that was gone as she continued dancing.

I'd seen this routine in her tryouts but I had her stop at the gymnastics outfit. This was different. The effect of her totally nude performance on the male audience was fascinating. It varied from clapping and whistling to silence as she performed some of the more difficult flips and twists. She had them eating out of the palm of her hand, although other body parts might make a better analogy.

As the music wound down she reached into the pile of costume pieces she had amassed at the back of the stage and produced a much smaller red ribbon. She strutted to the center of the stage and mimed taking a shower then drying off with the three-foot ribbon, rubbing it over every inch of her body.

She held the ribbon over her head by one end and with her other hand rubbed her fingers together in the international sign for money. The bidding started at fifty but quickly escalated to four hundred thanks to a drunken bachelor party. The winner dropped the money in the tip bucket between her feet.

She kissed the ribbon then placed it against his lips.

The crowd—as they say—went wild.

A blue-ribbon performance with a red ribbon.

I beat her to the dressing room. When she walked in carrying the pieces of her costume and the giant red ribbon, I said, "We need to talk, Jasmine."

Her eyes almost came out on their stalks. "I knew that Jasmine thing was a stupid idea." With irritation in her voice she said, "Mind if I get dressed first?"

That attitude wasn't going to work with me. I glared at her. "You're playing a game that can't end well."

Her composure crumbled. She dropped everything and covered her face with shaking hands. The saucy stripper morphed into a frightened child. Tears leaked from beneath her palms. "Everybody's against me."

Softly I said, "I'm not against you. I look out for my people."

She lowered her hands. "I know that. All the girls love you."

"But you have to be honest with me."

"I need to get some clothes on. I feel so naked."

"We'll go somewhere to talk, then I'll take you to your car."

She opened her mouth to speak. I put a finger to my lips and scanned the ceiling. She got my message and silently dressed.

Nick's righthand man Andrei came in and gave Desiree her share of the tips. He turned to me and said, "I told Nick you were here to make sure everything was cool. He told me to give you this—out of our share."

He handed me a hundred-dollar bill.

"It's a pleasure to work with a smart businessman like Nick. Give him a hug for me." I looked Andrei up and down. "On second thought, don't. You could crush him and whoever takes his place might not be so generous."

He roared. "You're something else, Sabrina."

"Would you make sure nobody's lurking near the back door."

He led us to the exit, checked, and motioned us on. I waved at him as he closed the door behind us. Blowing a kiss would be too much for the ice queen. We walked through the shopping plaza and stepped over the low wall into Jack & Mack's parking lot.

All my surveillance senses were on alert.

Surveillance senses I didn't know I had before today.

Somebody might be out there.

Desiree and I piled into my car. Instead of going out to the main drag, I turned down the side street which dead-ended a block ahead. I kept an eye on the rear-view mirror. Nobody behind us, but I wasn't going to take any chances. At the dead end I made a hard left onto the street paralleling the main drag and floored it. I flipped the switches to shut off my taillights and brake lights. Another glance in my rearview. Was that a car without headlights back there?

Reflectors a block and a half ahead marked another dead end. We were pushing ninety-five as we approached it. I stood on the brakes, released them, and made a left turn with my foot on the gas. The tires and suspension did their jobs as I came out at fifty without a wobble, accelerating hard.

Desiree slapped the dashboard. "Wow! How did you do that?"

"Magic."

I switched my taillights and brake lights on, slowed to a crawl at the stop sign, and hung a right into light traffic on the main drag.

She fanned herself with her fingertips but with a smile on her face.

Not easily scared. I reflected on her standing up to the cop earlier. There might be more to Desiree than I thought—in more ways than one. "Where's your car?"

"At the Stopped Clock."

Yikes!

CHAPTER FORTY-TWO

Dark Evader

HIM

My eyelids were drooping. I kept second-guessing myself about not slapping a GPS tracker under the Zapper's bumper. How long could it take? Park next to her car, get out, and do it. But there was the video camera factor. Jack & Mack's looked like the kind of place that would have functioning equipment. If for some reason the illegal tracker ever came up, there I'd be on tape....

Movement at the side door of the Naked Truth. The Zapper and the stripper who was possibly an informant emerged and rushed across the shopping plaza parking lot. The Zapper tripped as they stepped over the low wall into Jack & Mack's lot. The stripper steadied her. They got in the Zapper's car.

I started my engine. Would she go left or right?

Damn! Neither.

She took the side street I was parked on but headed away from me. She'd be able to spot any vehicle following her on that quiet street. She was very tail-wise. I wouldn't pass up another chance to put a tracker on her car.

When she neared the end of the block, I rocketed across the main drag with my headlights off. She made a left. I floored it and made the same turn less than twenty seconds later with my tires squealing. Could that be her with no taillights a block and a half ahead already? Her headlights reflected off the windows of a corner house as she turned back toward the main drag. No matter what her car looked like, she wasn't driving an average Chevy.

I stomped on the gas then came to my senses. Streetlights showed a number of homes needing paint and landscape work. The X-rated activity on the main drag a block away had the older residential area in decline. But some houses were decently maintained indicating they were occupied by people pissed off about the neighborhood. The kind of people who'd call 911 about street racing if they heard the Zapper roaring by. A likely strong police presence in an area like this would result in a quick response. The second speeder—meaning me—would get nabbed.

Time to shut it down. I braked hard, made a quick three-point U-turn, turned on my headlights, and drove—meticulously obeying the residential speed limit of thirty-five—to Jack & Mack's. A police cruiser went by as I pulled into their parking lot.

I had a fifty-fifty chance the Zapper would pass this way. Possibly better because it was likely she laid a false trail on the back street and would turn my way when she got to the main drag.

One minute of waiting blew that theory out of the water. No sign of her. I texted Jamie and told him to call immediately if she showed up at the Ibis Inn or Panty Free Zone. I went by the Jumbo Shrimp where this leg of our cat-and-mouse game began except the mouse didn't know the cat existed. No cars around. Even the staff was gone.

I decided to cruise the area in the direction she went—not expecting to find her and proving myself right. The way they left the Naked Truth and hurried to the Zapper's car, I didn't think they'd be hanging around.

Who the hell was the Zapper?

I'd seen her with two strippers and both times she acted like she was protecting them.

The strippers didn't act like trafficked girls. They had freedom.

And the Zapper didn't look like their housemother.

But she was connected to the Russian mob and the Catalina family.

And she had eluded me again.

In her dark car with dark windows.

The Dark Evader.

I was about to give up when a quarter-mile ahead of me I saw a shopping plaza not totally shuttered for the night.

A dark gray sedan was jockeying into a parking spot.

Its left taillight was a little dim.

I grinned.

CHAPTER FORTY-THREE

Spy vs Pie

HER

Taking Desiree directly to the Stopped Clock wouldn't be smart. I borrowed a few techniques to expose a tail from TV cop shows, basket weaving two blocks with a couple of last second turns as the traffic lights changed to red.

Maybe that hadn't been a car with no headlights behind me. At the time I was too focused on my driving for more than the quickest glance in my rear-view mirror.

Now on to the Stopped Clock. Why in the hell had Desiree picked that place to leave her car? Not nearly as safe as an all-night grocery or big box store. A twenty-four-hour diner with a mixed-bag clientele. The problem was at the other end of the shopping plaza, where the sleaziest strip club in town operated until five in the morning.

A few years ago I checked it out. No place for Sabrina's Showstoppers. The dancers were biker chicks complete with facial hardware and vicious-to-vulgar tattoos. Some had a reasonable number of teeth. Often their old men visited the diner to satisfy their munchies, mixing with people out on the town who wanted a late bite.

Judging by the cars, the Stopped Clock was doing a good business for a Monday night, now Tuesday morning. I parked several rows back in the shadows of trees blocking the parking lot lights. Cameras could be anywhere. I said, "Not the safest place to stash your car."

She laughed. "It is for me. The owner is the best friend of my big brother, so I'm his little sister. When you meet him you'll see why I feel very safe here."

We walked into the shotgun-style diner. A counter with round stools sat to the left with the cooking area behind it. Tables to the right against the windows. Beyond them, two rows of booths extended to a short hallway leading to bathrooms in the rear.

Behind the counter a tall muscular Black guy with hard eyes in a white tee, blue head bandana, and formerly white apron said, "Sis, give your order to Sally and hug me later."

"We're just here for coffee, Cube. We'll be in the back booth."

I scanned the patrons. Pretty well-dressed except for three bikers wearing leather vests emblazoned with their club's logo. They sat at the counter, staring at us. Cube slammed his spatula down. "That's my sister. Capeesh?"

They swiveled back to their plates. The big bald guy in the middle said, "We know that, Cube. And like I told you before, she don't look anything like you. But that don't mean she ain't worth looking at."

Cube nodded with a hint of a smile, pointed the spatula toward the rear, and spoke to me. "Coffee's on the way. Sis takes hers black. Sugar's on the table. Cream for you?"

I shook my head. "No, thank you."

Usually I didn't drink coffee this late, but I'd need help getting back to Crooked Foot Key. I took the side of the booth that gave me a view of the restaurant and the front door. Sally had steaming coffees in front of us by the time we settled in.

Desiree touched the waitress's arm. "I think I need a piece of key lime pie."

Sally nodded and returned with a huge slice nearly as quickly as a magician pulling a rabbit out of a hat.

Desiree smiled sheepishly. "I get hungry when I'm nervous."

I sipped my coffee with caution then said, "Cube? As in sugar?"

"As in Rubik's. He solved it in seconds when he was a kid. He was happy for the nickname instead of his given name Percival."

Not the handle a guy would want but in an undesirable appellation contest a distant second to Missy's real name Beulah Mudd.

"After a growth spurt the Percival name disappeared completely. Even his parents call him Cube."

"And the badass bikers dancing to the tune of his spatula?"

She shoveled a forkful of pie into her mouth and talked around it. "They follow his rules. Who knows why? Maybe respect for his time in the Special Forces. I never asked."

I was positive she was holding back. It didn't matter. We weren't here about Cube. But her connection to a guy like him made me wonder how much I hadn't discovered during our interview sessions.

"Desiree, I'm not against you but I want to know what's happening without going through a Q and A about you posing as Jasmine and meeting with a cop. You either trust me or I walk—and my guess is I'm the only person willing to help you."

She teared up but didn't cry and with another huge forkful demonstrated why it's called a piehole. "I mostly told you the truth when you interviewed me. I left out the part about my ex-boyfriend being a druggie, dealing to support his habit, and hiding his stash in the trunk of my car."

I didn't respond. It wasn't the first time I heard a poor-little-innocent-me story.

More pie. "Don't look at me like that," she said loudly. "It's true. I don't use. Anybody who does is crazy." She looked around then continued in a quieter voice. "Orlando DEA told me I could avoid arrest if I'd go to Tampa and work for a task force investigating the Russian mob. Sort of exciting."

"Exciting?"

And more pie. "Yeah, like a spy. I was done with Orlando anyway, and Cube was here to help me get set up."

"What does the Russian mob have to do with going to the Jumbo Shrimp as Jasmine?"

And yet more pie. "I've met three members of the task force. They all think the Russians couldn't be trafficking girls without the Catalina family getting something out of it. Speaking of Russians, that Nick really gives me the creeps. His super-smoothness makes it worse, like pasting a smiley face on a rabid baboon."

I couldn't contain my own smiley face. "Perfect description."

She scraped up the last of the graham cracker crumbs. "One of the task force guys—a Tampa cop—is positive respectable businessman Tony is the connection to the Russians. Another one—an FBI agent—is convinced Tony's the never-identified hitman for the family."

Uncle Tony a hitman? How about Santa Claus a mad bomber?

"Since I'd never get close to Tony because of your rules about not mixing dancers and models, they came up with the stupid Jasmine idea."

"Don't let them know you've been burned. Keep doing what they tell you until I can figure a way out of this for you."

I also had to decide the best way to handle this with Uncle

Tony. I sipped my coffee and looked over the rim at the commotion at the front door.

My hand jerked.

Coffee slopped onto my chin and clothes.

CHAPTER FORTY-FOUR

Dead Man Riding

HIM

I waited just inside the entrance to the plaza with my lights off until the women walked into an all-night diner at one end named the Stopped Clock. The only other place open was at the opposite end. I drove that way. A strip joint named Strip Joint.

Everybody's a comedian.

Fifteen or so vehicles—chopper-style motorcycles, rough pickups, and beat-up sedans—were parked near the Strip Joint.

I eased down to the Stopped Clock. About the same number of vehicles parked there but much nicer including some worth a second look. A restored '57 Thunderbird, an absurdly powerful Dodge Hellcat, and a rare Slantback Hummer H-1—a civilian adaptation of the military Humvee and nothing like the civilized H-2 and H-3 that GM marketed. Hipsters grabbing a late bite?

I parked and thought about going inside. The women didn't know me but if they saw me here, they might recognize me someplace else and conclude—correctly—I was tailing them. There wasn't much to be gained by going in other than a better look at them. The smart play was to move my car and follow them when they left.

Fate—in the form of one of the greasiest bikers ever—rode in. The colors of a motorcycle club I never heard of were stitched on the back of his denim vest. He got off his chopper and staggered toward the door. About my height and 240 girthy pounds, a black T-shirt under the vest. A drooping chain ran from his belt to a wallet sticking out of his back pocket.

The handle of a Marine KA-BAR type of combat knife protruded from a sewn-in scabbard on the right thigh of his jeans. He touched it as if to reassure himself it was there.

That changed my decision. I slid out of my car and went through the door two steps behind him.

I spotted the women I was tailing in a booth at the back of the diner. The brunette was facing me but a coffee cup obscured her face.

Greasy walked toward three bikers sitting at the counter. He stopped behind the large one in the middle with a shaved bald head and growled, "Granger, you dissed my old lady for the last time," he said as he reached for the knife.

I stepped forward and delivered two hard knuckle punches to his kidney. He faltered. With my right hand I yanked the wallet from his pocket, wrapped the chain around his wrist, and jerked his arm up to the middle of his back. He yelped. I twisted his long greasy hair with my left hand and pulled his head back. "Don't make a sound. I'm walking you outside."

A big mahogany-skinned cook grabbed a cast-iron skillet. I shook my head. "Let's move him outside."

"Good thinking." He dropped the skillet, came around the counter, and said to the three bikers, "Stay here. I don't want to see your asses outside."

The cook put Greasy's free arm in a lock and we marched him out the door past the first row of cars. The cook dropped the arm and took the knife out of its scabbard.

I released Greasy and spun him around. "Are you too drunk to think or just naturally stupid? Stab a guy in front of a diner full of witnesses so you can spend the rest of your life in the slam?"

He pressed his left hand against his lower back and rotated his right arm carefully. He wheezed, "It's about honor, man."

"Why didn't I think of that? There's a lot of honor in stabbing someone in the back."

The cook squeezed Greasy's jaws with his huge mitt. "I'm keeping Granger here for five minutes. Your bloody body in the parking lot would be bad for business." He pushed Greasy's face away. "Here's some free advice. Get the hell out of town. Way out of town. Like off the planet."

"How about my knife? It cost me eighty bucks."

The cook and I stared at him silently.

He walked to his bike, hunched over with his hand on his back. He roared out of the lot like he was being chased. I didn't understand why he wasn't.

The cook stuck out his hand. "Can't thank you enough, guy. Call me Cube."

"Tom." We shook.

After a closer look at him, I knew who owned the Hummer.

"If he stabbed Granger..." Cube shook his head. His dark skin paled a bit as he thought about it. "The Stopped Clock would be a stopped clock. People'd be afraid to come in. Why'd you do it?"

A tough question. I shrugged. "Why aren't Granger and friends out here?"

"It's a long story but they listen to what I say."

I had a feeling the story wasn't all that long but I didn't care all that much. I just wanted to wash the hair grease off my hand.

"Tom, whatever you want is on the house. I can't offer you champagne and pheasant-under-glass but I serve the best sirloin burger south of Kansas City and the best key lime pie north of Key Largo."

I wanted to turn him down, but I was mousetrapped. Why was I here if not to eat? Saying I was stalking two women wouldn't get it. And my last meal was the seafood omelet at Grams'. "Thanks but first I have to get the crud off my hand."

He grinned. "That guy probably hasn't washed his hair this year and won't get the chance to now. He's a dead man walking. Bathrooms are all the way back."

We went inside. Granger and his buddies had swiveled around from the counter and were staring at me.

Cube pointed at the large bald biker and said, "Granger, don't be badassin' this guy. He just saved your butt. This is Tom."

The guy stood and held out his hand. "Sorry, man. Wasn't sure if you were with that sonofabitch and chickened out or what. Let me buy you a beer."

"A beer from you and a burger from Cube. Damn near makes it worth grabbing that flea-infested rat's nest. Men's room first."

He gave me a small heh, which I suspected passed for a laugh with him. "You're a cool hand, dude." He gave me a speculative look like he still wasn't sure about me. "Didn't break a sweat jerking that lard-ass around."

I headed toward the men's room. Evidently the brunette was in the ladies' room because her side of the last booth was empty. The blonde in the other side of the booth smiled at me.

After I washed my hands, I texted Jamie that we were done for the night and I'd call him in the morning. When I came out of the bathroom both women were gone. I walked to the counter.

After Granger toasted my fresh bottle with his near-empty, he thumped my shoulder and left with his compadres right behind him. A minute later the explosive sound of multiple Harleys starting simultaneously at the far end of the parking lot reached my ears.

I watched the entrance to the plaza through the window. A half-dozen motorcycles blasted out onto the street. Greasy *was* a dead man walking—now riding.

Cube set the promised sirloin burger in front of me. He didn't exaggerate. It had to be the best south of Kansas City—or north or any other direction.

He watched me take my first bite and nod my approval. "Save room for the key lime pie. My ninety-year-old great aunt makes them. He kissed his fingertips like a TV ad chef. "Says she's leaving me the recipe in her will."

I swigged my beer. "You know the women who were in the back booth?"

"The blonde's like my little sister."

With a grin he held out his arm to emphasize the color of his skin. "Of a different mother. You unattached? That's a good woman who could use a good man.

"Appreciate the vote of confidence but I have a thing for brunettes."

"Really? Kind of plain compared to Desiree but—hey, whatever you want. I'll get you her story and if you're still interested I'll set up a meet."

A double-sized piece of his great-aunt's pie just about did me in. We talked while I pigged out. Cube was an enigma but a genuine guy. We exchanged phone numbers.

I was certain he'd hook me up with Coffee Cup Face.

The Dark Evader.

The Zapper.

I suppressed a smile.

CHAPTER FORTY-FIVE

The Morning After

HER

Did Tom recognize me at the Stopped Clock?

That question kept me tossing and turning all night. I got home too exhausted to do anything but clean my face, wash out my favorite undies, put on my pajamas, and fall into bed.

Then stare at the ceiling. And fret. And fret. And fret.

After a squawking seabird brought me out of a fitful doze, it was my first thought.

I felt worse than if I violated my absolute maximum three-margarita limit.

He had to recognize me.

Or not.

A pair of glasses kept Clark Kent from being recognized as Superman. But this wasn't a comic book story. My disguise was more than a pair of glasses. Hair color and style. Eye color. Baggy clothing to hide my body. My lower face hidden by a coffee cup.

Tom had one quick look at me before he and Cube dragged the nasty-looking biker outside. I was certain he'd wash his hands after handling that guy. I rushed into the ladies' room but left the door cracked. I watched until he went into the men's room. My chance to hustle out of the diner with Desiree in tow.

No, he couldn't have recognized me.

Maybe.

I quit worrying about that and switched to my other worry. Why was Tom in the diner?

Following Desiree?

Following my alter ego Sabrina?

Meeting Cube?

I could eliminate that one. It was obvious Tom didn't know anybody in the Stopped Clock when he tamed that big drunk.

Maybe he was an undercover cop as Uncle Tony suggested. That could fit with Desiree's information about the task force thinking Uncle Tony was a mobster, even a hitman. If Tom was one of the cops digging into Uncle Tony, he knew about Sabrina's models and dancers.

Maybe he even knew about Sabrina's corporation.

Maybe he even knew who Sabrina really was.

That would mean he was toying with me all along.

Surely not. That electricity between us couldn't be faked. Could it? How about if he was really good?

I rubbed my temples.

It didn't matter. I had to keep him at arm's length until I found out who and what he was.

After Desiree and I exited stage left at the Stopped Clock and she drove off, I moved my car into the shadow of some trees in the far corner of the lot. A few minutes later the three bikers ran from the diner to their motorcycles at the other end of the plaza. Three more bikers rushed out of the strip bar. All six sped out of the plaza.

After another ten minutes I decided Tom was staying for a while and left. What was going on in there? Desiree could find out from Cube, but she was already puzzled by our quick departure so I couldn't ask. I had a good feeling about her but didn't trust her that much yet.

I closed my eyes but with my mind and stomach churning, sleep wasn't about to happen. Maybe a shower would revive me. I padded to the bathroom and set my phone on the vanity. I changed my mind about the shower, turned on the tub, and added citrusy bubble bath. The hot soak relaxed my body but not my mind. Tom joined me in the bubbles.

Why was he at the Stopped Clock? Was he a cop as Uncle Tony suggested? He handled that drunk effortlessly. The same way he did everything—including taking control when we were together. So annoying. So irritating. So...so...I pulled the plug and stood.

Uncle Tony. I had to call him. He'd want me to drive to Tampa thanks to his phone paranoia—which I now understood was justified. That would add up to more trips to Tampa in a couple of days than I usually made in a month.

First I needed to talk to Missy. Maybe she'd give me some perspective. I was hungry—make that ravenous. Grams' Coffee Spot was in our future. I grabbed my phone from the vanity with my dripping hand.

Her phone rang and rang. I was about to give up when she answered. "My word, I hope this is life threatening. Do you have any idea what the time is?"

"Time to get up?"

"Five-thirty."

"Damn! Sorry. I had a bad night and a worse evening. I need to talk to you. Grams' at eight?"

"Mmmff."

I took *mmmff* as a yes and clicked off.

With a forty percent chance of rain, my Chrysler might get wet while squiring Tom around today and going to dinner tonight. Maybe the cool front would pass through early and be dry.

Better yet, maybe it would pass through late with a downpour then Tom and I couldn't take that drive I promised. What the hell was I thinking when I did that?

I played the Sabrina game for years with no problems. Two days of Tom hanging around and it was in danger of collapsing. Was he the Lois Lane to my Clark Kent?

When the tub finished its slow drain, I turned on the shower and washed my hair.

I lathered my body.

And thought of Tom.

Damn.

CHAPTER FORTY-SIX

Oyster Tip

HIM

I sprang out of bed and raced to the bathroom.

The fog in my head lifted as pressure from beer, coffee, and club soda consumed at the Stopped Clock decreased. I staggered back to the bedroom on unwilling legs and checked the bedside clock. Less than two hours in the sack.

Fifteen minutes after I left the Stopped Clock at two in the morning and headed to Crooked Foot Key, the tracker on the Borismobile alerted. The signal showed he was probably headed here also, but I had to be sure. I stayed on the monitor until his car stopped at the Crooked Foot Sands Resort where he was staying. I hung on for another fifteen minutes until I was reasonably sure he was in for the night. All it cost me was another hour of badly needed sleep.

I was worn out but there wasn't a chance I'd be able to go back to sleep. And I had a lot to do before I met with Freddi and Missy this afternoon. I used the in-room coffee maker to brew a decent cup, shaved—contemplating if I should cultivate a Tom Selleck mustache—and parboiled myself in the shower followed by a cold rinse.

While standing under three pulsating showerheads—one of many special features of a spectacular but affordable Beachsider luxury accommodation—my contemplation switched from a mustache to business. I'd soon know the Zapper's identity thanks to Cube. The mystery of Freddi and Missy and their involvement in all this—not so easy. But I had this afternoon and evening to work on them.

Dark gray sports briefs, my favorite black golf shirt, khakis, and boat shoes. I glanced in the full-length mirror on the bathroom door. Ready to spend the day and evening with Freddi and Missy. But first—Madge. I wanted to get to Grams' before it opened at six-thirty in the hope I'd have a chance to talk to her before she got busy.

My phone emitted a resigned sigh. The Squid's ringtone. Six o'clock in the damn morning. I snapped, "Do you—"

The Squid finished my sentence. "Know what time it is? It's update time. Last I heard, you were chasing after homegrown and Russian mobsters. Then you don't bother to call?"

"It wasn't a dangerous situation. I was following a couple of women around."

"Sure. Just like tea and crumpets with Misha."

Not unexpectedly, he followed that with a snort and continued to snort as I recounted the night's action ending with Boris apparently returning to his room. During the Greasy incident he sounded like *el toro* in the ring. Finally he spoke. "Rocking along on everything except the job we're being paid to do."

I was ready for that. "It's all intertwined. This morning while Boris is catching up on sleep—like I should be doing—I'm working on the diamond scam Madge overheard Boris and Natasha talking about. Ralph Miller is either conspiring with them or is their intended victim. Before Grams' opens I'm going to catch Madge to get more details about that conversation. Immediately after that I'll see Chad about Ralph and Rita Miller."

"Chad the bartender?"

"The very same. You haven't lived until you've had beer on your corn flakes."

"The only reason I tolerate your bad lines is you're an almost mediocre investigator when I can get you to do some work."

"Chad said he knows a lot about Rita. I made a mistake about Freddi and Missy being a good way into Boris so I need to work the Miller angle to get to the scam. If Ralph's in on it, maybe I can be a potential victim and run a sting on him and Boris. If he's a victim, I'll try to get him to work with the police to run a sting on Boris. Either way, Rita is the key."

"Rita is the key?"

"From what Chad says, Ralph's not going to do anything without her approval. I hope to catch Chad at the beach. He works as a cabana boy during the day."

The Squid snorted one last time and clicked off.

I drove to Grams' but bypassed the spaces in front as well as the city lot. I parked in the spot on the side street I used for surveillance yesterday. At six-twenty the restaurant door banged open. Madge came out with a broom and began sweeping the sidewalk. I strode over and braving the cloud of dust said, "You can't make a sidewalk shine, Madge."

She spun around, squealed, and hugged me—with an accidental whack on the side of my head with the broom handle. "Magnum! I knew you'd be back."

I followed her inside. We slid into a booth. She waved at the cook and said, "One black."

He came out with a large cup, clunked it in front of me, and hustled back to the kitchen. She put her elbows on the table, made a chin rest with her hands, and looked at me expectantly.

Something about her made me want to smile. "I'm here to confess. I'm a private investigator."

A smug expression settled on her face. "Shocking."

"And I need some Russian translated to English at the rate of a hundred bucks an hour for your time."

She gave me a Cheshire Cat grin.

I slipped her the flash drive with the conversations on it. I couldn't tell which made her happier—the money or the chance to kick some Russian ass again.

"These recordings aren't very good. Needless to say, you can't tell anyone—even close friends—about them."

"After six years in intelligence I know how to keep a secret."

"What else can you tell me about the diamond scam and Ralph and Rita?"

"I already told you everything significant that I heard about the diamonds. Rita I don't know much about. She's not from around here and we don't travel in the same circles. I've known that sleazebag worm Ralph since grade school, but we'll have to talk about him later. In case you haven't noticed, we're getting stampeded."

A steady stream of bleary-eyed coffee-deprived zombies kept the door banging. A thin fiftyish blonde waitress was servicing the tables and trying to cover the counter, smiling all the way but glancing at Madge frequently.

Madge stood. "I have to handle the counter, not to mention keeping an eye on the kitchen. I'll have Agnes bring you breakfast—not the triple-bacon, tower-of-flapjacks special—one that will help you keep that physique trim." She gave me a bawdy wink and rushed off.

While I waited I replayed my encounter with Misha several times, hoping he would be an asset in freeing the trafficked girls. The clatter of plates, the aroma of bacon, friend-to-friend greetings across the room, and jabbered conversation made it hard to think.

Agnes quietly set a plate in front of me and refilled my coffee. She gave me a long look and said, "Madge is right. You do look like Magnum."

The plate held a huge egg-white vegetable omelet plus reputed aphrodisiacs—three raw oysters on the half shell with a dash of hot sauce on each. I looked at Madge behind the counter. She rolled her eyes toward the ceiling.

I laughed out loud. Never had a raw oyster for breakfast before, but what the hell. I conquered the hubcap-sized omelet and finished my breakfast oysters without a single *urp*. The counter stools were now filled hip-to-hip with people chowing down like they were late for work. Madge came out to assist Agnes with clearing the tables and taking orders.

She wrote on the back of a Grams' Coffee Spot business card. "My cell. Talk to you later, Magnum."

I slid out of the booth. "Here's my card and a fifty for breakfast and—let's call it an oyster tip."

She patted my cheek, rushed back to the counter, and started clearing plates.

I walked to my car. Not a bad morning's work on a few hours of sleep.

Got Madge on board and found out that—like beer—oysters aren't just for breakfast anymore.

All before seven-thirty.

Timing is everything.

If my timing held, Chad would open his beach business early and I'd talk with him before he got busy.

Then it would be Miller time.

Rita Miller time.

CHAPTER FORTY-SEVEN

Frozen

HER

I drove into the municipal lot next to Grams' Coffee Spot and straddled two spaces to protect the paint on my 300F. I was fifteen minutes early but loped to the café like a lioness homing in on prey to feed her cub.

Starving and absorbed in calculating the miles I'd have to run to burn off a pre-breakfast biscuit, I nearly collided with the Wicked Witch of Crooked Foot Key. Rita Miller scowled at me and—always the charmer—snarled, "Watch where you're going."

"Sorry, Rita. Rushing to a business breakfast." I didn't see any reason to tell her I was trying to get to some food before I ate my leather purse.

I nodded toward the takeout bag and cardboard tray with two large coffees she was carrying. "Looks like you and Ralph will be basking in the ambience of your office while you dine."

She looked down at the food and coffee like she was surprised they were there. "No. Yes. No. I mean yes. Work is piling up. No time to waste in a restaurant."

Obviously flustered, she turned away and hotfooted it to her car, which was parked on the street a few spaces away. That showed how focused I was on food. I hadn't noticed the Ritamobile, as I dubbed it—her bright red Mercedes convertible, the only one in town as far as I knew—right in front of me.

Something was nagging at me other than Rita being flustered. She was usually so annoyingly smug and condescending that I wouldn't have thought *flustered* was even in her vocabulary. Then it struck me. Ralph didn't drink coffee. It bothered his ulcer.

Rita also got flustered yesterday when I pressed her about Jules Armand. Could Armand have left Tammy Yates at the Ibis Inn and come back here to rendezvous with Rita? Busy boy. I had to assume she was going to meet him somewhere private like a motel—particularly if she was shtupping him.

Missy and I needed to know what was up with Armand, especially since she had threatened him for both of us in public. Also, I wasn't sure we were clear of him on the condo contract yet, regardless of Ralph's assurances. And what was Armand doing at a motel next door to one of Nick's strip clubs with the woman who had followed me all day?

Ignoring my growling stomach, I called Missy instead of going into Grams'.

Missy sounded very cheery when she said, "Good morning, Freddi. Be there in five and looking forward to a divine egg-white veggie omelet. I might plunge off the deep end and have a piece of whole wheat toast with it."

"Uh, breakfast is going to be delayed."

I gave her a quick rundown on Armand and Tammy Yates hooking up last night. I explained my suspicion about Rita going to meet Armand now. Missy could best help by immediately going to see Ralph about something then discreetly watching for Rita to show up.

"Please spare me, hair gods," she said. "I don't think I can handle a crooked toupee this early."

"I'll switch to a less conspicuous vehicle to search for Rita and Armand. I can bring you a Grams' On-the-Run Biscuit Sandwich if you'd like."

"Lord no. Better to be hungry than have to do a dozen extra workouts."

I rushed to my car then sped to our office and parked in the small lot behind the building. I was in luck. Our landlord's car—a blend-in-with-the-traffic silver Honda—and his white panel truck were both there. Aaro was a handyman and did almost all of the repair work on his properties. His office was the smallest of the three in the building. I went around to the front and stepped into the North Pole. He was sitting behind his desk, possibly frozen in place.

"Damn, Aaro, it's even colder in here than in our office and probably Finland in the dead of winter."

"Ah, the lovely Fredricka. Always with the jokes. Everything okay? Is something broken?"

"My convertible just started making a funny noise. I don't want to drive it till I have it looked at and Missy and I have four hot prospects this morning. Two each."

"You need a ride home to get your Chevy?"

"I had to put it in the shop yesterday. Murphy's Law. Could I please borrow your car for a few hours?"

"Who is this Murphy and what is my name? It is Aaro Haataja—not Hertz, not Avis."

"Murphy's Law is an Americanism. I'll fill the tank before I return it."

He smiled. "For you, my lovely Fredricka, anything. Unfortunately, I must have my car this morning but my panel truck you can use."

I couldn't imagine why he needed his car. Mostly it was his transportation between home and office. He used the panel truck to visit and maintain his properties. Then I realized I no longer had his undivided attention. I looked down at where he was staring. The frigid air had my thermometers poking against my thin bra and top. He handed me the keys and I left through the back door.

His panel truck smelled like stale cigar smoke. I lowered the windows, walked to the rear, and opened both cargo doors. The Gulf breeze blew through from back to front and took the smoke smell with it.

Shelves neatly stocked with parts, tools, and toolboxes lined the sides of the cargo bay. A stack of coveralls in a clear plastic bag sat on the floor behind the passenger's seat. I closed the doors, got in, and started the engine. Then I knew why he loaned it to me instead of his car. The tank was less than a quarter full and would cost a fortune to fill.

I was had.

Maybe Missy was doing better with the ever-despicable Ralph Miller.

CHAPTER FORTY-EIGHT

Lolita

HIM

Two meager hours of sleep after chasing the Zapper around had my eyes drooping as I parked at the Beachsider Resort. If Chad was working the beach already, as I hoped, I should have time to catch some Zs after I talked with him. I walked around the building, stood on the patio, and surveyed the beach.

The morning was gorgeous, sunny with a few wispy clouds and a steady cooling breeze off the Gulf. Rain was predicted, but it looked like the cool front was going to come through dry. A number of large umbrellas shading beach chairs dotted the sand. My guess was Chad would do a good business today. His rental stand—protected from the sun by a blue canopy attached to the building—was at the other end of the patio. But no Chad.

As I worked my way through the umbrellaed tables and chairs crowding the patio, he wheeled a huge cooler out of an Employees Only door and maneuvered it behind his stand. He looked up and said, "Hey, it's you. Tom, right? Want a beer?"

Well, what the hell? Breakfast oysters needed to be washed down with a breakfast beer. And it would help me sleep later. "Got one of those Cigar City lagers?"

He rooted around in the cooler, found a bottle, popped the top, and handed it to me. "Let's take this table so if an early customer shows up I'm like right here to handle it."

We sat and I said, "Was that Rita coming in as I left yesterday?"

He nodded. "To kiss and make up. Not this time. She went too far."

That sounded like a guy who wanted to talk. "Something to do with a Ralph deal? A guy I've worked with down south is trying to get me into a Tampa real estate development that Ralph's in."

A frown of surprise showed on Chad's face as his head jerked back. "I've never heard of that dude doing anything outside of Crooked Foot Key where he's a big fish. If he cuts too many corners, he can squirm out. Be careful of him handling the money. You should like count it before and after—and during. But Rita wasn't here about real estate."

"So Rita wouldn't be a part of it? I thought you said she was the power behind the throne."

"She is. Whatever Ralph does, Rita's pulling his strings. What he does and when, where, and who he does it with. She's street savvy and has him wrapped. Nothing surprising there. That's her talent."

If Chad was right, Ralph couldn't do anything with Boris without a stamp of approval from Rita. But where was Chad coming from?

"How has she gone too far?" I said. "I need to know. This is a make-or-break situation for me."

He tried to hold my gaze but after a second looked down and softly said, "I want to help you but..."

His emotions were in play so I went into it obliquely. "How long have you known her?"

He took a deep breath and held it a few seconds like he was making a decision. "When I was five and she was six, her family moved in next door to mine in a little town about a hundred miles from here, close to Fort Myers."

Back to when he was five? This wasn't going to be quick. I sipped my Cigar City.

"She was a vamp."

I choked on my beer. "At six?"

"Dude, I was five."

"Ah yes, the older woman. You're right, a vamp is in the eye of the beholder."

"The next day—the day after she moved in—she showed me hers and demanded I show her mine. I wasn't exactly sure what it all meant but she said it would be our little secret. That was the beginning. We were only six months apart so we were in the same grade. Whenever she needed something, she'd arrange for us to have another little secret."

He rubbed his hand across his face. "As soon as I reached puberty she taught me how to make it a big secret. She had me so wrapped I didn't like figure out I was wrapped until I was fourteen. By then the hormones were running hard."

"Yours or hers?"

"Both—but mine weren't in the same league. She had the body and moves of a woman. At fourteen she got involved with a successful—for that town—businessman. He was in his forties. She bled him dry. Besides the Lolita thing hanging over his head, he couldn't get enough of her, no matter how risky. He was addicted to her. It went on for years."

"How did a forty-year-old get hooked up with a fourteen-year-old girl? Did she babysit his kids?"

"She took an after-school job at his jewelry store. They *played* after the store closed. She progressed from cleanup girl to records keeper to salesperson by the time she was sixteen. High commissions, their cover story for her spending money and being able to afford a car. She had a better one than her sugar daddy, who was slowly going broke and maybe crazy too."

That surprised me. "Going broke? How much does a high school girl need? Was she supporting her parents?"

"Not her parents. Her bad boy. When she was fifteen she fell for Erik, an outlaw fresh out of jail for stealing cars. She was as hooked on him as her sugar daddy was on her. Erik went from riding a ratty Harley and sleeping on friends' couches to a muscle car and an apartment."

"Rita paid for it with sugar-daddy money?"

"Erik didn't believe in work unless you count stealing. Mean as a snake. He was twenty at the time, at least six-foot-four, all muscle, lightning bolt and barbed wire tats on both arms, bushy red hair and big droopy mustache. Like a Viking. Even his name—Erik Thoreson. I told you Rita looks like a Norse goddess. In this case the goddess worshipped the Viking. He treated her like dirt."

"How do you know all this?"

Chad lowered his head. "I spied on her whenever I could. Even worse, she told me a lot of it."

He lowered his head farther. "There were times she wanted something from me or just to talk and we renewed our secret. I couldn't stop myself from doing whatever she wanted—to settle for her scraps. I guess that made me worse than her sugar daddy because at least he didn't know she was doing other guys."

"You were just a kid."

"When it first started—but it hasn't ended yet. The day after we graduated, she like took off with Erik, but she always let me know where she was. It wasn't long before Erik went to prison again—a hard fall this time. Every place she moved she found a new sugar daddy. I'd move to that town to do her bidding and take her scraps. Pathetic."

He looked off in the distance. "When you're dealing with Ralph, you're dealing with her. Ralph is the only sugar daddy she ever married, maybe because she's getting older. I have to break free of her. And this latest thing is too much so maybe this will do it."

"What does she want you to do?"

"Something illegal." He shook his head like he couldn't believe it. "She got wind of a guy trying to unload stolen diamonds. Right up her alley. She's an expert from her years in the jewelry store, and she has lots of shady contacts. She'd get Ralph to buy them and I'd be the go-between to deliver them to whoever she sells them to."

"Except you aren't going for it."

"Hell no, I'm not going to prison for anyone. I'd be the one at risk, not her. So she was like pissed at me. Then yesterday she comes in here and says everything is okay. All that means is something's changed and she doesn't need me for that anymore but she wants to keep me on the hook for future use."

He rubbed his eyes with his thumb and forefinger. "But I'm not falling for it again. I'm finally done with her. I'd move away but I have too much going on here. I'm making more money than I ever have with bartending and my half of the beach concession."

"You've saved me, Chad. My next deal has to be a winner. I can't afford to be associated with Ralph and Rita and her games."

"I never told anybody around here that Rita and I grew up together. I'm trusting you to keep it confidential. I don't need any trouble."

I made a zipping motion across my lips and gave him two fifties. "Again, a little something for looking out for me."

We stood. He said, "The beer's on me. We like had a reverse

role. The customer listening to the bartender's troubles."

I gave him my card. "If you see or think of anything else, there's more where that hundred came from."

Walking to my room I thought about Rita being a jewelry expert and Ralph buying stolen diamonds. It seemed Ralph was going to be the victim of Boris's scam with an unintentional assist from Rita. Or *was* it unintentional? With the devious Rita in the mix, it was too soon to approach Ralph about working with law enforcement to bring Boris down.

Time to update The Squid and grab some badly needed sleep. I had to be sharp if I was going to pry anything out of Freddi later.

I was almost certain she and Missy weren't criminally involved with Boris.

On the other hand, why was Natasha following her?

CHAPTER FORTY-NINE

Rita's Romp

HER

I called Missy.

She answered on the first ring. "I saw Ralph—thank God his rug was in place—and told him I must have gotten confused about where to meet you, his office or ours. I said I didn't want Rita to catch us in there alone and give her the wrong idea. That brightened his beady eyes. He said Rita had gone to her hairdresser in Tampa. I skedaddled out of there and am now sitting in front of the T-shirt shop up the street. I don't think she's coming here, at least not for hours."

"I borrowed Aaro's panel truck," I said. "Let's cruise the area and see if we can spot Rita's car. She must be fairly close or she wouldn't have gotten hot coffees at Grams'. I'll start at the old resort a few miles north of the Royal Squid and work my way south to our office."

"In that case, I'll check from here to the south end of the island. You do remember we have a showing at ten?"

"That gives us almost two hours. Keep an eye out for Armand's black Lexus. And Rita might be parked near a motel, rather than in the lot."

As I passed the Royal Squid, I started feeling good about my chances. The landmass necked down to a spit barely wider than the highway and stayed that narrow until it flared to make space for the most bizarre structure in the area, the Paradise Resort.

Exotic and luxurious in its day but ugly to the bone. A sort of Ali Baba look with domes and spires on top of a standard Florida two-story rectangular motel with external walkways. A courtyard swimming pool with an elaborate sliding board setup. A little seedy now but still attractive to families because of the pool and the Gulf.

The north side of the property—increasingly popular with the hookup crowd—was bordered by mangroves, which prevented the parking on that side from being visible from the highway. What better place for the Ritamobile?

I caught myself humming the theme from *The Pink Panther* as I left the highway. I went past the front of the building, then turned left into the secluded parking area. Nine rooms on both the ground floor and the second floor faced the parking area.

Parked in front of the middle room was the Ritamobile. I would have done a fist pump except the TV detectives I watched never fist pumped. Was she in that room or any of the rooms on that side? The parking spots weren't marked with room numbers. Jules Armand's black Lexus wasn't around. Damn. Who was she with? Was there yet another player in this whatever it was that Missy and I—and Sabrina—were caught up in?

My problems just multiplied. I went from simply verifying Rita had something going with Armand to learning who she was with, then determining if he was a part of Armand's game. Or was he involved in Nick's organization and whatever was going on between Nick and Armand?

I had to try to see Rita's playmate and get his tag number for Uncle Tony to feed to his magic connections. I called Missy with the news. She said she'd cover our ten o'clock alone if I couldn't make it.

An equipment enclosure sat at the rear edge of the parking lot, close to the mangroves. An eight-foot chain-link fence adorned with *DANGER* signs surrounded a ten-foot-tall shed, yellow pumps, and heavy-duty pipes. I had no idea what it was, but a panel truck wouldn't look out of place. I backed in and parked with a perfect view of the Ritamobile. The bad news was the shed blocked my view of half of the rooms and parked vehicles.

My dark blue pencil skirt, cream-colored V-necked silk top, and dark blue medium heels would be wildly out of place here. I turned and looked at the plastic bag I noticed earlier. It was a gift from the gods—a stack of several freshly laundered tan coveralls.

I hunched over, stepped between the seats into the rear, took off my skirt and top, and put on a pair of coveralls. Aaro had an inch or so and maybe thirty pounds on me, so the fit was baggy and long but the cuffs covered my high heels. I grabbed a painter's cap hanging from a shelf, pulled the brim low, and got out. I hoped nobody would pay attention to a worker in coveralls servicing the whatchamacallit.

The sun was beating down so after I discreetly snapped a pic of the Ritamobile, I went around to the other side of the shed. I was reasonably comfortable there in the shade with a nice breeze off the Gulf. I noticed a fixed ladder on the back side of the shed to provide access to some gizmos on the roof. At this time of day and this time of year, that side was in the shade also. I could peer around the sides of the shed and if I saw something that should be photographed, scoot up the ladder and shoot over the roof.

If I were on the inside of the fence.

The gate in the chain-link fence had the Big Ben of padlocks on it, but the top of the gate was a steel tube, not twisted wire like the fence. I could do this. I was a strong and fit dancer. I zipped my phone into a pocket, put my fingers and one toe into the links, and after two quick steps gripped the top of the gate with both hands preparing to haul myself over the top.

A giant palmetto bug ran across my left hand.

I shrieked, shuddered, and yanked my hand off the gate and shook it like crazy. I hung by one hand like a chimp mugging for a photo op. All I needed to do was roll my lips. I opened my right hand and dropped to the ground. When I straightened up I was next to the giant padlock. In frustration I slammed the damn thing with the side of my fist. It popped open.

Like they say, bigger ain't always better.

I went through the gate and up the ladder to check the vantage point. A clear view of every room and car. Perfect. I was about to go back down the ladder when the door to the room in front of the Ritamobile swung open. I activated the camera in my phone. Rita came out in a rush, opened the trunk of her car, grabbed a small travel bag, and pressed the button for the trunk lid to close.

Click, click, click. Got it all, but nearly missed the main event.

A man emerged from the darkness beyond the open door. Shirtless, muscular, barefoot, frayed jean shorts, at least six-foot-four, barbed wire and lightning bolt tats, bushy reddish-blond hair and thick droopy moustache. *Click. Click. Click.*

Who the hell was this?

He stepped two parking spots toward the beach and stopped by a battered orange Ford Mustang with hood scoops then popped the trunk. *Click. Click. Click.* He reached into a cooler and produced a bottle of champagne. He showed it to Rita as they went back into the room. Champagne for breakfast. She kissed his bare shoulder. Rita was ready for a romp.

I went to Aaro's panel truck, changed into my clothes, neatly folded the coveralls, and returned them to their plastic bag. Using Cellphony I texted Rita's playmate's tag number to Uncle Tony.

I called Missy on my real phone. "Mission accomplished, and we have time for breakfast before our ten o'clock."

"My stomach will be eternally grateful."

This was way too lucky.

Something bad was sure to balance it out.

On the way to Grams', I called Uncle Tony on Cellphony.

"Tomorrow," he said. "Can Sabrina come here tomorrow? We have two big catering events tonight and a birthday luncheon in the banquet room at noon."

"Perfect. She has appointments later and what she has is important but not urgent."

Missy and I had a quick breakfast and I brought her up to date on the happenings at the Stopped Clock last night. We finalized the sale of a condo at our ten o'clock. I gassed up Aaro's panel truck and returned it. I met Missy at the gym. After a hard but fast workout I told her I'd see her at the office at two when we were scheduled to meet Tom. I dashed home, took a quick shower, and set the alarm for an hour nap.

I needed to be at the top of my form for seven or eight hours of mental jousting with Tom McCall.

CHAPTER FIFTY

Tie Game

HIM

At two o'clock I walked into Bikini Realty. The tropical furnishings and colorful prints on the walls were attractive. The two babes rising off the couch to greet me with warm smiles made it the most beautiful office I'd ever seen. No wonder Boris got so bumfuzzled when he was negotiating with them.

I felt much better. A few hours of snoozing had helped overcome the sleep deprivation I suffered since arriving in Crooked Foot Key. Hugs from Freddi and Missy briefly pushed Boris and Nick and diamonds and trafficked girls from my mind. Was there a little extra oomph in Freddi's hug? Or had I done that? Or both of us? Or was it my imagination?

The weather was sublime. A weak cool front had pushed through, lowering the temperature and the humidity to chamber-of-commerce levels. As before, I got in the backseat of Freddi's convertible. Too much sun to drop the top but Freddi had me unzip the rear isinglass window and she lowered the others. Shade and invigorating flow-through ventilation. My guides didn't seem the least bit concerned about the wind blowing through their hair.

The fresh air configuration made conversation challenging, but Freddi and Missy provided a running narrative about the area as we drove from place to place. I wasn't able to ask questions that could give me insight into Freddi. We looked at sites and structures on Crooked Foot Key and in run-down—or in their words, "as-yet-to-reach-their-potential"—areas on the mainland.

The weather held but the atmosphere heated up every time I caught Freddi's glance in the rear-view mirror or we accidentally bumped each other checking out a property.

We stopped at a defunct ranch about halfway to Tampa. We drove the roads within the property boundaries then stopped at the badly damaged main house and got out. Missy said, "As you can see there's no point in going inside. It might even be dangerous. A few years ago, a small twister paid a visit and showed that Mother Nature is boss."

Freddi pointed to a crushed place in the center of the gable roof. "A huge oak tree fell there. After it was removed, the owner had it chopped into firewood for revenge."

"Sounds like he's a character," I said.

"He's more interested in what happens to the property than he is in selling it. He put a lot of restrictions on the sale, including his approval of the buyer's plans—which is why it hasn't sold yet. That's also why we have the listing. We're known for working with responsible developers—selling already-built condo units for Ralph Miller notwithstanding. These restrictions might scare off your investors."

"Not the guy I have in mind." Time to move this feel-good-about-the-planet stuff to info I needed. "Do you ladies have anything closer to Tampa?"

"This is the closest," Missy said. "Every once in a while we connect a buyer to a realtor there and get a split commission. Usually we do our dead-level best to stay away from that mess up there and count our blessings for Crooked Foot Key."

That made sense. Not likely that these Crooked Foot babes

would be working the Tampa market an hour away. So what was Freddi doing there with Natasha tailing her?

I looked at Freddi. Worry showed on her face but she quickly covered it with a smile and said, "Ralph's enough of a headache without going all the way to Tampa to add to it."

Something was bothering her. Something in Tampa? After spending hours with her, that was all that I learned. Maybe I'd do better tonight.

My phone vibrated. Text from Jamie. *Came in early. Something happening. Seven men in and out of alley at PFZ. No sign of Borismobile. Natasha's car gone from Ibis lot.*

Freddi raised her eyebrows. I smiled at her. "No problem. Just a friend busting my chops about the NFL draft in a couple of weeks." I swept my gaze across the horizon. "Tomorrow I need to learn more about the restrictions and get a map of this property for my client."

"I have to say we don't have any other suitable possibilities to show you today," Missy said. "If you've seen enough here we can go to our office, go over everything in detail, and still be on time for our reservation at the Royal Squid."

After Jamie's text I needed to have my car with me. I shook my head. "I'm tired and dusty. If you ladies drop me at the Beachsider, I'll revive myself with a quick shower and meet you in the bar for a cocktail before dinner. Is ten o'clock tomorrow morning a good time for me to get the info about the ranch?"

"That would be a delightful time. We'll have coffee brewing," Missy said.

My phone buzzed again. Another text message. My eyes almost popped out of my head when I saw the first line. *This is Misha.* It was the big Russian who confronted me at the Valley of Love. *Action tonight. Contact later.* The long shot paid off. Or he's setting me up.

I felt Freddi's stare. She said, "More football?"

"Latest rumor about the Dolphins first-round pick."

Our conversation during the trip back consisted primarily of Freddi probing. I stuck to my cover story and ad-libbed generalities that couldn't be easily proven or disproven. No information flowing from me to her—or her to me. Tie game. Extra innings tonight if play wasn't called because of Misha or Boris or Nick or trafficked girls or the Zapper or...

When they let me out I said, "See you at the Royal Squid. I'm looking forward to the fabulous food—and special company."

A shower was a good idea, not just an excuse. I was still dragging. First I checked the tracker on the Borismobile for the hundredth time today. No movement. A quick shower, fresh clothes, and a call to Jamie.

No changes on his end. He was worried about the earlier activity. It was the most he'd seen since the day the trafficked girls were moved.

I plonked onto a stool at the Royal Squid bar at six-fifteen. To my surprise Chad grinned at me from the other side and stuck out his hand. "The regular guy is off sick. My business partner is handling the beach this afternoon, and this is my day off at the Boardroom so when they called me, I could cover."

He looked around at the nearly empty room then spoke quietly. "Hot news. I saw Rita today with a guy I've never seen before. They were in her car—a bright red Mercedes convertible, and I mean bright—must be a special paint job. Top down so I got a good look at him. Dark wavy hair, brushed back, sat taller than her so maybe around six feet."

That had to be Boris. "Where were they?"

"Driving by the Beachsider as I was crossing over to the

employee parking lot around two. After they passed me I watched her turn into the Sands, two resorts up the street."

The Crooked Foot Sands—where Boris was staying. Definitely had to be Boris. Part of the diamond deal or hanky-panky? "Do you know if she stayed?"

He shook his head. "She came back out onto the street about fifteen seconds later, just enough time to drop him off." He leaned toward me and spoke even more quietly. "And then it gets better. Do you remember her bad boy?"

"Of course. The Viking."

"Rita goes by me, turns at the corner, and gives a thumbs-up to a ratty orange Mustang headed the other way, driven by none other than Erik Thoreson."

"Are you sure?"

"Once you see Erik, you never forget him. And speaking of people you never forget..." He nodded toward the door.

I slipped him a fifty as I swiveled my barstool and watched Bikini Realty walk in and light up the room.

CHAPTER FIFTY-ONE

Beach Formal

HER

Tom had a good idea about freshening up before dinner—although I was suspicious of his motive. He didn't say anything until shortly after he got that text. Now he'd have his car at the restaurant in case he decided to rush off like he did Sunday night.

I didn't have any success pulling information out of him during the tour while I was dressed professionally. Maybe something sexier would distract him enough to lower his guard. But not too sexy. I already stupidly said he could drive my 300F, which to me was more intimate than a French kiss.

As I stood in front of my closet considering my options, Missy called. "Any idea what you're wearing tonight?"

"Still trying to decide."

"Mercy me. What *are* you thinking? Beach Formal, Beach Formal, Beach Formal. If it doesn't make that man's jaw drop open and the words flow like syrup at a sugar cane mill, what is going to? And I have this fetching little frock that hasn't seen the light of day yet, other than the bulb in the closet."

I laughed. Beach Formal was our term for clothes to seal the deal when a recalcitrant buyer needed a nudge. I said, "Tom's not a buyer at this point."

"No, but you should be. Reel him in, no matter who or what he is. The intensity in his eyes—My, my! That's a *man*! And don't pick me up, you hear. I'll meet you there. After you take him for a ride in your convertible, he might even it up by taking you for a ride. My mama would tan my hide for not having good sense enough to be out of the way."

Missy had a way with words. I fought back another laugh and said in a strangled voice, "That's not going to happen. However, we do need to crack the Tom McCall code and figure out who he is, what he's doing, and why he's hanging around us."

"Maybe he's what he says he is."

"No way, not after he showed up at the Stopped Clock. I'll meet you outside the bar at six forty-five so the Bikini Realty tag team can enter together to maximize the Beach Formal effect."

I grabbed my best Beach Formal from its hanger—a form-fitting halter-topped dress with spaghetti straps and an almost-not-there built-in bra. The dress didn't come close to the tops of my knees with a slit up the right side to the middle of my thigh. The black silky material had a faint pattern of lavender orchids in a line extending from the right breast past the left hip. Strappy but casual black heels and wispy black panties—that Tom would never see—completed my outfit.

Uncomfortable thoughts flashed through my mind as I dressed. Tom could be investigating me. He could be trying to pin something on Uncle Tony. He could be a married man with six kids. I vowed to keep him at arm's length until I solved the riddle of Tom McCall.

Missy was there when I arrived. She was spectacular in a strapless gold print sarong that stopped four inches above her knees. We walked into the bar. Tom's face showed Missy was right about wearing Beach Formal tonight. His lingering hug was the hardest yet. I couldn't stop myself from returning it.

We had a repeat of our Sunday night drinks but didn't have time to finish them before our reservation was called. We carried our rum-spiked Arnold Palmers to our table. Tom was taking charge again, but this time it was fine with me. I wanted him comfortable and confident and off-balance under the influence of Beach Formal.

"I know the Snapper Française is terrific," Tom said. "Should I order it again, or do they have another dish you recommend?"

"An easy-to-eat Frutti di Mare," Missy said. "The shrimp, scallops, clams, and mussels are out of their shells. With fresh snapper chunks. The white wine sauce is to die for."

"*Da morire* as they say in Italy. I'll get a bottle of Vermentino—one of my favorite Italian whites—if they have it and if you two are agreeable."

"*Da morire*?" I said. "Do you speak Italian?"

"A phrase here and there. I spent a summer near Milano when I wore a younger man's clothes."

Tom had wasted no time. Before the menus arrived, we had our meals and wine chosen. But the bit about Italy showed he was opening up about his past. Except he wasn't. When I asked about his time in Italy, he spoke vaguely about being there as a student fifteen years ago.

Most of the evening he subtly guided our conversation toward Missy and me and Bikini Realty. When Missy got into some funny anecdotes about Ralph Miller—including his toupee—she mentioned Rita. He seemed to take a slight interest in her but nothing that couldn't be attributed to idle curiosity about that odd couple.

He expressed amazement that I was still so close with my college roommate in Tampa. That led to other questions about Tampa, which worried me. Did he recognize me up there? I had no idea how or why he was in the Stopped Clock thanks to his conversational elusiveness. So much for Beach Formal. It wasn't working on this guy.

Despite that, it was a great evening with fantastic food and wine, incredible weather, and fun conversation with Missy in top comic form. And as much as I fought it, the heat continued to build between Tom and me. The last thing I wanted—at least until I knew what he was up to. I wanted him to be what he said but there was the Stopped Clock to explain.

Missy finished her espresso and got up. "Tom, thank you so much for another absolutely delightful evening. Enjoy your test drive in Freddi's baby. The last time she let someone drive it was... never." They hugged and she waggled her fingers at me as she left smiling.

Tom turned toward me. "You don't have to go through with it."

"I always do what I say I'm going to do." I stood. "I'm stopping at the ladies' room. Meet you at my car." I walked away very conscious of the meager built-in bra and the slit in my skirt, chastising myself for having made the commitment for him to drive my 300F.

In the bathroom I said, "Mirror, mirror on the wall, who's the most nervous person of all." I brushed my teeth to nullify the garlic. "I can handle this." The mirror didn't respond so I went to my car.

"It's a gorgeous night," Tom said. "Shall we drop the top?"

I breathed a little easier. He was only interested in driving my classic beauty. "Great idea. Here's the key. Go north. Toward the end of the island, we'll run out of civilization and come to the curves I told you about."

CHAPTER FIFTY-TWO

Illegal

HIM

Freddi's car was going to be a treat. I drove a number of cars from its era back when I worked at the restoration garage. Never a 300F with Ram Induction carburation and torsion bar suspension.

I turned north on Gulfway Drive and was instantly lost in the moment. Beautiful Freddi beside me, a spectacular moon above, and a fabulous car purring down the road. I passed the turnoff to I-275 on the right and a mile later the Paradise Resort on the left. We crossed a small bridge a half-mile farther on. Gulfway Drive morphed into Crooked Foot Preserve Trail.

The road narrowed and curved right and left as it wound along a ridge of ground between bogs and sloughs. The aroma of the Gulf and natural vegetation added to the primordial atmosphere. Freddi picked a good road. The car handled it smoothly as I pushed well above the speeds posted on the curve-warning signs.

I was enjoying the drive and thinking about Freddi. Her letting me drive this car, so near and dear to her heart, had an intimate feel to it. The heat, the electricity between us was palpable. The knee bumping at dinner and the hugs had me feeling like a teenaged boy anticipating a first-date kiss. I was almost certain she wasn't involved with Boris or anybody criminally, but what was she doing in Tampa with Natasha following her?

And her dress—which had to be illegal in at least fourteen

states—with Missy in that equally illegal tropical getup. Is that how they fried Boris's brain? They might not be criminals, but something was up. Especially with Freddi. I had to stay away from her until I figured it out.

Before I knew it, we were near the end of Crooked Foot Preserve Trail. Through the trees the headlights reflected off the dead-end barricade around the next bend. A damaged curve-warning sign lay in the muck to my right. Gravel from the shoulder had been kicked up on the pavement.

I stood on the brake until I was about to skid. I released the brake and went into the curve. More gravel. No way to stop before the barricade. I used the slipperiness of the scattered gravel to help me as I cut the wheel and powered through a skidding one-eighty that had the Chrysler sliding backward. I watched the barricade growing larger in the rearview mirror.

CHAPTER FIFTY-THREE

Dead End

HER

From the start it was obvious Tom was a top-notch driver. He had my baby hugging the road through the curves. Usually when I was on this road, I was in my Chevy, keeping my skills sharp.

I was enjoying the exhilarating ride under a beautiful moon when we reached the last curve before the dead end. He went into it scary fast. Gravel that shouldn't have been there was scattered across the road making it even scarier.

After a masterful job of threshold braking, controlling a gravelly skid, and powering through a one-eighty, we slid backward toward the barricade, tires screeching.

We weren't going to make it.

With only a couple of feet left between the rear bumper and the barricade, the tires caught and we shot forward, heading back the way we came.

I exhaled.

He pulled off the road into a clearing facing the Gulf. He gripped my hand. "Sorry about that. The loose gravel made it more exciting than it needed to be. But your baby performed beautifully."

The rush from the near-crash and amazement at his driving and calmness had me speechless. Who was this guy?

CHAPTER FIFTY-FOUR

Overwhelmed

HIM

I gripped the steering wheel firmly. The tires caught a few feet from the barricade. We shot forward. An observation point on my right overlooked a bog and the Gulf beyond. I pulled in and stared at Freddi. She seemed a little stunned. Not as much as I expected. A very cool lady.

I took her hand, squeezed it, and tried to keep things light. "The loose gravel made that more exciting than it needed to be."

The warmth of her hand and staring into her eyes overwhelmed me. I didn't care if she was an axe murderer or plotting to set off a nuclear device in downtown Tampa. My hand—unbidden—raised hers to my lips. I kissed her fingertips then her palm. She shuddered. We leaned across the armrest and kissed.

CHAPTER FIFTY-FIVE

Moonlight Madness

HER

He lifted my hand and kissed my fingertips and my palm. He leaned across the foot-wide armrest separating the bucket seats and kissed my lips.

Whether it was the rush, the electricity between us, the passionate kiss, or Cupid's arrow—no matter who or what he was—I needed him desperately.

The fantastic full moon shined brightly on us.

It was madness.

I needed him now. Right now!

The armrest kept us apart.

I broke the kiss and thumped the armrest. It raised and pivoted on a hinge toward the backseat revealing a flat panel.

"What's that?"

"My favorite uncle did it."

"Uncle?"

"He's a worry wart even though he's a race car driver. That panel slides open. It's a gun compartment."

"Are you going to shoot me?"

"Only if you don't get it."

"Get what?"

I put my hand behind his neck.

"The armrest is no longer in our way."

CHAPTER FIFTY-SIX

Separation

HIM

Freddi's molten stare burned away any microscopic shred of caution that might have remained in my professional ethics.

With the armrest out of the way there was nothing separating us.

Soon, not even clothing.

The most incredible passionate experience of my life.

CHAPTER FIFTY-SEVEN

Prom Queen

HER

Crazy. I just made love in a car like a virginal prom queen who decided that after the dance was over she and her boyfriend would change the virginal part.

Even crazier. The best ever.

We were still coupled tightly across the seats. Tom was the lover in the Pointer Sisters' classic song about a man with a slow hand, a lover with an easy touch. My body continued to pulse.

I didn't want to move but we had to before we were discovered by hordes of mosquitos or a bored deputy looking to roust teenage lovers.

How embarrassing would that be?

I violated my resolve to keep him at arm's length. He could be a cop, a con man, a thief, a killer, a married man with six kids, a butcher, a baker, a candlestick maker. I didn't care. I had plans for him. Pick up his car at the Royal Squid and go to my place.

Time to find out how much stamina Mister Calm, Cool, and Collected Tom McCall had.

But for now, a little more here—just like this.

I wouldn't have thought it possible, but I was on the verge of another bonus.

CHAPTER FIFTY-EIGHT

Mood Interruptus

HIM

We lay across the seats, Freddi's lips on my neck. The moment too intimate to speak.

Pure bliss.

A poet might say it was a melding of souls.

She pushed against me. Her breath caught.

My phone buzzed.

Text message.

CHAPTER FIFTY-NINE

New Driver

HER

I tried to keep my fingernails out of his back but my bonus was near. I vaguely heard the buzzing of a cell phone. His arm moved and he started fumbling around in his clothes on the floor.

What the hell?

I moved my mouth from his neck. "Are you thinking about reading that text?"

"I have to. This could be life or death. If you knew the situation you'd want me to—"

An instant volcanic reaction. I was fuming. This was nothing to him. "Sure—a life-or-death situation that didn't show up until after I made a fool of myself."

I grabbed my clothes from the pile on the floor, grateful for the built-in bra, and stuffed my panties into my purse.

"Freddi, sweetheart. Trust me. This is real—"

"I just trusted you and look what it got me. Rejection, embarrassment, and a mosquito bite on my butt. I was dumb enough to think it was real."

"It is real. I've never—"

"Don't say another word. Get dressed. I'm driving."

I dropped the armrest into place.

CHAPTER SIXTY

Sound of Silence

HIM

Now I understood the cliché about the silence being deafening. Freddi was pissed and sped through the curves even faster than I had. She didn't speak a word. Her driving spoke for her. She wanted to get rid of me as fast as possible.

I didn't speak either. I started to, but Freddi shot me a withering look before my opening *ah* got completely out of my mouth. I wanted to know what the text message said, but if she saw me reading it she'd go ballistic. Well, she was already ballistic. Was it possible to go ballistic-er? The message didn't matter at this point. There wasn't anything I could do about it until I got to my car—which wouldn't be long the way she was driving.

I was totally bummed out, as Chad might say. I had the most incredible experience of my life with this woman, and judging by the scratches—gouges—on my back, it was pretty good for her too. Yet here we were, not uttering a sound.

What could I do? She already accused me of coming up with the life-or-death situation only after we made love so anything I said along those lines wouldn't work.

I couldn't tell her the truth about why I was in Crooked Foot Key. I didn't know her game. She was connected with Ralph and Rita Miller. As well as Boris—Jules Armand to her. And Natasha was following her around. It seemed remote that Freddi was involved in the diamond scam but I couldn't eliminate her one hundred percent. I intuitively believed she wasn't a crook, but women had fooled me before—including my ex-wife.

As I thought about our evening, some facts bubbled through the lasciviousness. Her favorite uncle was a race car driver. She was driving like a professional on this winding road. Had she gotten that from her uncle?

I didn't really care where she got the skill. What other woman had I recently encountered who could drive like this? The Zapper. Something bothered me from the first time I saw her on Jamie Bond's video screen. Something was almost familiar about her.

Freddi had ash blonde hair in a long shag cut or whatever it's called. The Zapper had straight shoulder-length black hair. A wig would explain that.

Freddi was a little taller than the Zapper. Except for our first encounter on the beach, Freddi always wore heels. The Zapper wore flats.

Freddi had a great body. The Zapper's clothes were so loose it was hard to judge what was hidden under them—but it could be a great body.

Freddi didn't wear glasses. The Zapper did. So what? Glasses were easy to come by.

They walked differently but that was easy to fake.

What wasn't easy to fake was overall body carriage. Freddi's and the Zapper's were similar, which might be what seemed familiar to me.

That realization made my stomach flip. Getting involved with Freddi—a potential witness if not more—was unprofessional and inexcusable. I never lost control in any situation. Until her.

If she turned out to be the Zapper and tied into Nick the Russian and Smiling Tony Catalina criminally, what I did could—at a minimum—muddy the water if charges were ever filed. Unforgivable and would cost me my job.

I glanced at her behind the wheel. Not a hint of a smile. Total concentration as she navigated the tricky road. I was overwhelmed by her again. Her touch, her warmth, her sensuousness flooded my mind. Please don't let her be a part of any schemes or scams. Then I'll find a way to bring her back to me.

We crossed the bridge onto Crooked Foot Key.

In a few minutes I'd be able to read the text.

Was it from Jamie or Misha?

CHAPTER SIXTY-ONE

Nightcap

HER

I took Tom to his car in the non-valet parking lot at the Royal Squid, stopping barely long enough for him to get out. I mentally gave him a shove with my foot. He tried to speak. I squealed my tires getting away from him.

And that was another thing. Why didn't he valet? The way he squandered on dinner, it couldn't be a matter of money. Did he want to be in position for a fast getaway?

I pulled into my garage and buttoned up my convertible. I looked at the front seats. The armrest moved out of the way replaced by intertwined bodies. I shook the mirage out of my head. Next I'd be seeing an oasis. I went into my house, stopped in the kitchen to pour a glass of sauvignon blanc, and carried it into my bedroom.

A sip of wine. I stripped off my dress and dropped it on the chair by the closet. A second sip, a little larger. I dug my panties out of my purse and threw them in the hamper. Another sip, more like a gulp. I started shaking and sat on the edge of the bed.

I intended to shower the memory of that bastard off me but the rush I felt in the car with him came back. The vision of us lying on the seat returned along with the exquisite pleasure in the moonlight.

Did I overreact? Maybe he was a cop like Uncle Tony suggested. Life and death? An exaggeration if not a fabrication. Even so, it should have been all about us at a time like that—at least for a few minutes. He was so aggravating anyway. Always in charge without even trying. And he might be a better driver. So aggravating. What was I thinking when I moved the armrest out of our way?

I finished my wine, unmade the bed, and slipped under the sheet, too exhausted to even brush my teeth. I no longer wanted to wash him off me. I wanted him for the night.

The remnant of our one-off interlude.

CHAPTER SIXTY-TWO

Switcheroo

HIM

I watched Freddi speed away. A hollow feeling engulfed me. But I knew the pain in my heart wasn't forever. We'd be back together. The connection was too strong. If only she wasn't such a pain in the ass.

Her car was out of sight before I read the text message. Not Jamie. Not Misha. But Madge, my interpreter and source of local information. *Call me before eleven. Important.*

Not an emergency. It wasn't ten o'clock yet and all I had to do was make a call. Madge was interpreting two-day-old conversations. Unlikely she'd have anything that required my immediate attention like Misha or Jamie might.

If Freddi hadn't gone off the rails, we could have...

And I wouldn't feel like...

Time to suck it up. I had a job to do. There were trafficked girls who needed help.

I walked to my car, settled into the driver's seat, and phoned Madge.

Her usual cheerful voice filled my ear. "Hello, Magnum. I mean Tom. Hope I didn't interrupt anything important."

If only she knew. "Not at all. What's up?"

"According to my software I've achieved ninety-seven percent translation with a ninety-four percent accuracy rate."

"What does that mean? Ninety-seven percent of what you can sort of hear?"

"Ninety-seven percent of the whole enchilada."

That surprised me so much that I blurted, "How did you manage that?"

Before the words left my mouth I realized what a stupid question that was. How she did it was nothing that should be discussed on the phone. Fortunately she ignored it and said, "Can you be at the restaurant at five-thirty? That will give us a half hour before anyone else gets there."

I wasn't going to be able to sleep anyway. "If you'll have the coffee brewing."

She hesitated. "I had expenses."

No hesitation on my part. "Covered."

Her expenses had to be for upping The Squid's fifty percent of the audios being intelligible to Madge's ninety-seven percent. No sweat for a former intelligence officer who intercepted Russian communications if she still had contacts.

She giggled. "Magnum always gets the job done no matter what it takes. I'll have a fresh pot in hand."

I drove to the Beachsider. The king-size bed in my room looked as empty as my post-divorce bank account. Sleep didn't come. I thrashed around—conflicted and regretful. Unprofessionally succumbing to her babe power then spoiling everything with my dedication. Foolishly thinking I'd be able to resist if I toyed with our attraction while allowing suspicion to interfere with it. Cognitive dissonance?

Maybe the minibar would help. I rolled out of bed, fixed a Jack Daniel's on the rocks, and stepped onto the balcony. Glistening foam on the crests of the small waves dying on the beach brought back memories of the most pleasurable night of my life—but without the pleasure.

The ice clinked as I chugged my drink then returned to bed. I finally dozed slightly when I imagined her tucked into my shoulder.

At five, I hit the shower, finishing with a cold rinse. I dressed and took a final look. The me in the mirror was far more energized than the me inside. I hoped Madge's coffee would give me a boost.

True to her word, she opened the door to Grams' with a pot in her hand and a big grin. She held out a cheek to be kissed. We sat in the booth closest to the counter.

I felt like I should apologize for the indiscreet question. I was happy that she hadn't lost confidence in me. She let me off the hook.

She winked and smiled at me. "Magnum knows my secret, doesn't he?"

"It's safe with me. I'm lucky you have the contacts to get it done."

She put her hands together on the table. "My friend didn't do anything illegal. It was your data and not connected to national security. Technically, maybe unauthorized use of equipment. Her mother—who's like a second mother to me—is battling cancer. I planned to give her my translation fee if you couldn't cover it." Madge's normal cheerful countenance was spoiled by glistening eyes.

I patted her hands. "Would Magnum let you use money you need for Grams to cover a business expense?"

Her smile returned. "What was I thinking?"

She removed my flash drive from the pocket of her apron and put it in my hand. "In addition to what was on here, it now has my enhancements, the audio translations of them to English, and the transcripts of the translations. I didn't print anything because I assumed you didn't want sheets of paper floating around."

"The old translation information was limited and sketchy."

She nodded. "Boris was dazzled out of his mind by Missy and Freddi. He's not the first. Who's this Nicolai character?"

"Russian mob boss."

"Phew! Glad it's Boris in trouble with him and not me. You already know about the condo fiasco with Freddi and Missy. There's much more. Boris lost the seed diamonds for a scam on a gem dealer in Boca. They were Nicolai's diamonds. When Boris returned the stones, the mark—a guy named Xanos—did his own switcheroo and gave Boris fakes—then the mark backed out of the deal. Do you know Xanos?"

"I call him X. So Boris was running a variation on the old bait-and-switch where the bait was a sample of the mother lode. X did his own switch and Boris didn't catch it?"

"Boris threatened X unsuccessfully, so he's trying to get Tanya to worm her way back into him."

"How?"

Madge shrugged. "Unknown. She's fighting Boris on it. She thinks she might be killed if she goes back in. He tried to get Nicolai to send some muscle to get the diamonds back. Nicolai told Boris he had to solve his own problems—either get the diamonds back or pay him for them."

I didn't bother to mention X was our client. "Natasha—I mean Tanya—is daring to resist Boris?"

Madge laughed. "Boris and Natasha. I get it. You are such a kidder. Do they throw bombs that look like a bowling ball with a wick in it? Their relationship goes way beyond the scams, which gives her some leverage, or at least she thinks it does. My opinion is Boris would drop her into a snake pit without a second thought to save his own ass. He has Natasha following Freddi and Missy around because he thinks they might be connected to X. Are they?"

"No. No possibility. That's Boris's paranoia caused by Nicolai breathing down his neck."

"I knew it couldn't be. Those girls are the best."

"This is all in the translations?"

"Those plus the conversation between Boris and Natasha I eavesdropped on."

"Their conversation? You said you told me everything you heard."

"Everything *significant* I heard. Most of what they said wasn't significant because it didn't make sense until I heard the audios. Boris has a big score coming up so he'll be able to pay Nicolai for those diamonds, but he needs to get more seed diamonds from Nicolai—who is holding back—to pull it off. Originally the scam was going to be a bait-and-switch on Ralph Miller. Boris made the connection through a friend of a friend of a friend of Rita."

"Did he say the friend's name?"

She shook her head. "I forgot to mention I included a transcript of their conversation here in the restaurant—as I remember it—on your flash drive. I have a nearly photographic memory."

Madge never ceased to amaze. "You said *originally*. The scam has changed?"

"The condo fiasco spooked Ralph. He doesn't trust Boris so he nixed the deal. Ralph's a sleaze, but he can smell a rat a mile away. Maybe because he is one."

"So the deal's off."

She shook her head. "Rita wants to do it without Ralph. She has access to one of his investment accounts and has the contacts to move the rocks immediately. The money will be back in the account before Ralph knows anything. Boris and Natasha laughed about that. There won't be any money to put in the account."

That jibed perfectly with Rita trying to involve Chad the bartender as a go-between in a diamond deal. Then Rita's old flame Erik Thoreson showed up so she didn't need Chad anymore.

"Madge, sweetheart, you did a terrific job. How many hours?"

"Five."

"That's only five hundred. Not enough money for what you've done. I'm giving you three grand to share with your friend as you see fit."

A huge grin split her face but with tears in the corners of her eyes. "Oh, Magnum, you don't know how much this means."

We got out of the booth. She gave me a fierce hug. I said, "I might be able to get you more money." That earned me another hug.

As I walked out the door, my phone vibrated.

A text message before six in the morning?

Either very good news like Freddi saying come here immediately, all is forgiven.

Or very bad news like Jamie Bond whacking another pole.

CHAPTER SIXTY-THREE

Leapin' Legumes

HER

Missy's call woke me at 7:30 a.m. I mumbled some sounds into the phone, surprised that my voice wasn't working.

"Freddi, are you okay?"

I cleared my throat and croaked, "Everything's good. A little groggy is all."

"We didn't make plans, but I thought you might want to meet at Grams' before our ten o'clock."

The mere thought of Grams' heavenly coffee picked me up a little. "Moving slow. Eight-thirty."

I trotted to the bathroom. Brushing, flossing, and gargling helped. A test count of one to ten got my voice working. On to the kitchen. I popped a high-test in my Keurig with an ice cube in the cup to ward off tongue burn, drumming my fingers while it brewed. Back to the bathroom. I took quick sips of the coffee while the shower warmed up.

Finally, I had to do it. The water was ready. I stepped in and washed Tom off me but not out of my life. I couldn't because Missy and I were involved in negotiating the ranch deal with him. I could wimp out and let Missy handle it or hang in and act like last night meant nothing to me.

After I was out of the shower and towel drying my hair, I leaned toward the mirror. No crow's feet yet. Were my eyes sort of weepy? Was I going to cry? I rarely cried. If he made me cry, I'd be even more pissed at him.

I got control of myself and dressed in a vibrant burnt orange blouse, which went well with my ash blonde—not dishwater, thank you very much, Mister Tom McCall—hair. I paired it with a white skirt and slipped into white medium heels. This was going to be a cheerful day if it killed me.

Missy beat me to Grams' and secured the coveted corner booth where it was possible to speak softly without being overheard. Missy was ready for me to spill the beans. Before I was fully seated she said, "How was your ride last night?" with a grin and strong emphasis on *ride.*

Madge slapped a coffee in front of me. "Be back to chat later." She zoomed off.

My voice came out in a near whisper, much quieter than necessary. "Incredible." I felt a tear forming. Damn.

Missy peered at me. "So why the face like someone just ran over your kitty cat?"

"I don't have a cat."

She scrunched up her face and stared at me with one eye. "Don't get cute."

Of course not. If I couldn't talk to Missy, who could I talk to? And she'd lend a sympathetic ear. The legumes leapt out of the can—totally. To my credit, without shedding a tear.

After my monologue Missy shook her head. "That was dumb as dirt."

I jerked up straight. "A little harsh don't you think?"

"You—the smartest person I know—dump a guy perfect for you. So he checked a message. What if it was crucial? You said Uncle Tony thinks he might be an undercover cop."

"If he's not who he says he is, that makes it worse. He can't level with the woman he's in bed with?" I thought for a second. "Actually, in car with."

Missy giggled.

That made me smile. My first smile since last night.

"So how are you going to handle Tom coming in this morning about the ranch?"

"Business-like. But he probably won't show."

"I declare, your mind is not inside your head this morning. I would bet dollars to doughnuts no matter who he really is, he'll be at our office at ten like he said. If you're shaky about being there, don't worry. I can handle it even though I've never seen you run from anything."

Missy was so obvious. Baiting me because she hadn't given up on Tom and me being a couple. That wasn't going to happen. "I wouldn't miss it," I said.

Madge buzzed up to the table. "Sorry I haven't had a chance to gab. Say, have you gals met this guy Tom who's been in here a few times? Looks like Tom Selleck and a real nice guy."

"He's coming to our office in an hour," Missy said.

Madge smiled. "Should have known the Bikini Realty team would be on it. One of you should take a close look. He might be a keeper. Gotta run." Madge hustled off.

Was this a conspiracy? I glanced at Missy. She shook her head and shrugged like she had nothing to do with Madge's comment.

It didn't matter. My plan was to be cool and professional when he came to the office.

Like I never felt the warmth of his body crushed against mine.

And never would again.

CHAPTER SIXTY-FOUR

Good News, Bad News, No News

HIM

Agnes—the waitress who served me Madge's special oyster breakfast—was entering Grams' as I was leaving. With a wry grin she said, "Did you go for a dozen this time?"

I laughed and shook my head. "Tomorrow—with extra horseradish."

My phone gave me a reminder vibration about the text. Misha. *Will call before noon.*

Sure, same as the call he didn't make last night.

So much for my theory about the text having to be very good or very bad news. I left out inconclusive.

I got into my car, drove to the Beachsider, went to my room, and sat at the desk. I wanted to go through the transcripts word by word, but first I had to call The Squid. Our client was playing games, games that put my butt on the line against the Russian mob. I wasn't happy with him. Because of the trafficked girls I'd be going against the Russian mob anyway, but X didn't know that.

The Squid picked up on the second ring, slow for him. I braced myself for his melodious "What?"

When it came through, I was ready. "Our client's a fraud. X ripped Boris for seed diamonds and probably called you when he realized he was screwing with the Russian mob. By the way, I spent three thousand dollars for a nearly one hundred percent audio enhancement and translation of Boris's calls and a transcript of the conversation Madge overheard. My suggestion is to squeeze this expense and all the money you can out of X *now*."

Mister Congeniality grunted. "That's a helluva by-the-way."

"I'd like to give Madge another grand or two. That was some really good work."

The Squid grunted again. "I checked X out before I agreed to take him on as a client. He's slippery but not violent. I don't know why Natasha would think he is."

"It might be an excuse. There's more to Boris and Natasha's relationship than frauds. He wants her to go back to X to get the seed diamonds. She doesn't want to. I haven't been through the transcripts yet to get the details. I wanted you to know about X's game ASAP.

"So where do we stand?"

I gave him a rundown on Boris's problems with Nick and the seed diamonds and the new scam targeting Ralph—now Rita. Then I said, "My plan to identify Boris's next victim and convince him or her to work with law enforcement to nail Boris in mid-scam is now almost out the window. Rita isn't likely to cooperate since she's going behind Ralph's back. She'd probably walk away from the deal rather than expose that."

The Squid grunted his grunt that meant continue.

"Last night Chad the bartender told me about seeing Rita's heartthrob Erik Thoreson in Crooked Foot. Rita might be doing this to get Erik some money. That's her history. If I can locate him, I'll put a tracker on his car and see what that gets us."

"I'll work up a complete background and text you his tag and local credit card charges."

"One last thing. Misha texted that he'll call me later. Maybe something's happening with the trafficked girls."

"Be careful. That's dangerous doo-doo. Even more dangerous if Jamie Bond and his cannon are with you."

"Nobody's going to be with me. As soon as I get solid information, I'll turn it over to the cops and be out of it."

"I hope so. Just be careful."

"Yes, Dad."

I called room service to order a Greek omelet and settled in with my flash drive plugged into my laptop. Three hours later, I had the transcripts burned into my brain, a text from The Squid with Erik's tag number and a credit card charge at the Paradise Resort, and a clean breakfast plate—which would have made Mom proud...and Madge too.

Time enough to go by Erik's motel and still be at Bikini Realty at ten. I trotted to my car and headed north on Gulfway Drive. I passed Paradise Resort last night when Freddi and I were headed to the dead end—in more ways than one. I snapped my attention out of the clouds and onto the road.

I turned into the resort entrance and went to the north parking lot, planning to work my way south and out if his car wasn't there.

Bingo! In the row of parking next to the building sat a beat-up performance Mustang—orange with black hood scoops. Erik was here. Checking the tag wasn't necessary, but I did it anyway.

I scanned the next row. Bingo again! Rita's screaming red Mercedes convertible. Her heartthrob wasn't an old flame. He was burning brightly.

Maybe Rita was trying to do more than finance Erik. Maybe finance their great escape.

I parked my car and walked down the first row. I stopped at Erik's car, bent over as if to tie my boat shoe, and slipped a tracker under his rear bumper. I cut over to the second row and kneeled by Rita's car. Any boat-shoe-wearer watching my actions would understand about needing to retie that often. I slapped a tracker under her bumper.

Nine forty-five. Got in my car. Checked my Tracker Phone. Both devices working.

Onward to Bikini Realty to discuss the restrictions on the sale of the ranch.

Would Freddi be there? Of course. She'd act like nothing happened.

She was tough. One of many things about her that attracted me.

If only she wasn't such a pain in the ass.

CHAPTER SIXTY-FIVE

No Goodbyes

HER

I paced the floor in the Bikini Realty office. Missy sat on the couch as we usually did when waiting for a potential buyer to arrive. She wore a cheerful yellow sleeveless dress. I glanced at the wall clock and said, "I told you he wouldn't show."

She rolled her eyes. "Hush. He's only two minutes late. If you can't handle this, let me take it. We need to move that ranch property."

"I can handle it," I snapped. "Sorry, didn't mean to sound so...so..."

"Bitchy?"

I let out a short laugh as I took my place on the couch. "I don't know why I couldn't come up with the word. I'm okay. I'll hold up my end of our tag team."

A half minute later, the jerk walked through the door, looking his usual calm self, like last night never happened. We stood. Missy gave him a little cheek-to-cheek hug. He tried to add body into our cheek-to-cheek but I stiffly resisted. That didn't stop the tingle. Damn.

If only he wasn't so annoying, so...so...I was having trouble with my vocabulary. I didn't have any idea of what the right word was for last night.

He glanced at my cheerful orange blouse then at Missy's dress. "Ladies, as always, you are spectacular. Forgive me if I wax poetic, but I feel as if I'm engulfed by a magnificent sunrise."

A line only he could pull off without sounding corny. I thought Missy was going to swoon. I wanted to bop the jerk.

What could we say to that? We each murmured a demure thank you. I walked to the desk and lifted three sheets of paper. "These are the restrictions. Please sit here so you can make notes and we'll answer any questions you have."

I returned to the couch. Missy and I fielded his questions. He had so many I began to believe he had a real client who might be interested. Many of them concerned our opinions about why the owner wanted this restriction or that restriction. Like he was trying to get inside the owner's head. Maybe that's what he did with me.

He turned to page three of the restrictions. A double ding reached my ears. I froze. Sabrina had a text from Uncle Tony on Cellphony. With everything that was going on, I had to check the text. It could be urgent. Both my cell and Cellphony were in my purse on the far edge of the desk. No way to handle it casually.

I stood and stepped toward the desk. Tom grabbed my purse and handed it to me with an intense stare.

My face got warm. I went back to the couch without comment and fished Cellphony out of the depths of my purse. *Can Sabrina come to my office around three?*

Tom continued to stare at me. I sent Uncle Tony a thumbs-up then smiled at Tom—extra-sweetly—and said with an edge in my voice, "Not the same situation." I didn't want him to even begin to think my text was letting him off the hook.

He smiled at me for about ten seconds before going back to asking about the restrictions. He finished and looked at the clock. "I'll send this to my client and talk to him in depth. If he's interested in pursuing it, I'll have to meet the owner." He stood. "For now, it's getting close to lunchtime. If you have a beachside lunch spot where we can enjoy this gorgeous weather, it would be my treat in exchange for all your time this morning."

Before I could make an excuse and without looking at me Missy popped off, "The Pirate's Booty where we first met has good food."

"I'll see you there. We're early enough to beat the lunch crowd if they—"

The buzzing of his cell phone interrupted him. He looked at his text message. His expression became very serious. "Sorry, ladies. Maybe tomorrow. I'll be in touch."

He rushed out without any goodbye pleasantries.

Missy and I looked at each other.

What the hell?

CHAPTER SIXTY-SIX

El Escorpión

HIM

I trotted to my car, slammed into the seat, and reread Misha's text. *Call me before noon. New girls tonight.*

A body blow. A setup? Could be. I didn't think so. There was a soldier in this guy wanting to be honorable or at least semi-honorable. I had to chance it.

Misha answered immediately and spoke in hushed tones. "This is too much. New girls, younger than ever, younger than my daughter in Russia. I saw pictures."

His American accent was perfect and neutral. He could have been from Iowa. Was he a product of the infamous Russian spy *Charm School*? He said, "I must protect my family in the Motherland. If I tell you this, it has to die with you."

"Tell me where to look. I'll find a way to uncover the information independently before I pass it on. And I'll keep myself out of it. The link will be completely broken."

"You're not a cop?"

"Ex—now private—which is good. Makes it easier to hide you."

"If you're not a cop, why are you doing this?"

"Same reason you're talking to me. These girls. You have my word your information dies with me."

He was silent for an eternity. Had I lost him? Was he going

to back out? Finally, "You already have shown me the kind of man you are."

Tension drained out of my body. "You texted me yesterday."

"They were to be delivered last night but the truck was delayed."

"Truck?"

"We're running out of time. Nicolai has a club near Ybor City."

"The Old Town section? The club named Barely Here?"

"That's it. On Porto Avenue. Go north past the club three blocks to the free public parking lot on the right side. I'm driving a black Suburban. How soon can you be here?"

"Less than an hour if there aren't any accidents to screw up traffic and no troopers who want my autograph."

"Tight, but it will work. If you have a problem call me."

I headed toward Tampa and called The Squid. "I put trackers on Rita's and Erik's cars."

"Hold on. I'll check their signals. I'm bringing up the app now. Got 'em. Good work. Have you checked on Boris lately? He just parked close to Erik and Rita."

"Maybe they're meeting about the diamonds. I'll check it out later. On a different subject, the real estate ploy I've been using to stay close to the Bikini Realty gals might have paid off."

"Investigatively? Or for you personally?" Is there such a thing as a snide grunt? A sound something like that came through the phone.

"Investigatively is a dead end. Their involvement with Boris was selling him the condo. Period. Nothing to do with the diamond scam. The real estate ploy payoff is for you. I think I ran into a deal that might interest you."

"How do you know what would interest me?"

"Like you said, my internet investigation lessons have paid off. I think you have your fingers in more pies than Sara Lee."

I spent a few minutes describing the ranch and the sale restrictions imposed by the owner. While he was mulling it over I said, "By the way—"

"Please tell me this isn't as expensive as your last by-the-way."

"I'm on my way to Tampa to meet Misha."

"Whaaaaaaaat?" he bellowed. "Are you crazy?"

"Maybe. But I have to do it." I told him about the call with Misha. "If he's on the level, this is our chance to shut down the traffickers."

The Squid huffed and puffed and made me promise to text him before the meeting and after—if I lived through it. I knew he'd be hacking every camera he could find in the area.

When I got to Tampa I worked my way to Porto Avenue and turned north. A half mile later I passed Barely Here on my right. I glanced at its parking lot. Was that the Zapper's car? I slowed way down. Not hers. It had a primer spot on its trunk lid that had been repaired but not yet painted. I sped up. In my rearview mirror I saw a man who might have been Nick watching me.

At twelve-thirty—fifty-two minutes after Misha and I hung up—I arrived at the lot. It took up over half of the block and went through to the street behind it. I spotted a black Suburban in the next to the last row. Now I'd find out if my long shot miraculously paid off or I was in a world of hurt. I parked in the row in front of the Suburban and texted The Squid. *About to meet Misha.*

The Squid texted back. *Looks like Boris heading for Tampa. Rita and Erik not moving. Be careful.*

I walked to Misha's passenger door. The lock clicked open and I got in—without so much as a glance in the back seat—a poker face belying the trepidation in my gut.

Misha nodded and held out his hand. "You have stones, Tom."

We shook. "I know a good man when I see one."

A small sardonic smile flashed across his mouth.

He pointed straight across to a narrow alley that dead-ended into Porto Avenue. "The building on the right side of the alley belongs to Nicolai."

"Looks like some kind of an art store."

"On the ground floor—but it's not important. There's a restaurant upstairs that is important. The owner is half Mexican and half Chinese. Looks like a pissed-off cross between Pancho Villa and Fu Manchu. The truck that was supposed to deliver the girls yesterday? If the drivers don't have a good reason, they'll have new scars courtesy of *el Escorpión*."

It didn't take a Rosetta Stone to make that translation. "The truck is coming from Mexico?"

"Texas. Nicolai has recruiters in the old Soviet Bloc countries. Some of the girls the recruiters buy from orphanages and foster homes. Others, the recruiters convince the parents the girls are going to have good lives as au pairs, even models, in the US, and pay the parents for them. They ship the girls to Mexico. *El Escorpión*'s people smuggle them across the border and bring them here in a twenty-foot U Move rental truck."

The story sounded believable but so do most yarns spun by criminals. It still could be a setup. "You've known about this. Why are you talking about it now?"

"You. I also know a good man when I see one. You're my chance to stop this and stay out of it. The girls keep getting younger. Nicolai makes big money on the young ones, especially the virgins. Of course, most of them are virgins many times, until it's obvious they aren't—a condition Nicolai personally determines."

My stomach burned. "Where do you fit in?"

"I don't. He keeps the club operation separate. I was brought here to keep them running smoothly. Nicolai knows I don't like the trafficking, but he doesn't hide it from me. Sometimes he gets a nasty customer I have to reason with. I've seen things—like the buildings being set up for the girls—and heard enough to piece together what I told you."

"How many buildings are set up for the girls?"

"Nicolai calls a building for the girls a *dacha*, which is more-or-less Russian for vacation home. The girls live and work as prostitutes in the dacha. I'm sure you see the irony. He only operates one at a time—usually six months to a year—for tight control. The dachas are always within a couple of miles of one of the strip clubs. They have garage doors large enough to accommodate the moving trucks. The doors are also used for vehicles that ferry customers to and from their cars."

"Where are the girls being delivered tonight?"

"The Valley of Love dacha. I'll give you the address. It's going to be shut down in a few days and the operation moved to a new one a couple of blocks from here on Rail Avenue, the street behind this lot. From here go north, cross Boney Road, and it's on your right about halfway up the block."

"So why am I here looking at the rear entrance to Scorpion's restaurant?"

"He'll be here soon. He takes his restaurant seriously, comes in early every afternoon to get his cooking and cleaning crews working for the four o'clock opening. He's usually here by now. I want you to see him because he'll oversee the transfer of the girls."

"Transfer?"

"After the new girls are trucked here Nicolai sells *el Escorpión* the girls he no longer wants. The used girls are taken away in the same truck. That's the transfer."

Rage threatened to overcome my poker face but I held on.

"He has at least a dozen illegals here at all times to handle narcotics and they're always in the area when the transfers happen."

An iridescent-blue mid-engine Corvette with a wide spoiler entered the lot and parked in the second row.

"*El Escorpión* has arrived."

A big man unwound himself from the eye-catching car. "Not a subtle guy."

"Arrogant—but dangerous."

I watched him stretch. Over six feet, broad shoulders, shaggy salt-and-pepper hair covering most of his ears, sparse Fu Manchu mustache. The Asian and Mexican heritage blended into a mean face. He wore a tan Western-style sport coat, black shirt, bolo tie, and jeans. I couldn't see his feet but my money was on cowboy boots. A studied border outlaw look.

"The Scorpion. Riiiiight."

"Don't sell him short," Misha said. "He always has two guns and two knives on him. He told me one night trying to impress me with how tough he is. That was after I stopped him from bothering one of Sabrina's dancers."

"Sabrina?"

"An agent for some beautiful strippers. Nobody can touch her girls and they don't touch anybody. He grabbed the dancer's wrist and bare ass trying to convince her to leave with him. I had to explain the rules to him."

I bet he did.

Scorpion swaggered across the street into the alley like he was going to the dumpster beside the building.

Yep, cowboy boots.

Before he got to the dumpster, he turned into the building and went up a set of steps.

"Where's he going?"

"That's an open staircase to a hallway leading to back doors of the upstairs businesses."

"What's up there besides his restaurant?"

"A martial arts dojo. And Nicolai's business office."

"Business office?"

"An office for Nicolai when he doesn't want to use one of the club offices, so he calls it his business office. It's where he and *el Escorpión* plan their trafficking operations. The business office led to *el Escorpión* having his restaurant here. Previously it was a Cuban restaurant. *El Escorpión* decided it was perfect for one he wanted to open. And excellent cover for meetings with Nicolai—who agreed and forced the Cubans out."

Misha turned toward me with sadness in his eyes. "I've heard *el Escorpión* has used some of the girls he bought in snuff films."

I didn't know how yet, but the human trafficking days were over for Nicolai Hutchko and *el Escorpión*.

CHAPTER SIXTY-SEVEN

Brush Off

HER

Missy pursed her lips. "Was it something we said? He flew out of here like the ladybug in the nursery rhyme with her house on fire."

"He probably had his usual emergency. Even EMTs don't get called out as much as private investment counselors. Just as well. I would have gotten indigestion eating with that jerk."

She rolled her eyes.

I stood. "The text I got was from Uncle Tony. He wants to see Sabrina at three o'clock. Fortunately we don't have anything scheduled this afternoon, but I'm tired of driving to Tampa."

"I'm surely sorry you have to go, but it's one more reason for you to take and throw that business in a bayou where it belongs."

After last night I didn't need that. I gave her the hear-no-evil fingers in the ears—but with a smile—and left. I went home contemplating stretching out on the bed for an hour or so but I wouldn't be able to sleep. Damn that Tom. Who was he?

My energy was at the basement level. I was physically, mentally, and emotionally depleted. Regardless I had to go to Tampa. I owed it to Uncle Tony to tell him everything I learned in the past day and a half including some cops thinking he was a hitman.

Tagphony was still mounted on my Chevy. All I needed to do was cream off my light makeup and don one of my drab

Sabrina outfits, brunette wig, brown contacts, and eyeglasses. I could be in Tampa long before three o'clock.

I double-checked the Sabrina Showstoppers schedule. The dancer whose cha-cha was the center of attention at the Panty Free Zone on Sunday night was working the lunchtime slot at Barely Here. It would be good to ensure Brandi was okay with her first gig since the incident. Then I'd go up to Ybor City for lunch in one of the many Cuban restaurants there.

When was the last time I ate knock-your-socks-off Cuban food? I could taste the *bistec de pollo* now. I smiled. I was okay, more than okay, Thomas J. McCall.

Traffic was light. Just before one o'clock I parked in the Barely Here parking lot. A burger-and-fries fast-food truck was next to the back door. Nick rotated different trucks at this location for lunch. Today, patrons of the arts could order a gut-bomb and crinkle fries from a diaphanous-clad waitress while Brandi made their mouths water. Plus a 20 percent discount on lap dances was available from non-Sabrina strippers.

The door bouncer nodded at me and I stepped inside. The joint was full, which was the reason Nick contracted for a Showstoppers dancer for his food truck feasts. It changed a dead time into a profit center. Brandi wasn't onstage. I waved at the inside bouncer and walked to the dressing room.

Brandi was in her *Swan Lake* costume. She hugged me and said, "Thanks for coming by. I'm over the Sunday night thing. I'm sorry to be so much trouble. The manager told me Nick will be here soon to make sure I'm okay and apologize."

Humanitarian Nick. More than likely he thought while she was off balance he had a shot to smooth talk her into dinner followed by breakfast.

Such a sleaze. With luck I'd be gone before he showed

up. Brandi and I talked for a minute then said our goodbyes. I rushed through the club and out the front door—but not fast enough. Nick's black sedan—a gigantic older Lincoln Town Car that was probably bulletproof—pulled into the loading zone.

Nick got out and spread his arms wide. "Ah, the lovely Sabrina. My lucky day." He gave me a quick cheek-to-cheek. "Brandi?"

I nodded. "I was going to babysit her if she was the least bit shaky. I didn't want her to be a problem for you. Fortunately she's fine."

"You are so conscientious. Are you sure I can't convince you to come to work for me?"

Nick never gave up, but he seemed distracted and on edge instead of his usual nauseating overly suave self.

"Sorry, still not interested."

I was sure he didn't hear my answer. He was looking at the bouncer who swung the door open.

Nick took two long strides and was gone without a goodbye. The bouncer closed the door behind him.

Had I just been brushed off? My day for it. First Tom. Now Nick.

I was puzzling about it as I got in my car and drove north on Porto Avenue toward Ybor City's vast array of Cuban restaurants. Three blocks later I was looking ahead at a parking lot entrance to be sure an idiot wasn't going to blast out without looking. What did I see? Tom McCall walking through the lot. He knelt by an electric blue Corvette. I passed him but watched in my mirrors. He stood then walked toward the rear of the lot before I lost sight of him.

The mystery of Thomas J. McCall continued. His text

message must have caused him to come here. Probably to meet someone. If he came straight from our office, he had about forty-five minutes to accomplish whatever it was before I saw him.

Because he was able to follow Sabrina and Desiree to the Stopped Clock, he knew my Chevy. I had to keep it out of sight. That didn't mean I couldn't try to get a glimpse of where he was going. I turned left at the corner onto Boney Road then left again at the next intersection. A half-block farther on the left was an alley that would give me a view of that parking lot.

A one-way alley. One-way against me. But plenty of room even with the dumpsters and trash cans lined up against the left wall.

What were the chances of somebody coming in the other end?

I turned into the alley. I had a clear view of the lot when cars weren't whizzing up and down the street. When I got to the end, I should be able to see the parking lot exit. With luck that would be about the time Tom was leaving. I almost made it when a large black sedan pulled in and stopped.

Nick's large black sedan.

CHAPTER SIXTY-EIGHT

Home, Not-So-Sweet Home

HIM

I slid out of Misha's car and into my own. He drove off. I thought about Nick using dacha—the Russian word for vacation home—for any building where trafficked girls lived and were forced to work as prostitutes. Home, not-so-sweet home. And definitely not a vacation for them.

Tonight's transfer would happen at the Valley of Love dacha. Exact time unknown because the delivery was a day late but probably after midnight. Scorpion would be there. He was at every transfer.

In a few days the girls would be moved into the new dacha near Barely Here and have a life of hell there.

That was Nick's plan. It wasn't mine.

If Scorpion was going to be at the transfer, his car would be there.

I watched the Corvette for ten minutes after Misha left. I scanned the area one more time then walked up to it with my last GPS tracker. The low-slung design made the installation tricky, but after a few fumbles, I managed to attach it. I went to my car, checked that the tracker was operational, and called The Squid.

A guy can't have too many *whats*, grunts, or snorts in his life.

After I told him about the tracker on the Vette and Misha's information, The Squid said, "Okay, Scorpion's Vette is online here too. Hold a minute." When he came back on he said, "I'm having trouble finding a camera with a view of the Valley of Love dacha. I have a couple of intermittent signals at the one near Barely Here."

"I'll check out Valley of Love first and see if I can build probable cause for a search warrant to feed to the police. I need strong probable cause to convince them to dedicate the manpower this is going to take."

"Who are you going to call? I have contacts—"

"With cops, person-to-person works best—by far. Let me see what I can come up with."

"Okay but I'm going to have some equipment delivered to you to overcome this camera deficiency and help you with the PC. Be back in that parking lot in one hour."

I drove to the exit. A black sedan pulled into the alley across the street. I recognized it from Jamie Bond's videos. Nick's Town Car. I was amazed. Was Nick meeting with Scorpion? Had something gone wrong? I turned right and got the hell out of there. The Valley of Love awaited.

Twenty minutes of moderate traffic later, I was in a light industrial area, parked on Gemmler Avenue looking at a building at the intersection with Hammer Drive, four blocks from the Valley of Love. This was the dacha where the transfer was to take place tonight. The sign above the oversized garage door was lettered Marks Brothers Roofing and Trusses.

I hoped The Squid's equipment was top drawer because I couldn't sit here long without getting burned. I was about to leave when a white van with magnetic signs saying W & Z Supplies rolled past me to the dacha. The garage door went up and the van entered. I moved my car to a driveway hidden from view of the dacha. A minute later the W & Z van drove by.

Was that a pickup or delivery? Or both?

I gave the van half a block then pulled out. I stayed well behind it to avoid being spotted. Better to lose it than get burned. The van went about a mile and dropped a morbidly obese passenger at a big box store. I drove by the guy as he struggled into his car. I repeated his tag number three times to be sure it was in my memory bank then texted it to The Squid.

The Barely Here dacha was next on my to-do list. I pushed the speed limit driving to Rail Avenue, the street on the back side of the parking lot where I met Misha and my equipment was to be delivered. I turned north on Rail, passed the parking lot on my left, and crossed Boney Road.

The dacha was on my right on the east side of Rail Avenue in the middle of the block north of Boney just like Misha said. No sign on the building and no activity, but the oversized garage door was obviously new. Horses on the other side of the street drew my attention to a carriage ride business. My hour was almost up. At the end of the block, I turned left then left again on Porto Avenue, continued south across Boney then left into the parking lot.

The Squid called. "Where'd you get the tag number you texted me?'

I told him the story. He said, "You hit pay dirt. The guy's a pedophile and registered sex offender."

"Pay dirt, but it makes me a witness if the police use it for probable cause for a search warrant. A problem for a lot of reasons—including keeping Misha as far away from this as possible."

"The new equipment should take care of that. A state-of-the-art battery-powered camera with a half-mile range that doesn't rely on cell towers and a receiver/recorder that will operate on battery or the power outlet in your car. Also a high-resolution dashcam and recorder is coming to you."

"Beautiful. Everything will be on flash drives for law enforcement to use for the probable cause."

A van with five antennas on the roof and the words *Esquire Security and Alarms* on the side entered the lot.

The Squid—Roy Alan Squire—was a man of many companies and secrets. I said, "Esquire Security. Really? You have me using junk equipment when you own a high-tech company with who knows how many offices around the state—or world for that matter."

"Hey! You save money where you can, something a spendthrift like you wouldn't understand."

I lowered my window, waved at the van, took possession of the equipment, and returned to the Valley of Love dacha. I found the perfect spot for the camera on a pump at a defunct gas station on Gemmler Avenue with a clear shot to Hammer Drive and the building masquerading as Marks Brothers Roofing and Trusses. I parked on a parallel street a block over from Gemmler and turned on the monitor.

When the screen showed the W & Z Supplies van leaving the dacha, I moved into position with the dashcam running. Over the next several hours I videoed eleven johns being transported to their cars and texted their tag numbers to The Squid. Ten of them checked out to be registered sex offenders, pedophiles, or pending prosecution for child porn arrests.

Nick had built a specialized clientele. I would have loved to give him a specialized beating into the ground. I'd have to settle for the satisfaction of having a hidden hand in his downfall tonight.

By four-thirty, my stomach thought my throat had been cut. I called Bond, Jamie Bond, to relieve me. He said, "Boris is back at the Ibis Inn. So is Natasha's car."

I wasn't sure what that meant beyond the obvious boy-and-girl stuff. Maybe Boris talked Nick into providing the seed diamonds and wanted to be near the Panty Free Zone to pick them up.

Jamie and I met at a convenience store five blocks away from the Valley of Love strip club. I explained what I was doing at the dacha and moved the equipment to his car. He said he would absolutely not get burned. He promised to text me any tag numbers he got and not to shoot people or lampposts. His .44 Magnum bulged under his suit coat.

I shuddered as I turned him loose and started my engine. A gigantic lunch was on my mind. Maybe a Cuban sandwich with a side of black beans and rice.

My phone vibrated. A text from Cube. *Your girl is here.*

Even my fingers were smiling as I tapped *On my way.*

The Zapper at last.

Maybe I could grab one of Cube's sirloin burgers while I was there.

CHAPTER SIXTY-NINE

Pleased to Meet You, Very Pleased

HER

Nick's car had me blocked in. I could back all the way down the alley but I had to say something to him first in case he recognized my car.

I came to a stop about fifteen feet from his bumper and got halfway out. I stood on one foot behind my open door and waved. "Sorry, Nick."

He walked around the front of his Lincoln and spread his arms. "Sabrina. What are you doing here?"

"Trying to take a shortcut to the lot across the street."

At that moment, I saw Tom drive out of the lot exit. Nick turned to see what I was looking at and said, "You know that guy?"

I shook my head. "There must be a million cars like that on the road."

"But only one driven by that guy. An hour ago he was eyeing my club and now he's here. You were just at my club and now you're here. Pretty suspicious, huh?"

I was truly perplexed. Nick acted strangely at Barely Here and now this. Was paranoia consuming him? "Suspicious? Nick, this is Sabrina. We've worked together for how long? Three years? More?"

He shook his head and smiled. "You're right. I'm having some business problems and trying to blame them on anything I can. Next thing, I'll be firing my astrologer."

He laughed. He always played the comedian, but this didn't seem real. He was trying too hard to be his normal self. He was still leery of me. Weird.

"Traffic blocked me out of the parking lot entrance. I was working my way back to it and took this alley as a shortcut. I wanted a quick bite of Cuban before I checked on a couple more of my girls."

Noise on the steps to the left caught our attention. A guy dressed like a honky-tonk cowboy set to barhop on Saturday night clomped into the alley in snakeskin boots. "The damn truck broke down again. I told my mechanics to stay with it all the way here. Tonight for sure or..."

He finally noticed Nick nodding his head toward me and turned, showing me a venomous face. "Who the hell is this?"

I wondered if I could get to my stun gun in time.

Nick immediately tried to smooth it over. "This is the lovely Sabrina, agent for some of my dancers. She took a wrong-way shortcut." He sounded like a guy with a pit bull he wasn't sure he could control.

The honky-tonk cowboy continued to stare at me. "Are you sure?"

"Yes, I'm sure. Are you doubting me?" Nick sounded irritated.

I got in my car, closed the door, waved at Nick through the windshield, and backed down the alley.

What the hell was that?

Over the years, some of my girls heard vague rumors about Nick using his clubs to find customers for trafficked-girls prostitution. If that guy in the alley didn't smuggle women across the border, I didn't brush my teeth every morning and Thomas J. McCall wasn't a jerk.

And where did that jerk go?

My appetite was gone now that I had myself sufficiently worried about the safety of any woman near Nick—including my other two dancers working this afternoon. I decided to check on them before I saw Uncle Tony.

Once I determined everything was okay with my dancers performing at Tangy and Naked Truth, I calmed down. Maybe I overreacted. My appetite returned with a vengeance. Unfortunately, by then, it was time to meet Uncle Tony.

On to the Jumbo Shrimp. Uncle Tony led me to his office, gave me one of his gentle hugs, and said, "Let's talk."

I told him everything—with the exception of the moonlight madness of course.

He listened quietly, asked questions when I didn't make it clear, and actually chuckled when I told him about the hitman allegation.

When I told him about my now strong suspicion that Tom was a cop, he smiled and said most cops were good people.

He was troubled by my account of the confrontation in the alley and warned me to stay away from Nick except for Sabrina's Showstoppers business.

There was no doubt in my mind that Uncle Tony was the Uncle Tony I'd known for years. Not a mobster. Not a hitman. A damn good man to have looking out for you and to consider you a part of his family.

I was a little bit drained by the time we finished. My cell phone beeped. A text from Desiree. *Meet me at Stopped Clock at five? Important.*

Desiree was waiting for me outside when I got there. We waved at Cube and went to the same back booth. We were ahead of the supper rush.

She looked harried. "I talked with my law enforcement contact this afternoon. The pressure is on. Gino says I have to produce something. I'm dancing in Nick's clubs and working for you but we have nothing new on Nick or Smiling Tony."

"There's nothing new to get on Tony Catalina. He's a straight businessman with some bad relatives. However there might be something happening with Nick. He was strange today. I'll tell you about it, then we'll figure out how you can pass it on without it coming from me."

We talked and speculated about Nick's actions and his involvement with the violent honky-tonk cowboy.

Desiree abruptly changed subjects. "That reminds me there's something else I need to tell you. Did you get a good look at that stud who handled the violent drunk in here last night?"

Where was this going? "Not really. I was in the bathroom and then I thought we should leave in case a motorcycle gang war broke out."

"I don't think that was anything to worry about with Cube and that guy here."

Unbelievable. Another female fan of Tom.

"Anyway, he told Cube he wants to meet you. I should be so lucky."

Uh oh. I wanted to help Desiree but it was time for me to get out.

I looked up and the door was closing behind Tom. His voice carried to our booth. "Cube, good seeing you, my man. Could you whip me up one of your incomparable sirloin burgers?"

Cube slapped his spatula on the counter in a form of Morse

Code *you betcha* then pointed it in our direction. "Have a seat. Desiree, look here. This is the guy. Tom's his name. Introduce him to your friend."

Tom looked at me. He knew who I was. And he knew that I knew that he knew.

Maybe I blacked out but he was beside me before I could blink. I stood, trying to escape to the bathroom. Bad move. That jammed me into him.

From a million miles away I heard Desiree say, "Tom, this is Sabrina."

To my shock, he kissed me passionately. I struggled for a second then melted into his body with my arms around him, kissing him back as passionately. I couldn't resist him. Flames surged through my body. It would be so embarrassing if he undressed me on the spot.

Desiree's faraway voice came through. "Wow! Do I know how to make an introduction or what?!"

CHAPTER SEVENTY

Hand Off

HIM

I strode into the Stopped Clock and saw the Zapper and Desiree in the same booth as last night. Without slowing down, I asked Cube for a sirloin burger and vectored in on the Dark Evader. I didn't need direction from Cube's spatula and I didn't need an introduction by Desiree.

The Zapper was the dancer agent who Misha called Sabrina. My first good look at her face confirmed what her driving skill told me. Sabrina was Freddi. My emotions pinballed.

She jumped up and slammed into me. We were mashed together just like at the Pirate's Booty except we weren't in bathing suits. The heat couldn't have been higher if we were naked.

The next thing I knew I was kissing her. How did that happen? And she was kissing me back. The blood roaring in my ears masked something Desiree said. I eased Freddi into the booth and crowded in next to her. She stayed glued to me for a few seconds then slid over an inch.

I held my hand out. "Nice to meet you, Desiree."

She shook my hand and said, "Why don't I get the same greeting as Sabrina?"

We laughed then Freddi said to me, "You already knew. What gave me away?"

"I wasn't positive until I walked in here, but I was pretty sure after you drove me back to the Royal Squid last night. Not many women—not many people—can drive like that. It's against all odds I'd run into two in the space of a few days. And of course, the physical similarity."

"You could have saved both of us grief if you'd told me why you had to read the text.... Wait a minute. You still didn't trust me even after..." She huffed but didn't move away from me.

"Desiree," I said, "I have something for you much better than a kiss."

She looked puzzled but shifted her gaze to Freddi and said, "I don't have any idea of what's going on, Sabrina. Obviously you know each other and maybe just patched up a lover's spat, but I didn't know he would be here."

Freddi smiled. "Everything's good, Desiree. I'm sure you didn't know. I'm happy about it."

I felt Freddi was only partially happy and trying to put Desiree at ease. Freddi and I could work it out later.

Desiree returned her attention to me and I said, "I'm going to get you off the hook. What's the name of the cop you're working with?"

Now both of them looked puzzled. Freddi said, "How do you know—"

"I saw the same exchange you saw outside the Naked Truth."

Desiree shook her head slowly. "I should have sold tickets to the event."

She was smart and quick, qualities that could be of value, but I wanted her safely out of this.

"Desiree, we're short on time. Tell me about the cop who's working you and how you got jammed up."

The girl could talk. She started with how she got into dancing and finished with getting blamed for her boyfriend's drugs.

Cube delivered my burger personally and interrupted Desiree's story. He said, "Everything okay here? I saw you had a successful intro to Desiree's friend." He grinned.

"Very successful. Meet Sabrina. Sabrina, this is Cube."

"Nice meeting you, Sabrina. Tom told me the other night he wanted to meet you so when you came in with Desiree, I called him. I might be wrong but it seems like you're glad I did."

Freddi nodded. "Very."

I saw her eyeing my burger. "Another one of these please, Cube. One isn't going to be enough for both of us."

"And a piece of key lime pie," Desiree said. "You know how I have to eat when I'm nervous."

"Is this guy making you nervous?" Cube said. "You couldn't be safer—unless you're thinking about stabbing someone." He walked off laughing.

I pushed the plate to Freddi. "Ladies first—that is, first bite."

Freddi chomped and chewed and said, "I don't care how many hours this takes to work off in the gym, it's worth it." She took another bite before reluctantly sliding the plate to me.

Before I took a bite—knowing I'd have plenty of time to chew once Desiree got going—I said, "About the cop, do you think he's a straight shooter?"

She started with coming to Tampa to be a spy—as she put it—and ended with the call from Gino this afternoon.

A waitress came to the booth, gave Desiree a big smile, and set a piece of pie in front of her. She placed a plate with our second burger on it between Freddi and me and winked at me before she walked away with our empty plate. Evidently she witnessed our *introduction*.

Freddi grabbed it. "Ladies first."

I shifted my attention from the burger to Desiree who was forking a sizable bite of pie into her mouth. "You still haven't told me about the cop working with you."

She managed to swallow the pie. "Gino's okay. He has a job to do, but I can tell he's not convinced he should be spending his time on Tony without more to go on. He's a state agent assigned to this task force, but I don't think it was his choice."

I glanced at Freddi who gave me a sheepish smile and grudgingly slid the plate over. "I have a lot of people to protect—including you and Sabrina—from some very bad actors. Do you trust Gino? Will he keep his word?"

She shrugged. "Seems like he would."

"Let's hope so. Call him and hand me your phone so I can talk to him."

She unearthed her phone from her purse, called Gino, and handed me the phone.

Freddi leaned over and put her ear next to mine.

Gino answered with, "Desiree, why are you calling? Are you okay?"

A good sign. His first concern was for Desiree. "Gino, my name's Tom. I had Desiree call so you wouldn't have my number."

"What the hell is this?"

"This is about trafficked girls—and I do mean girls. I'm a former cop. I ran across this operation in the course of my work as a private investigator."

"So why the backdoor approach instead of meeting me heads up?"

"I have the life of an informant to protect. These are dangerous people. If you don't know who I am or even see me, there's no way the information can be connected to my informant. The link is broken regardless of pressure from defense attorneys, your supervisors, or judges."

"This isn't going to work. If you were a cop, you know information doesn't convict people. I need evidence."

"I have videos you can use for probable cause to get a search warrant. The videos speak for themselves. You don't have to know anything about me. Once you serve the warrant, you'll have all the evidence you need to take down the Russian mob you've been working on, including Nicolai Hutchko—especially if you hit at a critical time."

"And when is that?"

"Tonight, in a matter of hours. If you organize a raid, I'll be able to tell you exactly when to move in."

"Tonight? Man oh man. If I go along with this, what do you want out of it?"

"Three things. This takes care of Desiree's beef. You close her informant file and bury it. And you never mention her in connection with this. The second thing is you stick with the story of an unknown person giving you the flash drives."

"That's easy. You *are* an unknown person. What's the third thing?"

"Make sure the girls you rescue are treated well. They're victims, not criminals."

"I would have done that anyway. How do I get the flash drives?"

Freddi put her hand over the phone and said, "I'll meet him in the West Tampa Library lobby. He can view the videos on a computer there. I'll call you on the untraceable phone I use as Sabrina so he won't need your number."

Brilliant. Desiree—the only one of us Gino knew—would be out of it.

I moved Freddi's hand from the phone. "An unknown person will meet you in the lobby of the West Tampa Library. She's a brunette and wears glasses. Just make her an unknown person in your reports so it sounds like you were dealing with one person."

"Twenty minutes?"

Freddi nodded.

"I need a few minutes to get the flash drives to her. Better make it six-thirty."

Everything was going better than I could have hoped.

I was handing off the ball to Gino.

Freddi was safe. She was taking the flash drives to a cop, then she was out of it.

Desiree was safe. She was out of it.

Misha was safe. The link was broken. Gino didn't know who I was.

Operation Kick-Nick's-Ass was rolling.

CHAPTER SEVENTY-ONE

Game On

HER

I watched Tom as he called someone named Jamie and asked him to meet at the place where Boris ate Monday night.

"Huh?" I said, "Who's Boris?"

Instead of answering my question, he turned to Desiree. "You've been a big help, but for your own good, forget all this. Some Russian mobsters are going to be very pissed, off and you don't want them to suspect you were involved."

"But it sounds like you two are going to have some fun."

Tom sounded irritated when he said, "It's not fun. Lives are at stake here."

Desiree's nonchalant reaction irritated me also. She was smarter than that. I said, "Besides, you're scheduled for the Naked Truth at nine."

Tom glanced at me, then said to Desiree, "The best thing you can do is put this out of your head, go there, and dance as usual."

Her expression was close to a pout. "You have to promise to give me the details tomorrow."

"Tomorrow," Tom said, "you'll see it on the news. Now let's get going."

As we passed the counter, Cube said, "Tom, your money's no good here."

Tom dropped a twenty. "Thanks, Cube. Something for the waitress. And thanks for the intro."

Cube grinned and waved his spatula at me.

I waved back then walked Desiree to her car. She said, "I'm going home to get my costumes, then come back here to Uber to the Naked Truth."

"Call me before you call Uber. If I'm not tied up I'll take you to work."

We watched Desiree drive away. I said, "I'll feel better if I know she gets there safely. Where are you meeting Jamie, whoever that is?"

"At the McDonald's not far from here."

"I'll have to follow you there to get to the library by six-thirty."

Tom nodded.

"You still haven't told me who Boris is."

"He's a Russian you know as Jules Armand. I'll tell you about it after we finish with Gino."

Talk about being floored! Jules Armand was a Russian named Boris! That kept my mind in turmoil on the way to Mickey D's.

Traffic was amazingly light. Tom pulled in next to a ten-year-old oxidized Buick. I stopped five spots away. A small guy with a large weapon—or serious deformity—under his suit coat stood by the Buick. Tom switched some equipment from it to his car and motioned me up.

He handed me two flash drives through my driver's window. "These are the videos that Gino can use for probable cause. I'll be waiting for your call after he views them."

The traffic stayed light and I made good time, but Gino was pacing in the lobby when I arrived. He looked me over. "Are you Tom's associate?"

I felt Mata Hari-ish as I scanned the area then quietly said, "Let's go to the computer room. I have what you need."

We sat side by side as he toggled through the videos. He talked to somebody on his cell each time he saw a tag number—in flagrant violation of the sign on the wall forbidding cell phone use. He continued watching the videos as he waited for a response. Almost every time he got one, he gave a fist pump and a barely audible *yessss.*

After fifteen minutes I realized that one way or another this was going to be a long night. Tom wasn't going to let the girls be trafficked—and neither was I—whether Gino went for it or not. I thought about calling Missy in case I couldn't work tomorrow.

My phone vibrated. Think of the devil. Text from Missy. *Call. Urgent.*

"Gino," I whispered and put my hand to my ear in the phone call sign.

He nodded. I walked outside and called her. Missy said, "I'm on surveillance."

That flabbered my gaster. "Where? Why?"

"After dinner—a very light dinner because we've been indulging at Grams' and the Royal Squid way too much of late—I got to pondering about Rita always trying to make trouble for us and her being tied in with that weasel Armand. It was downright obvious we needed leverage on her with her new beaux. So I donned appropriate clandestine clothing and drove to the Paradise Resort where you last saw them. I was almost there when the Ritamobile—with the orange Mustang behind it—came out heading toward town. A quick U-turn and I was on them like white on rice."

"Are you sure they didn't see you?"

"I swear I love my black Beamer, but it doesn't stand out in traffic. And I watch almost as many of those cop and spy shows as you. I know how not to get burned even if I don't have all those switches on my headlights and taillights. Although I'm thinking I might have to have some put in."

"Missy, we sell real estate. I only have the switches because my uncle never obeyed a speed limit in his life and he used them to evade traffic cops."

"True enough, but this real estate deal has led me into a situation in which I dearly need switches like that. This might be the new norm."

I rubbed my eyes. "Where are you now?"

"On 275 to Tampa. Where are you?"

"West Tampa Library."

"Is there a book you need in a hurry?"

I told her everything from Nick and the honky-tonk cowboy and the trafficked girls to Desiree connecting Tom and Gino.

After I finished she said, "After I figure out what Rita's doing, I'll be there to help."

"What?!"

"You need help. You might could end up with dozens of terrified girls to handle. We're a tag team selling real estate. We can be a tag team with those poor girls."

"Weren't you listening? I told you Gino's going to handle the trafficked girls."

"Something always goes wrong. I'll be there for you and Tom."

Naturally, I argued. She defeated most of my arguments with my own words, particularly when I mentioned danger.

"You always say what you're doing in Tampa isn't dangerous. And I have weapons. You aren't the only real estate agent with a stun gun and a big golf umbrella."

"Yours is chartreuse. How are you going to surprise anyone with that?"

"And my karate skills."

"One lesson two years ago. How is that overwhelming?"

"I'll wear a tank top without a bra."

"How soon can you get here?"

We laughed, then she said, "I'm serious. Well, not about the tank top. I'm not taking no for an answer. Y'all gonna need my hep."

Her accent was worsening by the word, showing her stress level was climbing rapidly. I said, "When you're done with Rita, call and I'll tell you where I am. It's a fluid situation."

I went back into the library. Gino was finishing up.

He removed the flash drives, put them in a zippered jacket pocket, and stood. "I need to talk to Tom."

"Let's go outside. I'll call him. Are the videos enough?"

Gino smiled. "Game on."

CHAPTER SEVENTY-TWO

Candid Camera

HIM

Immediately after I handed Freddi the flash drives, she sped out of the lot, narrowly missing my toes. As I got in my car, Jamie climbed into the passenger side. "Please, Tom, please. You have to let me ride with you. I might have the chance to help those girls I failed before."

"Jamie, I'm handing this off to the real cops. I'm not going to be anywhere near the action."

"Please, please. Just in case. I'll follow all your orders—to the letter. Please."

Pathetic. What could it hurt?

"To the letter?"

"Honest."

"Okay. I'll pick you up at your office."

He was out of my car and into his in a flash. I followed him to Term Limits Pest Control, drumming my fingers on the steering wheel. No danger of him getting pulled over by a traffic cop. My great-grandmother would have urged him to speed up. Maybe I should stop for a mental evaluation on the way. I had plenty of time.

He parked in their lot and jumped in my car, all smiles. "What's next, boss?"

"Retrieve the hidden camera. I don't want to leave any

traceable loose ends. Your job is to be an extra set of eyes. If you see any suspicious vehicles or people, let me know and I won't stop."

The fastest way to get to the camera was to pull into the gas station like an idiot who didn't realize it wasn't open. Get out ready to pump, then notice the place was closed. During the charade I'd take the camera off the pump and leave using the side street. Only about twenty seconds of exposure. If Jamie warned me off I'd turn down the side street and try again in a few minutes.

I drove to the gas station with Jamie's head ratcheting around like the lamp on an old lighthouse. When we were close I said, "See any reason for me not to pull in?"

Jamie peered around the headrest again. "The W & Z van's not in sight. All clear. Go for it."

I wheeled in, stopped under the roof on the right side of the pumps, and bailed out. Nick's Lincoln went by. Damn. Did he see me?

He didn't slow down. A good sign. I was partially hidden by the pumps and in the shadow of the roof. If he did see me, would it matter? Would he change plans? He didn't know me. Earlier he eyeballed me passing the Barely Here strip club. Did that even register with him?

Ten seconds later I was back in the driver's seat with the camera in my hand.

I pulled straight ahead to the side street, hung a right, and got the hell out of there. "Jamie, you didn't think Nick's car was worth mentioning?"

He smacked his forehead with his palm. "That was Nick's car? I thought it was a car from a funeral home."

A funeral home. I hoped that wasn't prophetic. I had to find a place for Jamie out of harm's way—meaning doing me harm.

I returned to Term Limits and dropped Jamie off. To

accomplish this, I had to convince him that I wasn't ditching him, that I wanted us to have two cars available.

My phone rang. Sabrina's number showed on the screen, which meant it was Gino. He was enthusiastic to say the least. "Tom, this is dynamite. I was calling in the tags as they came up on the screen and almost all of them came back to pedophiles and—Wait a minute. You already knew that. How—"

"Not important. So you have plenty of probable cause without involving a human."

"Hell yeah. We'll match the video with mug shots and other photos and arrest records and nail it down tight."

"And you'll get Desiree off the hook."

"I always keep my word."

"I'm relying on that. The timing on serving the warrant is paramount. I should be able to give you a fifteen-minute notice on when to hit—as late as midnight, probably earlier. Stage your teams well away from the target, which is protected by electronic and video perimeter surveillance. If you get burned or mistime the raid, you'll miss the big guys and..."

I hesitated, trying to decide if revealing more would jeopardize Misha.

"And what?"

"A truckload of trafficked girls, most so young they'd be in middle school in this country."

He let out a whoosh then went silent.

Continuing to communicate with Gino through Sabrina's phone wasn't viable. I had another option. My desperation cell phone—to be used only in the most critical situations—was in my cargo pocket. The Squid had so many false trails on it that tracing true ownership was impossible short of the NSA. Trafficked girls were desperation enough for me.

I gave the number to Gino and had him call it from his cell. Our line of communication was established. It was now the Rescue Phone. He said, "I returned your associate's phone to her."

We discussed how soon he could have his troops in place and the safety of the trafficked girls after the truck arrived. He said, "As soon as we disconnect I'll call the brass to get them on board. They'll get the raid teams assembled. I'll work on the warrant and the tactical plan. When we roll I'll be the only one in contact with you. Everything you want to be secret will stay that way."

I didn't mention the new dacha near Barely Here or Scorpion or his Vette because that information could point directly to Misha. Besides, the new dacha wasn't in play and I had a tracker on Scorpion's Vette.

Now, what could I do with Freddi to keep her safe?

"Sounds perfect, Gino. Please have my associate call me."

Gino clicked off and a few seconds later my phone rang. Freddi said, "I'm here."

"Call me after you drop Desiree at work. We'll meet so I can update you."

"Where?"

I gave her directions to the parking lot across the street from Scorpion's restaurant. I'd be able to watch his car in case the tracker failed. This raid was too important not to have a backup plan.

Freddi chauffeuring Desiree would buy me time to think about how to keep her out of danger. She'd want to be a part of the diamond action once she found out about Boris and Rita.

I yawned. The night was just getting started. I was already bushed. I reached into the console and grabbed the Tracker Phone.

Rita's Mercedes and Erik's Mustang were moving north on

I-275.

The Borismobile near the Panty Free Zone and Scorpion's Vette in the parking lot—no movement.

I put the Tracker Phone in my left cargo pocket. I had the Rescue Phone in my right cargo pocket and my cell phone on my belt.

Three cell phones and four trackers in play.

I hoped my head wouldn't explode.

CHAPTER SEVENTY-THREE

Mushroom

HER

As I walked through the library lot, I called Tom. He said we should meet for an update—although I detected a reluctance in his voice—right after I took Desiree to the Naked Truth. He gave me directions to a Porto Avenue parking lot. It was the one across the street from the alley where I had my tête-à-tête with Nick and the honky-tonk cowboy. And where Tom took an interest in an electric blue Corvette.

I got into my car with time to kill before meeting Desiree. I didn't want to wait for her at the Stopped Clock because I might succumb to another of Cube's sirloin burgers. I already had some extra hours in the gym ahead of me. I sat and thought about the complicated mess Tom was going to have to explain.

The minutes evaporated and it was time to go. Before I fastened my seat belt, Desiree called. "Sabrina, Cube's going to drive me to the Naked Truth and stay to take me home."

"You didn't say anything to him about Gino and tonight's action, did you?"

"What could I say? I know nothing. I'm like the old joke about being a mushroom kept in the dark. Cube called me to see if everything was okay—I think mainly because the introduction today was unusual, to say the least. I told him things were strange, but I was going to go to work anyway. He asked if Tom would be there."

"Why did he ask that?"

"I have no idea. Cube is a genius. He understands things most people don't. He knows the Russian mob runs the Naked Truth. That worries him as much as my dancing. When I said Tom wouldn't be there, Cube said he would. You don't argue with Cube."

I didn't realize how concerned I was about Desiree until she told me about Cube. I didn't know the full story yet, but nothing was going to happen at the Naked Truth. Tom wouldn't let her walk into trouble. However with Cube there, she'd be safe if things went totally off the rails.

Since I wasn't taxiing Desiree, Tom would have a lot of time to update me, as he put it—or move me off the mushroom farm, as Desiree might put it.

I called Tom to give him the news. He didn't seem all that thrilled, but after a long hesitation—with a *hold-on-I'm-thinking* feel to it—he said he'd meet me in about half an hour.

The first time I ever saw him close to indecisive.

"One other thing—when you get there, hide in the back. We don't want to be seen. And here's a news flash. Rita and Erik are headed to Tampa."

"How do you know that?"

"I'll tell you more when I get there, but I have trackers on their cars."

That shocked me but I could top it. "There's an additional tracker on them."

"What do you mean?"

"Missy is following Rita and Erik. She decided it was in our best interests to try to learn what they're up to."

A long pause followed before Tom said, "How did she know where—"

"I found them at the Paradise Resort this morning."

"Tell her to break off and go home. If she gets burned, it'll kill the deal."

"After Missy ends her surveillance, she wants to come here."

"Why in the hell would she do that?"

"In case we need help with the trafficked girls."

"I told you we're out of that. It's in the hands of Gino and his task force. Tell Missy to go home where she'll be safe."

Tom sounded stressed, so I didn't mention she and I had already been through that. "I'll tell her."

He exhaled loudly. "You and I have a lot to talk about." He clicked off.

I drove to the lot, which was at least three-quarters full. I found a dark spot in a row near the back. The blue Vette didn't appear to have moved.

Missy called. "We're in Tampa on Hillsborough. Both cars just pulled into a diner."

"Don't get burned. Tom has trackers on both cars."

"Why—"

"I don't know yet. He's coming here to explain."

I gave her my location, lowered my windows, and let the evening breeze flow through. The breeze was cool, which was good because my temperature was rising as I thought about Tom hemming and hawing when we spoke.

Now that I knew about the trafficked girls I more or less forgave him for wanting to check his text message when we were barely out of—actually still in—the throes of passion. But was he trying to keep me in the dark about Boris and what was happening with the raid?

I studied the alley where I ran into Nick and the honky-tonk cowboy. To the left of the alley was a one-story building with a large neon sign identifying it as Beer-R-Us and smaller signs in the windows advertising beer brands.

Tom picked this parking lot for a reason. I had a feeling it had to do with the two-story building and the blue Corvette, not the beer joint.

Missy's car passed in front of me. She parked two spaces down and got out with her tightly furled chartreuse umbrella. She wore a black long-sleeved T-shirt, black tights, and black athletic shoes. She looked like a blonde ninja with a radioactive sword. She walked toward my car, then stopped and did some fencing moves with her umbrella.

She slid into the passenger's seat. "How was that? Swashbuckling enough for you?"

"If they ever make a *Three Musketeerettes* movie, Hollywood will be calling. As you can see, Tom's not here yet. By the way, he said I should tell you to go home where you'll be safe."

"I do believe you and I just had this conversation."

"I told him I'd tell you and now I have."

I pointed across the street. "I'm thinking about checking out that building to determine where the cowboy came from."

"A marvelous idea."

I closed my windows, turned right out of the parking lot, then left on Boney Road. Earlier I hadn't paid attention to the building as I was rushing to the alley to see what Tom was doing.

Missy peered past me. "The art store downstairs appears to be closed for the night but upstairs..." She clapped her hands together. "Look at the windows. Taekwondo and Brazilian jujitsu. A martial arts school. Maybe I can get a quick lesson in case my umbrella isn't enough."

We laughed as I made another left. Two men in white karate outfits with black belts were entering a doorway leading up to the dojo. The downstairs was also dark on this side, except for the entrance to the Blue Moon Restaurant. Light came through all the restaurant windows upstairs. A sidewalk sign announced it was open from four to ten.

I drove past the alley where I ran into Nick and the cowboy then circled around the Beer-R-Us building back into my same slot in the parking lot. I said to myself as much as to Missy, "The honky-tonk cowboy had to come from the Blue Moon Restaurant this afternoon."

What did it mean? I had no idea, but investigating was way better than sitting and waiting for Tom to show up.

I was not going to be a mushroom.

And Tom was in for a surprise.

Missy!

CHAPTER SEVENTY-FOUR

Riot Squad

HIM

Freddi's Sabrina cell number popped up on my dashboard screen. I answered hands-free wondering why Freddi was calling. She wasn't taking Desiree to the Naked Truth so we could meet now. The walls were closing in. I told her about Rita, Erik, and the trackers. I was even more unhappy after she told me about Missy following Rita and Erik.

There was plenty of time for Missy to turn back and stay far away from this mess. I told Freddi to send Missy home. I wanted Freddi to return to Crooked Foot Key also but couldn't come up with a reason that would be immediately acceptable to her. I said I'd be there in thirty minutes, resigned to telling her the full story and hoping to convince her to go home. I clicked off. Where were Boris, Rita, and Erik going to do the diamond deal?

My Bluetooth alerted again. Misha calling. I prepared myself for bad news. "Problems, Misha?"

"You know Boris Nabokov?" He sounded stressed.

"Why?"

"He led you to Nicolai, didn't he? A private eye isn't likely to investigate trafficking on his own. You ran across it doing something else. The only other thing Nicolai's into right now is a scam that this screwup is trying to pull off. If Boris is going to be arrested tonight, I don't want to go down with him."

"Misha, everything is cool. You aren't going to be arrested. As for the trafficking, the cops don't know my name let alone yours. You're completely out of it like I promised."

"Sorry, Tom," he said in a calmer voice. "Nick's been strange for a couple of months, and he's even worse today. Maybe it's rubbing off on me. Originally I was to be at the Valley of Love club tonight to be near the dacha in case *el Escorpión* needed to be stomped on during the exchange. Nicolai doesn't trust that crazy bastard."

"You said *originally*."

"My orders just changed. I'm to guard diamonds for Boris to use in his scam and stay with him until the scam's over."

"Perfect."

"In one way, yes. I won't be anywhere near the transfer of the girls. But if Boris is going down tonight and I'm there..."

"Where's there?"

"The building on Porto Avenue I showed you this afternoon. Boris is going to meet me at the Panty Free Zone and follow me to the lot where you and I met. We'll go up to Nicolai's business office. After Boris sets the stage, he'll call the mark who'll be waiting in the same lot and tell her where to find us. It's set for ten o'clock."

"I'll be there, but I don't have enough to get Boris arrested yet. Maybe after tonight I will. Once it all hits the fan, slip out of the office. I'll keep you out of it. I might need to take the seed diamonds for evidence."

Misha let out a one-ha laugh. "Boris has experience at losing them."

"It sounds like Boris's scam should be over before the U Move truck gets here. Will you have to check in with Nicolai when it's done?"

"He won't be thinking about Boris. Nicolai is always edgy about transfers, but he's more nervous than usual. I don't know why. Maybe it's an extra-large shipment of girls or maybe just the way he's been lately. He's bringing in extra men. If anything changes—and I hope not because this is complicated enough—I'll text you."

Misha was right. This was complicated, and he didn't have Freddi to deal with.

I called The Squid and told him about the diamond scam. Unfortunately, he didn't have any suggestions on how to handle it. Even more unfortunately, neither did I.

Jamie sat in his car, his eyes riveted on me like he was afraid I'd drive off at any second and leave him behind.

I texted Jamie the location of the parking lot where I was meeting Freddi and told him to go there. His tortoise style of driving would afford me at least five minutes with her in private.

Traffic was kind. I made up for the delay of Misha's call, entered the lot on time, parked five spots away from Freddi, and waved her over. Astounded didn't begin to describe me when I saw Missy with her.

They walked in sync as they came toward my car, each in dark-colored clothing, a large shoulder bag, and a furled umbrella pounding the ground every other step. A pretty good representation of a two-person riot squad—slightly spoiled by Missy's chartreuse umbrella.

I jumped out of my car. "Missy, what the hell are you doing here?"

"Delighted to see you too, Tom."

"I didn't mean it like that." I stepped forward to give her our usual cheek-to-cheek.

She gave me a hard full-body hug—umbrella and all. She leaned back and said, "I'm right sorry to surprise you. I was darn near here when Freddi allowed as how you had Rita and Erik on your radar. I kept on keeping on, dearly wanting to help. Please don't be angry."

We broke apart. I said, "I'm not angry but you—and Freddi too—need to get the hell out of here. Tonight's action—"

"And now," Freddi said in a sharp voice, "you have two of us to worry about. We're not helpless damsels in distress. We can do what needs to be done without you protecting us."

"Is that what you think, Tom?" Missy said, her voice as sharp as Freddi's. "That we're a burden?"

Not only did I have two of them to worry about, I had two of them to deal with. "I couldn't live with myself if anything happened to either of you. You'd be safer at home."

"So would you," Freddi said. "The trafficked girls are important to you. They're important to us. We're in as long as you're in."

I looked from Freddi to Missy to Freddi. "You have to promise if things get dangerous you'll do exactly as I say."

"We promise," Missy said.

"Scout's honor." Freddi held up her hand with three fingers extended.

Why didn't I feel reassured?

"Law enforcement is handling the rescue of the trafficked girls completely. My only role is to give them the cue to move in. The diamond deal is what's on my plate."

That got their attention. Missy said, "Diamond deal?"

"Which you two can't afford to be around because it could be a serious problem for you in Crooked Foot Key. Boris is going to run a stolen diamond scam on Rita. She has expertise in gems and thinks she can dispose of hot rocks through some shady contacts, all without Ralph finding out. The so-called stolen diamonds will be phonies. So if Rita sees either one of you..."

Freddi's eyes were wide. "How do you know this?"

"Get in and I'll tell you about it."

I sat in the driver's seat angling myself toward the back seat. Freddi and Missy walked around my SUV. Freddi slid into the passenger's seat. Missy jumped in the back behind her. I said, "I'm not trying to be mysterious."

"That's right admirable," Missy said. "Just how mysterious would you be if you were trying?"

It was going to be a long night. "In addition to you and Freddi staying away from the diamond deal, we all need to stay as far away from the trafficking as possible. Especially you, Freddi."

"You're still trying to get rid of us."

"It's for your own good. If you're anywhere near the rescue, there's a risk of exposure—both as Freddi and Sabrina. At a minimum, testifying against the Russians would wipe out Sabrina's business. Also it could endanger you. Right now you can say Bikini Realty sold a condo to Boris—actually Jules Armand—and he backed out. Period."

"I'm already involved beyond the condo deal. I met with Gino. Remember?"

"He doesn't know who you are and—"

"I know things you don't know, Tom. For instance, why are we in your car? Because Sabrina's car is known to Nick and his people, right?"

Freddi didn't give me a chance to respond. She said, "For your information, this car is known to Nick and so are you."

"How—"

"He asked me about you this afternoon."

She told me about her escapade in the alley with Nick.

I thumped the steering wheel. "I thought *I* was paranoid. How in the hell could he have made that connection? Something about working with Scorpion tonight has him on edge. He put a ridiculous two and two together and came up with an accurate four."

"My guess is I saw Scorpion earlier today," Freddi said.

"One more reason you and Missy should go home. He's dangerous. Very dangerous to women."

Freddi responded glibly. "I'm sure if it comes down to it, you'll shoot him for us."

"I'd be happy to—except I don't carry a gun."

"What?!" they replied in unison.

"You don't carry a gun?" Freddi said. "What kind of ex-cop private eye are you? I've seen hundreds of shows. They all carry guns. Some carry a bunch."

I explained my philosophy about not carrying a gun.

When Freddi said, "That's plain stupid," I was pretty sure she was less than impressed.

Missy put her hand over her eyes and shook her head.

"If you two insist on staying, I'm going to tell you things you have to forget—for the sake of the life and family of my confidential source."

Then I heard an unusual noise. "Do you hear that?"

"Hear what?" Missy asked.

I lowered the windows. Distant cheering and shouting. I said, "What the hell is that?"

Jamie Bond stuck his head through the passenger window opening.

Freddi shrieked.

Missy shrieked.

"I know what it is," Jamie said.

CHAPTER SEVENTY-FIVE

Aprilfest

HER

I shrieked. The same little guy who delivered the flash drives to Tom stuck his head through my window and startled the hell out of me. Lucky for him I didn't have my stun gun in hand. And what was that bulge under his coat?

"It's Aprilfest," he said in response to Tom's question about the distant noise.

Who cared? Tom was about to open up when this dweeb interrupted.

"Jamie, get in. We need to talk. By the way, this lady you are almost drooling on is the Zapper."

His face reddened. He stuck his hand out and said, "Pleased to meet you, Miss Zapper. Bond, Jamie Bond."

"Please, I only go by Miss Zapper in formal situations. My friends call me Sabrina."

Tom sounded like he was choking back a laugh, but Jamie said with a solemn face, "I'd be honored to call you Sabrina, Miss Sabrina."

I didn't want to pull this guy's leg, but if Tom didn't want him to know my real name, I'd roll with it. Part of Tom's compartmentalization?

Jamie opened the door behind me and almost catapulted himself into Missy's lap. He halted in mid-launch and stammered, "I...I...I'm sorry. I...I didn't know...this seat was..."

I hesitated then said, "Jamie, this is my friend..." I clammed up. I didn't think Tom would want me to say her name so I didn't know what I should call her.

The longer he looked at Missy, the more he melted and stammered. At this rate a giant spatula would be the only way to pry him off the ground.

Missy smiled and held out her hand.

Jamie's face quivered. "Pleased to meet you, Miss Friend."

They shook hands while Tom made another choking sound. Missy had to work her hand free. She patted the seat next to her. "I'd be most pleased if you'd come over here beside me."

He walked around the front of the car, his head bobbing like his legs were rubber. On his second attempt he managed to clamber into the back seat. He fell so far sideways his head bounced off Missy's shoulder. She helped him straighten up.

Jamie smiled sheepishly. "Thank you, Miss Friend."

"Did I hear Aprilfest, Jamie?" Tom said. "As in Oktoberfest?"

"Yes. The Nights Bavarian Social Club is on the street behind us, a block north. What you're hearing is Nights Bavarian."

Tom rubbed his face. "Like Knights Templar?"

"*Nights* without a *K*. Musical nights. The third Wednesday of every month they have an Oktoberfest-type celebration with traditional music and traditional performances. Next month they'll have Maifest."

"Sounds like the Social Club," Tom said, "is across the street from the new dacha."

"I do believe," Missy said, "I never heard that word before."

"That's Russian for vacation home," Tom said. "In this case, a place where trafficked girls are housed and forced into sex work. When I checked it out earlier, I was so focused I didn't notice the Social Club."

Jamie made a circular motion with his hand. "Understandable. It's a large building but nothing notable about it. The stable for Boomer's Horse-drawn Carriage Tours next door draws a lot more attention. Because the weather's nice tonight, Aprilfest is being held in the courtyard in back of the building."

With traditional bier to go with the traditional music, no doubt. I said, "Jamie, how do you know all this?"

"I'm on their email list."

Cheering and clapping from the direction of the Club hit a crescendo and an *oom pah pah* broke out. Evidently the band was back from break. Group singing accompanied the *oom pah pah*. Tom closed the windows.

"What's my assignment, boss?" Jamie asked with little-boy eagerness in his voice.

Tom massaged his neck. "The girls coming in tonight are to be delivered to the dacha you and I had under surveillance today. But—just in case—it can't hurt to have eyes on the new dacha on Rail Avenue."

Jamie held a finger in the air. "Ludwig's Schnitzel Shack is there just this side of the Social Club. He has the best schnitzel in Tampa. A window seat will give me a clear view of all the buildings on the other side of the street."

Tom nodded.

Jamie looked at Tom. "Should Miss Friend or Miss Sabrina accompany me—for cover purposes? A couple is less conspicuous than a single guy."

I almost smiled. That sly dog. There was more to Jamie than I thought.

Tom did smile, sort of a proud parent smile. He shot a quick glance at me then at Missy.

"Sorry, Jamie. I have other assignments for them. If you see anything, call me. Stay in your seat. Do *not* get involved. I'll alert the police so they can handle it. I repeat. Do *not* get involved."

"Definitely." Jamie opened the door and stepped down. "I'm on it, boss."

Tom shuddered when Jamie said *boss.* He watched Jamie trot out of the lot and shook his head. He turned to us and said, "Okay—"

His phone rang. Damn. Interrupted again just as he was about to open up.

He listened for a few seconds and removed a cell phone from his left cargo pocket. "I'm on the Tracker Phone now and seeing what you see. Rita and Erik are moving again. They were at a diner. My information is that Rita is doing the deal. Erik might be with her for protection, but why two cars?"

Tom glanced at his Tracker Phone again then stared out the window. "I'm positive the Vette hasn't moved. I'm looking at it now. I want to have an eyeball on it in case of a technical glitch. Scorpion's location is key to the rescue."

Now I knew why Tom was kneeling by the blue Corvette this afternoon.

Tom gave whoever was on the other end of the call a complete rundown on the trafficking situation. He ended by saying, "Gino and his people will handle it all. I'm completely out of it and the informant is covered up. I still don't know how I'll handle the diamond scam. Maybe Freddi and Missy will have some suggestions."

Grunts, snorts, and profanity exploded through the phone. Tom held it away from his ear. When it subsided he said, "Yes, they're with me. They're not in danger. I told you the cops are going to handle the rescue. It's under control."

Tom listened again. "I don't quite know how they ended up here, but if something goes wrong, I'll be glad they're with me. And before you say it, not just because they're gorgeous." He clicked off.

"That was your boss?" I asked. "Something else you never mentioned."

"Like you never mentioned Tony Catalina."

So he knew about Uncle Tony. We each knew things the other didn't. "I think we need to fess up."

"I agree. You and Missy go first."

CHAPTER SEVENTY-SIX

Andrei the Giant

HIM

Freddi smiled at me. I expected resistance to her and Missy going first. Instead she said, "How can we argue with a guy who launched a major police operation without identifying himself?"

"A backdoor way of asking who I am. My real name is Rick Dante but for this gig, let's keep it as Tom McCall and Sabrina and avoid using Missy's name altogether."

Freddi put her palms to her cheeks and formed a vertical oval with her lips. "Oh no, I went to bed with a man whose name I didn't know. Does that make me a round-heeled slut?"

"Absolutely," Missy said.

The Bikini Realty babes were something else.

Missy and Freddi tagged in and out—as I should have expected—while telling me about Jules Armand, who they now knew was Boris, and what they knew about Rita Miller and Erik Thoreson. Freddi told me the Sabrina story starting with college and Uncle Tony and finishing with Nick and Scorpion.

I told them about Boris's scam including Rita's Lolita background and Erik's history with her. They already knew about the rescue plans so I didn't bother with those. I also talked about the trackers and audio tapes but didn't mention Misha. I held off in case the diamond deal was moved at the last minute and they didn't see him.

While we talked, every trace of light left the sky. The streetlights in the area weren't that great.

Jamie called to say he hadn't seen any activity outside the dacha but there were lights on inside and the schnitzel was excellent.

I checked the trackers. Rita and Erik were about fifteen minutes out. The Borismobile heading to us from the Panty Free Zone was about five minutes away. The diamond scam was going to go down as Misha said. It was time to tell the Bikini Realty babes about him. "I have to tell you about one more person. I gave my word to him that he wouldn't be exposed, but you'll soon see him."

"So who's the mystery person?" Missy said.

"He's going to be in the office to watch over the seed diamonds because Nick doesn't trust Boris. I call him Misha. He has family in Russia who will be in jeopardy if his part in this ever comes out. He runs Nick's strip club operation."

"You're talking about Andrei," Freddi said. "I think of him as Andrei the Giant. Decent guy. Always a gentleman."

"We must protect him at all costs. Busting up the diamond scam should be a relatively low-profile operation, but Misha has to get away." As a joke I added, "So zapping is okay but don't shoot anyone."

"I couldn't if I wanted to," Freddi said. "My gun is in the hidden compartment in my 300F. I didn't see a need for it. I came up here to meet with Uncle Tony."

I rechecked the Tracker Phone. The Borismobile was almost here. Rita and Erik were closer but still ten or fifteen minutes away, depending on traffic.

"Ladies, this might happen a little earlier than planned. I have to recon the dacha. Stay out of sight and call me if you see any of the players."

"Aye, aye, sir," Freddi said with a smile.

I walked out of the parking lot to Rail Avenue as fast as I could, turned north, and crossed Boney Road. I passed a music store on the corner then Ludwig's Schnitzel Shack where Jamie sat in a booth by the window with an empty plate in front of him.

Oom pah pah filled the air.

The Nights Bavarian Social Club was next to Ludwig's, almost directly across from the dacha. A number of people—the men dressed in lederhosen, the women in dirndl dresses complete with aprons—were milling around on the sidewalk.

Past the Social Club was an old building that had been converted into Boomer's Horse-drawn Carriage Tours. Two tourist-filled four-passenger carriages—each drawn by a Clydesdale clopping southbound in a narrow lane reserved for them—were turning into the faux stable. A number of the Social Club revelers appeared to be waiting for their turns for a carriage ride.

Across the street, the dacha was closed up tight but light showed around the edges of the garage door.

Three inebriated men in lederhosen—one with a huge handlebar mustache—paced randomly and lackadaisically in front of the entrance to the Social Club. They carried three-by-five-foot flags embroidered with *Nights Bavarian* on thick eight-foot wooden poles topped with brass orbs. Handlebar Mustache stopped, leaned against the wall, and peered into his stein. I thought he was going to shed a tear.

I stepped up to him. "Want me to handle the flag while you get a refill? I'll even walk it down to the corner to drum up more business."

Handlebar Mustache slurred, "Where are your lederhosen?"

"Cleaners messed up. Can't get them till tomorrow."

He nodded wisely. "I'll only be a minute."

"Take all the time you need."

I walked rapidly, waving the flag like I was serious if anybody was watching or cared.

Not a great weapon but better than nothing.

Talking and trickery probably weren't going to be enough with Erik in the mix.

Maybe Freddi was right.

Maybe not carrying a gun was plain stupid.

CHAPTER SEVENTY-SEVEN

Battle Flag

HER

Tom walked away and I said to Missy, "I better get in the back too. We can't let Rita or Boris see us. We'll have to scooch down till this is over."

"I had to stop for gas after I, *ahem*, terminated my surveillance." She smiled. "I picked up two club sodas. I'll go get them."

Missy got out and I moved to the back seat. She returned, handed me a large cup, and said, "This could be a tad more serious than we're taking it. I'm glad Tom is here."

We slid down and watched the parking lot entrance.

A few minutes later, a giant driving a black Suburban pulled into the lot and parked near the entrance. I saw Boris's car on the street.

I called Tom. "Misha is here and Boris is entering the lot right now."

"In the Borismobile?"

"Of course, but it's funny you should call it that. I named Rita's car the Ritamobile."

"We might need group—small group—counseling."

"Boris parked next to Misha near the entrance. He's waiting for Boris to get out."

"I just checked Rita's tracker. She's only about a minute or two away. Erik's car stopped moving."

"Okay, Tom, they're crossing Porto Avenue. Now they're going up the stairs like you said they would."

"Once they've set the scene, Boris will call Rita to come to the office. I'm almost to the parking lot."

I swiveled my head. Tom was crossing Boney Road carrying a Nights Bavarian flag on a long pole. He lowered it and came to the car.

The Ritamobile rolled in. Tom squatted next to my window out of her sight line. She parked one row away from the entrance. Was everybody preparing for a fast getaway?

Rita stayed in her car. About five minutes later she got out talking on her phone. She dropped it into her purse, crossed over to the alley, and went up the stairs.

I started to tell Tom he nailed it but he was looking at his Tracker Phone. He said, "Erik's on the move. Rita must have just called him in. I have to see his play before I make mine. Who knows if his action will make Rita more likely or less likely to cooperate?"

A minute later Erik's beater Mustang muscle car parked two spaces away from the Ritamobile. He got out of his car empty-handed, wearing a black windbreaker. He looked around then walked out of the lot toward the alley.

Tom leaned through the window and spoke softly. "I don't have a good feeling. This is too fast if he's here to protect her after she gets the diamonds. You two stay out of sight no matter what you see or hear. If I'm not back in ten minutes, jump in your cars and get the hell out of here. I'll catch up to you in Crooked Foot."

Words fell out of my mouth. "Be careful, Tom. You coming back to me in one piece is more important than a Boris scam."

He patted my cheek then trotted across the street—carrying the flagpole like Sir Lancelot—and turned into the stairwell.

CHAPTER SEVENTY-EIGHT

A Farewell to Arms

HIM

Freddi's words echoed in my ears as I ran across Porto Avenue. I pushed her out of my mind. My flag and I reached the bottom of the stairs as Erik cleared the last step at the top and drew a Desert Eagle semiautomatic—a rival for Jamie's most powerful handgun in the world—from a hip holster. I was certain he had a body armor vest under his jacket.

I ran up the stairs silently two at a time and saw him throw the office door wide open, go in with his Desert Eagle in a two-handed grip, and say, "Freeze you motherstickers, this is a fuckup."

A desk faced the door. Boris sat behind it and Misha stood to his left.

Rita was sitting in a chair in front of the desk. She jumped up, took a small .22 revolver from her purse, backed up to the wall, and pointed the gun at Boris. She said, "Stickup!"

Erik turned his head in her direction. "Huh?"

She rolled her eyes. "Stickup! This is a stickup!"

He returned his attention to Boris. "Yeah. Stickup. Give me the diamonds."

I'd been worried about stopping Boris from scamming Rita but she'd been planning a rip-off the whole time.

Boris pulled his own Desert Eagle pistol from the desk drawer. Two of those uncommon Desert Eagles? Were they on sale someplace?

Erik and Boris deserved each other, but I couldn't abide bullets flying everywhere, hitting innocent people.

I extended the flagpole into the room with the flag between Boris and Erik so they couldn't see each other to shoot. That worked as well as a Chinese Rolex. They shot through the flag simultaneously. The noise was eye watering even from where I stood slightly outside the office.

Erik took one in his body armor, dropped his gun, and slid down the wall. If the vest stopped that powerful bullet, it would be paralyzingly painful, like getting kicked by a mule. If the vest didn't stop the bullet, he would be pain-free forever.

I lowered the flag. Boris's gun lay on the desk but he wasn't in sight. The wall behind the desk resembled a Rorschach inkblot test in red instead of black. Misha looked to his right and down. He touched the middle of his forehead. Boris had more than a flesh wound.

Rita still had her revolver pointed where Boris used to be but she was looking at Erik sitting on the floor. She spun toward him and accidentally pulled the trigger, harmlessly plunking a round from the small caliber gun into the wall above his head. She shrieked, dropped the gun, and knelt beside Erik, crying.

All the guns were out of play.

A farewell to arms.

Misha hadn't moved. I said, "Grab the diamonds and go."

Either he had some hearing left or could read my lips. He snatched a velvet bag with a drawstring off the desk, slapped me on the shoulder as he passed, ran down the stairs to the alley, and turned left toward the parking lot.

A few seconds later Scorpion charged out of the kitchen fire exit of his restaurant. He looked toward Nick's office with his right hand on a holstered gun exposed by his flipped-back sport coat.

He glared at me. I could have—and possibly should have—looked away like I had no interest in him. Instead I lasered him with my eyes.

We both knew what we knew.

He shrugged like it was Nick's business, not his, and let his coat fall over the gun. He swaggered down the stairs.

I waited until he was out of sight, hurried down, and peeked around the edge of the stairwell. Misha's Suburban was speeding away northbound and Scorpion was crossing the street. He walked to his Vette, looked around, and got in.

Rita stumbled past me, bawling like an abandoned calf. She caught her balance, ran to her bright red Mercedes, and screeched out of the lot southbound.

Scorpion's car didn't move. He was barely visible through the windshield, talking on his cell. I didn't dare move until he drove off.

Gino called on the Rescue Phone. "Are you sure about your information? We just reconned that building. Not a sign of life."

Scorpion pulled out of the lot northbound.

"Hang on, Gino. If there's been a change I'll know shortly."

I looked at the Tracker Phone. Scorpion's Corvette turned east on Boney Road.

That was the wrong way.

Was he headed to the nearby dacha?

He turned left on Rail Avenue.

Jamie called on my regular phone. "The garage door just went up. Two guys stepped out of the building. They're looking down the street. Now a snazzy Corvette is in front of the opening.

One of the guys is directing it inside. The door is closing. It wasn't open fifteen seconds."

I rubbed the back of my neck. Did Nick see me retrieving the camera at the Valley of Love dacha and change the location of the transfer?

"Good work, Jamie. Stay put."

That news was devastating. The search warrant was for the Valley of Love dacha.

Back to the Rescue Phone. "Gino, they moved the operation."

"That wipes out our warrant!"

"You'll have to go with probable cause and exigent circumstances."

"That's going to make it harder to keep you out of it."

"Just keep my associate and Desiree hidden. I don't want the Russians on their butts. If I have to testify, I'll do whatever it takes to avoid divulging the existence of an informant let alone the identity."

"Gotcha."

"The deal is going to go down at a new dacha on the east side of Rail Avenue, a half block north of Boney Road, across from the Nights Bavarian Social Club. The truck is still key. I'll be able to tell you when it arrives so you can move in."

I trotted to my car, leaned the flag on the fender, and got in. Freddi and Missy were still in the back seat. Freddi said, "What happened up there? I thought I heard an explosion. Next thing, Misha and Rita ran to their cars and sped away."

"Rita and Erik were trying to rob Boris." I gave them the Twitter version of the shoot-out, finishing with, "One of the shots ended your problems with Boris."

A simultaneous gasp. Freddi said, "That's terrible. We

wouldn't have wished that on him."

"Don't waste any tears. Boris was a heartless con man taking life savings from widows and retirees before he came up with his scams to rip off the rich and obscure.

I opened my door.

Freddi grabbed my arm. "Where are you going?"

"Scorpion's in the dacha that Jamie's watching, which means Nick has changed the location of the transfer of the girls. I need to get Jamie out of the restaurant. I don't want him anywhere close to the action. I'll have him come back to wait with you and Missy. As soon as I see the U Move truck at the dacha, I'll call Gino and join you here."

I got out of my car and snatched the flag from the fender.

Freddi got out with her umbrella. "I'm going with you. Don't argue. If it hadn't been for me introducing you to my dancer Desiree, you wouldn't be here."

That logic was so faulty it didn't merit a response—a response that would have been a waste of my breath anyway.

Freddi batted her eyes at me. "Besides—like Jamie says—a couple is less conspicuous than a single guy."

I slowly shook my head. "Missy, wait here for Jamie."

Freddi and I walked toward the *oom pah pah.*

CHAPTER SEVENTY-NINE

Ein Prosit

HER

I held Tom's arm just like the average couple on an evening stroll carrying a big flag. On my other side I had my oversized purse on my shoulder and my umbrella in my hand. Clouds had rolled in and blacked out the moon. It was a dark night—fortunately not stormy.

I heard running footsteps behind us. Missy caught up and took Tom's flag arm.

He leaned his head and spoke in her ear, but not softly. "Missy, you promised to follow my instructions."

"If things got dangerous," she said. "This isn't as dangerous as dancing in stiletto heels. And Fre...I mean Sabrina and I are a team. Now we're a team of three. Let me know if you need to borrow my umbrella."

I was sure Tom would have massaged the back of his neck if Missy and I weren't holding his arms.

We crossed Boney Road and stopped at the closed-for-the-night musical instrument shop on the corner. The backlit sign for Ludwig's Schnitzel Shack hung over the sidewalk two doors ahead.

Oom pah pah. The music was much louder than in the parking lot, and many people—including those on the sidewalk—were singing *Ein Prosit.*

Tom pulled us into the wide entrance to the shop. It was framed by glass windows displaying tubas, zithers, accordions, German bagpipes, and the like.

He stuck a finger in one ear and jammed his cell phone against the other. "Jamie, pay your bill and meet us at the music shop on the corner."

His face darkened. "I don't give a damn how good their Bavarian cream dessert is. Get your ass out here now. Right now." He clicked off emphatically.

Missy tugged on his arm. "Tom, what are those people singing?"

"A German beer drinking song. Very popular at Oktoberfest and—wild guess—Aprilfest."

The music coming from the Nights Bavarian Social Club got louder. The instruments began to overpower the singing. Reinforcement tubas? *Oom pah pah.*

Tom shook his head as Jamie stepped toward us in time to the music. Who would have guessed he could dance? Sort of dance. Okay, he didn't trip. Often.

I took my eyes off Jamie's jig and looked up the street. Next to the sidewalk a carriage from Boomer's Horse-drawn Carriage Tours clopped toward us in the narrow lane reserved for carriages. The passengers were two couples from the Social Club, judging by their garb and the bier steins in their hands.

In front of Ludwig's Schnitzel Shack the carriage lane was partially blocked by orange cones surrounding a storm drain under repair. To squeeze by the construction, the Clydesdale had to swing out, taking up part of the Rail Avenue southbound vehicle lane.

A road-rage driver in a Camaro about twenty feet behind the carriage shook his fist out of his window and screamed, "Hey you stupid beast, get out of my way," as he screeched to an unnecessarily sudden stop.

A Camaro convertible with the top down banged into the first Camaro. Airbags deployed in both cars. The convertible driver yelled, "The only stupid beast around here is the jerk who jammed on his brakes."

The first driver struggled out of his car, battling the airbag all the way. "You son of a—"

He wasn't able to finish because the convertible driver was out of his car swinging.

Southbound traffic behind the dueling Camaros came to a complete stop. Horns started honking.

Oom pah pah. Honk honk honk.

Missy and I readied our umbrellas in case the brouhaha spread our way. Tom rested his flagpole against the entry door and stepped out to the sidewalk, looking north with a pair of mini binoculars. His cargo pants pockets held more equipment than my oversized purse.

A Cadillac SUV behind the Camaros swerved into the northbound lane and scooted around the brawlers and the horse-drawn carriage, then ducked back into the southbound lane.

Four more cars followed suit, the last one nearly colliding with a northbound car.

The northbound car was a black Lincoln. Nick!

The dacha garage door was going up. The Lincoln didn't wait for the door to fully raise. It cleared by a skosh and made a hard stop next to Scorpion's Vette.

The passenger door flew open and a blonde woman wearing green slacks and a cream-colored blouse tried to jump out. Where had I seen those clothes? A short stocky guy ran to the door and snatched her up. He threw her over his shoulder. She kicked and beat on him weakly with her fists. The door started closing. Her captor turned enough for me to see her face.

Desiree!

My stomach roiled. Outrage was about to explode my head. It had to be my fault. I had done something to arouse Nick's suspicions, and he took Desiree as leverage.

Tom was still looking north through the binoculars. Just as I reached him, he pulled his buzzing cell phone off his belt and looked at the screen and then me. He said, "Cube. This can't be good."

He listened, his expression darkening before he spoke into the phone. "Are you sure? Why in the hell would Nick take her? He must be unraveling."

I pulled on Tom's shoulder and pointed two fingers at my eyes then at the dacha.

He silently mouthed, "You saw her?"

I thought about Desiree pummeling her captor and mouthed, "She's okay—so far."

Missy came up beside me.

Oom pah pah. Honk honk honk.

Tom switched to speakerphone. "Cube, she's okay. We know where she's being held. Meet me in the parking lot on Porto Avenue three blocks north of Nick's strip club called Barely Here. Come in from the south on Porto. Stay away from Rail Avenue—the street behind the lot. Traffic's already a mess there and bound to get worse."

I leaned in as Cube's voice came through Tom's phone. "I have Granger—the guy whose ass you saved from being carved up—coming to me. I'll redirect him to you. He's on his motorcycle so he'll get there first. Don't be afraid to use him. He has a few problems but he's a good man."

"This situation is FUBAR. We need the help."

"If anybody hurts a hair on Desiree's head, I'm not taking any prisoners."

I watched Tom's jaw set. His laid-back demeanor was gone. "Cube, I'm with you all the way. We'll get her back, brother."

Cube's voice got louder. "No matter what it takes."

Tom's eyes focused on infinity. "These are violent bastards. We'll kill whoever we have to kill."

CHAPTER EIGHTY

The Band Played On

HIM

Freddi squeezed my shoulder. "Don't blame yourself, Tom. There's no way you could have known."

I couldn't buy that. I mentally kicked myself for being a damn idiot.

Why did I tell Desiree to go to work tonight like business as usual? Nick was losing it and this proved it. Even if he suspected Freddi—Sabrina to him—of working against him, taking Desiree had no long-term value. But irrational people were unpredictable and dangerous.

Oom pah pah. Honk honk honk.

I herded Freddi, Missy, and Jamie to the back of the music store's entryway to minimize the racket. "Here's the story. Cube took Desiree to work and went into the club as a patron, not wanting to make problems for her. She was supposed to perform at nine. When she hadn't come out by nine-twenty, Cube went in the back and had a conversation with a couple of bouncers. It took a few minutes, but he learned Nick took her out the back door. Nick's car just went into the dacha's garage with her in it."

Jamie touched the bulge under his coat. "How do you know, boss? Let's get her."

The guy's heart was in the right place, but he was dangerous. "We know because Sabrina saw her. And we aren't going in for her. We wouldn't stand a chance and we'd screw up Gino's op, which will spring Desiree along with the trafficked girls."

My Rescue Phone rang. Gino said, "Any sign of the truck?"

"There's a possibility north of me I'm about to check out. But there's a new problem. Nick abducted Desiree and has her in the dacha. After the raid, shuttle her off to me and I'll take her away. That's our best chance of keeping her from being exposed as an informant. Also southbound traffic is a disaster because of construction and an accident. You better move in as close as you can."

"We already have. We're less than two blocks away. Call me when you see the truck."

I clicked off and said, "To cement Gino's probable cause, I need to spot the truck transporting the girls. A truck that could be a U Move is about ten vehicles back in this knot of traffic. Wait here."

After a half-dozen steps up the sidewalk, I felt like I wasn't alone. I stopped and turned. They almost plowed into me.

"Partner," Jamie said, "you need backup."

Missy gave me an innocent look. "I thought you might need to avail yourself of my umbrella."

I glared at Freddi. "What part of 'wait here' is too complicated to understand?"

"Nick might come after me. I was scared to stay."

Sure she was. After she surprised Nick with a jab of her umbrella, a jolt from her stun gun, and a kick from her strong dancer's leg that would make his private parts puff out his cheeks, she might whimper.

While I was trying to decide what to do with my crew and whether my stomach flipped more when Jamie called me partner or boss, the carriage passed us. It started a right turn onto westbound Boney Road but had to stop halfway through because several bier-drinking pedestrians were in the carriage lane.

I returned my binoculars to my eyes and my attention to the suspect truck. It was not a U Move truck. Another truck several vehicles behind it swung into the empty northbound lane with its left signal on. It was a twenty-foot U Move truck.

"Roll. It's here," I said to Gino on the Rescue Phone.

Instantly, the wail of sirens added to the cacophony on the street.

Oom pah pah. Honk honk honk. Wail wail wail.

The U Move truck was angling toward the dacha's garage door, which started opening.

Jamie ran by me screaming, "The girls," with the most powerful handgun in the world raised above his head. The driver saw Jamie waving the gun and ducked. The truck crashed into the garage door, which screeched and stopped about a foot off the ground.

I took off after Jamie, yelling, "Don't shoot!"

He blasted a round into the engine compartment. The engine shut down with a wheeze. Jamie was knocked on his ass.

The driver and passenger bailed out of the driver's door and ran north. Two more bad guys to worry about.

Jamie struggled to his feet and ran to the rear of the truck. I ran after him.

He put his gun against the padlock on the cargo door and pulled the trigger. The lock disappeared. Jamie spun around like a punch-drunk fighter who just took one on the chin—but he stayed on his feet.

The cacophony of *oom pah pah, honk honk honk, wail wail wail* was getting worse because the wailing was louder and the honking more frantic.

Oom pah pah. The band played on.

The cargo door clattered on its rollers as I threw it open.

I lit up the interior with my pocket flashlight.

Twenty pairs of eyes shined out at me.

CHAPTER EIGHTY-ONE

Mary Poppins

HER

Missy and I chased after Tom. After Jamie killed the truck, I saw a blonde head coming out from under the jammed door.

Desiree!

She was on her back with her hands on the bottom of the door, wiggling through the small opening. I grabbed her shoulders and tugged. She was almost out when two hands came under the door and grabbed her ankle.

Missy jammed the point of her umbrella with all of her weight behind it into one of the exposed wrists.

The hands sprung open, accompanied by a scream.

The umbrella also sprung open. Missy lifted it over our heads to get it out of our way.

The hand that was still working clamped the wounded wrist to stem the pumping blood.

Missy and I pulled a woozy Desiree to her feet. If a spy satellite was watching us, we were shielded by a chartreuse canopy with yellow smiley faces on it. Missy propped Desiree against my shoulder. "Hold her for a second?"

I nodded. Missy let go of her and—umbrella flapping—jumped on the hands with both feet, resembling a failed takeoff of a psychedelic Mary Poppins.

The crunching of hands generated another scream.

"Was that Nick?" Desiree said in a groggy voice, rubbing her jaw. "The slimy no-good sonofabitch knocked me out. I'm going to kill him."

She slumped against me and Missy stabilized her.

"Missy, take Desiree to your car and get down out of sight. Cube's on his way."

Missy and Desiree—with their arms around each other's shoulders like dawn drunks on New Year's morning—swayed and staggered toward the parking lot. Missy struggled to close her umbrella with one hand.

Ten feet to my right was a steel door bearing the word *Office*. Nick's men would be pouring out of there any second. I took three quick strides toward it and heard clicking like someone fiddling with a lock.

The door slowly opened a couple of inches. Sneak a free peek on my watch? No way. I grabbed the outside knob and yanked hard. A man I never saw before stumbled halfway through the opening with a gun stupidly pointed in the air.

A strong umbrella thrust into his paunchy gut stopped him cold. Before he could say *oof* I kicked him so hard in the groin he fell over backward into a dimly lit corridor. When his body and head slammed into the floor, his gun discharged putting a kill shot into the ceiling. Didn't even have to use my stun gun.

How many of them were in there? I had to jam the door. I was about to slam it when I saw the dead bolt had a key in it. It was a double tumbler lock, the kind that needed a key to lock and unlock it both inside and out. I pulled the key out and slammed the door. I locked it from the outside and left the key in the lock.

Jamie's cannon went off at the back of the truck.

Oom pah pah. Honk honk honk. Wail wail wail.

About five feet away the sidewalk was broken. I pried a chunk out with my umbrella. I used it to beat on the key until it snapped off at the shoulder, making it impossible to get a key into it from either the inside or outside. This door was out of commission.

I dropped the chunk and raced around the truck to Tom's side. "Desiree is safe in Missy's car. I jammed the lock on the other door with a..." I looked where Tom was shining his flashlight.

The cargo bay was full of girls. More than I expected. And it stunk. I was so enraged I could only sputter.

"How did you get Desiree... No time for that now. These girls have to be moved right now. These pissed-off traffickers might do anything. Gino's guys aren't going to be able to get through this mess anytime soon."

Mess was an understatement. The Camaros still had the southbound lane blocked. The U Move truck had the northbound lane blocked. Traffic was already backed up beyond the Boney Road intersection. Several drivers were out of their cars and jawing. Could more fights be far behind?

Honk honk honk. Wail wail wail.

What happened to the *Oom pah pah*?

Individual refrains of *Ein Prosit* came from behind me. I spun around. People were singing as they left the Nights Bavarian Social Club. Evidently the show was over.

A few went north but the majority streamed south. Some had to be going to the parking lot but others—based on the go-cups in their hands—were ready for more partying.

I turned back to Tom. "These bier aficionados must be headed to Beer-R-Us. If we use them as cover and walk single-file next to the buildings, we might be able to get the girls out of here."

One of Tom's two hundred cell phones went off. He looked at the screen and put it on speakerphone. "Gino, we have Desiree and we extracted twenty kidnapped girls from a truck. Pissed-off armed traffickers are going to be on us any minute. We need to get these girls into your hands before there's a bloodbath."

"TPD had a shots-fired call near you at a building owned by the Russians. I know the building. I've been there on surveillance. TPD's trying to respond now but uniforms are at a premium and traffic's a problem."

With a straight face Tom said, "I know the building too."

"The fastest way to get the girls into protection is to take them there. On the far side is the entrance to an upstairs karate dojo. If you beat the cops there, hide the girls in the stairwell. The sensei is a good guy."

"See if TPD can send a bus or paddy wagon or two. They'll have to transport twenty girls and an unknown number of scumbags. We need to get going. I'll call you in a few."

Tom clicked off and said to me, "Your way is our only chance. We'll use the partiers as cover until we get to Nick's building, then peel off and run to the dojo entrance. Jamie, lead the way. Sabrina, take the rear to keep the girls going. I'll hang back to slow the traffickers if they get out of the dacha."

"Slow them! How? Now what do you think about not carrying a gun?"

"As compared to the old *I left my gun in my other car.*"

So annoying. Tom took a step away. I turned to the faces in the truck. "Do you speak English?"

It sounded like at least half of them answered they did.

"We're taking you to a safe place. We don't have time to do anything but go. Follow this guy—single file." I pointed to Jamie. "I'll be right behind you."

Tom, Jamie, and I helped them out of the truck. Some were translating for others. They all had backpacks. Some had trouble standing. I said, "Jamie, go slowly till they get their land legs."

"You got it, Miss Sabrina. C'mon, ladies. After this is over I'll treat you to some authentic American gelato."

Our smelly ragtag group started trekking down the sidewalk.

CHAPTER EIGHTY-TWO

Migration

HIM

Once Freddi and Jamie had our human caravan underway, I called Gino to tell him.

His news wasn't good. "Our vehicles are creeping along even with the lights and sirens going. We'll keep trying to get the vehicles through, but most of the SWAT team is going in on foot from the north and most of the task force on foot from the south."

"Be careful. There are more girls in the building and my guess is every scumbag in there is armed and willing to shoot."

"TPD just reported the units responding to the shots-fired call are caught up in an unrelated traffic problem, which FHP is trying to clear. Two more units and a bus are being dispatched but you'll beat them to the dojo."

"I'm going to hang in here for a few minutes to slow anybody trying to get out of the garage. Tell your SWAT guys not to shoot me."

"I don't know what you look like."

"That is a problem." I paused. "Tell them not to shoot anyone carrying a Nights Bavarian flag. It's a long story."

A group of drivers gathered by the U Move truck to try to push the rear of it onto the sidewalk far enough for traffic to squeeze by. They did a one-two-three-push, barely moving the truck, but the garage door screeched. Once the wounded door had pressure relieved, it jerked open another foot.

Nick and Scorpion and about a dozen other traffickers skittered out from under the garage door like cockroaches when the kitchen lights come on. Without a giant can of bug spray, there wasn't much I could do.

Scorpion said, "Check the girls," as he got to his feet. He and Nick weren't going to be happy when they saw the empty cargo bay.

Honk honk honk. Wail wail wail.

I ran to the music shop, retrieved my pilfered flag, and raced around the corner.

Behind me Nick yelled, "Find them now."

I caught up with Freddi at the rear of our cavalcade of escapees—some limping, some crying. They had turned the corner and were westbound on Boney Road headed toward Nick's building. I told Freddi about Nick and Scorpion and a dozen others getting under the garage door.

She muttered something about a gun.

The cover was getting thinner. A number of people crossed Boney Road to the parking lot, weaving through stopped or creeping cars. The eastbound lane was at a standstill because of the plugged intersection at Rail Avenue. Westbound traffic was inching forward because dense southbound traffic on Porto Avenue was causing a delay at the light.

Fortunately some stalwarts continued to migrate to Beer-R-Us.

I left Freddi and pushed forward through the crowd. "Jamie, thread the girls through this stalled traffic on Boney. When we cross Porto we'll stay next to Nick's building and hotfoot it straight to the dojo entrance around the far corner of the building."

After I aggravated the crowd by working my way back, I said to Freddi, "Let's tighten this up. Tell them to get on one another's heels."

She whispered in the ear of the girl in front of her, who in turn did the same, and so on. Our line contracted like a caterpillar nipped on the butt by a beetle.

Honk honk honk. Wail wail wail.

Jamie cut through the vehicles on Boney—many of them pickups and SUVs tall enough to provide intermittent cover. I looked around and didn't see any Russians coming for us. Now all we had to do was get across Porto and haul ass down the side of Nick's building to the dojo.

Crossing Porto was going to be tricky. Southbound was creeping but northbound traffic was flowing fairly well.

Cube called my cell. "Just passed Barely Here. I'm less than three blocks away. Granger should be there any second."

"Desiree's safe in a car in the parking lot until you can take her the hell out of here. There's an alley across the street from the lot. When you get here... Hold on."

Jamie stepped in front of a taxi in the northbound lane holding his hand up like a crossing guard. He had his suit coat pulled back exposing his Magnum. The taxi rocked to a stop. Freddi ran up beside Jamie, pointing her umbrella at the driver. Jamie picked an opening between two cars in the snail-like southbound lane and led the girls through.

I looked ahead at the far end of Nick's building and saw five or six Tex-Mex coyotes facing us. Scorpion must have called in more men. I trotted past Freddi. "Get the girls on the sidewalk quickly. Jamie, change of plans. Turn left and go to the alley. We have to go that way."

When the last of the girls and Freddi made it onto the sidewalk, I ran toward the alley. Even with the flag in one hand and my cell phone in the other, I was moving faster than they were. I passed them and put my phone to my ear.

Cube was still on the line. "Tom, what in the bloody hell is going on?"

"We have twenty rescued girls we're trying to protect from smugglers."

"Where are you?"

"I'm by the building on the north side of the alley."

"I'll tell Granger."

"The plan is to take the girls up the alley to the police. Are you in your Hummer?"

"Yep, with some pretty powerful lights and speakers mounted on my roof."

I stopped at the alley, peeked around the corner, and saw another pack of coyotes at the other end.

"Cube, the game has changed. This could get messy."

A laugh that wasn't a laugh came through my phone. "It's a good night for messy."

CHAPTER EIGHTY-THREE

Showtime

HER

I almost ran into the last girl in line when Tom put his hand on Jamie's chest and stopped our procession short of the alley. Then he dialed a number on the cell phone in his hand. I moved up next to him.

"Update," Tom said. "At least a dozen bad guys slid out under that garage door. Scorpion has called in his coyotes. Both the street and the alley leading to the dojo are blocked by his men."

Gino's voice came through the speaker. "The task force is close to the parking lot. After the dacha and the girls in it are secured, the SWAT team will head your way too."

"We can't wait for the task force and damn sure can't wait for SWAT to mop up the dacha. These people are rabid, out for blood. Instead of getting their asses down the road, they're risking everything. This is mano a mano to both the Mexicans and the Russians. They're ready to shoot it out."

If Tom was worried, I was worried. This wasn't like handling a drunk in a parking lot or an idiot coming out a door with his gun pointed at a cloud.

"The only other option," Gino said, "is take the girls up the stairs in the alley and go to the back door of the dojo. I'll call the sensei and tell him you're coming."

"Are you sure someone's there?"

"They stay late several nights a week to accommodate cops who can't get there at other times."

"We'll be at their back door," Tom said, "before they can shout a *kiai*."

I peered through widening gaps in the *Ein Prosit* singers. A group of six or seven people in dark blue windbreakers trotted up the street beyond the parking lot. "Tom, the task force is less than a block away."

"The Russians are closer. I see at least a half-dozen men checking underneath cars in the lot as they come this way."

I turned my attention to the alley. The entrance was completely exposed but the dumpster would prevent the coyotes at the far end from seeing us. Tom said, "Jamie, duck down and take the girls up the stairs. Go to the dojo. Right. Now."

Jamie grabbed the hand of the nearest girl—about fourteen years old and weeping—and pulled her to the steps. Tom kept his head below dumpster level, stepped into the alley, and helped me shepherd the girls up the stairs.

The brightest light in the area was the one over the entrance to the stairs.

As I helped the last girl onto the stairs, Nick's voice boomed out. "They're in the alley. And that's Sabrina. I want that bitch!"

I shot him a bird and put my foot on the first step.

Tom smacked my butt. "Showtime, babe."

CHAPTER EIGHTY-FOUR

Physics Lesson

HIM

I slapped Freddi's ass like a coach sending a player into a game—which I was. She was tough, but she'd never been in a game like this. Neither had I. The worst of the worst teamed up with the worst of the worst. The Russian mob and Cartel coyotes. Armed, vicious, and homicidal.

A group of bier drinkers meandered close to me on the sidewalk. I kept low—and my flag lower—while I slipped out of the alley under their cover then sidled along the wall a few feet. Nick and Scorpion didn't notice me.

"I want that bitch Sabrina!" Nick screamed as he led his Russians through the migrating bier enthusiasts.

Scorpion pointed down the alley. "Go this way. I have men guarding the end. We go up through the restaurant. You get Sabrina and we take her and *las putas* out the same way."

Nick pointed to the stairs. "Leo. Georg. Vlad. They're trapped up there. Nobody up or down if you want to see the Motherland again. The rest of you, follow me."

Nick, Scorpion, and eight Russians raced down the alley.

I eased closer to the edge of the building and watched Leo, Georg, and Vlad form a line halfway across the alley next to the stairs with the dumpster five feet behind them. A deep rumble behind me rose above the other noise on the street. I turned and saw bier drinkers parting like the Red Sea as a motorcycle drove up the sidewalk. It wasn't like any motorcycle this side of a Batman movie.

The large rider wore a full helmet that extended below his chin—flat black with a blood red death's head on the face shield that faded to droplets on the sides. The flat black machine was a custom with a long rake and windshield-handlebar configuration that resembled the Batcycle.

Very badass.

Granger stopped beside me. Not quite as low-key as I would have liked.

"Cube says you need help."

"Up those stairs are twenty rescued girls. I have to get past those three Russians."

"Those guys are Russian? I speak Russian."

Who didn't? "I need them out of action."

"No problem. Why are you carrying that flagpole?"

"It's my weapon."

Granger laughed. "Like I said at Cube's place, you're a cool hand. If you can take the one on the right with your, ah, weapon, I'll take out the two on the left with the help of this baby." He patted the gas tank.

I patted the flagpole. "No problem. One more favor. After they're out of commission, cover my back. Don't let anyone but police go upstairs. If they question you, I'd appreciate it if you keep the description vague. Blame it on the bad light. I have a source to protect, and the best way is for the police not to be able to ID me."

"Lie to the police? Never." A gravelly *hah* escaped from his helmet.

He kept his head down as he maneuvered his motorcycle

until he faced the three Russians. They looked confused until he raised his head and they saw the blood red death's head.

They reached for their guns but it was too late. Granger popped the clutch, covered the fifteen feet in an instant, and split the space between the two on the left. He simultaneously kicked them in their stomachs, sent them airborne, and jammed on his brakes. His motorcycle stopped on a dime with the front wheel inches from the dumpster.

The kickees not so much. Both demonstrated Newton's First Law that a body in motion will stay in motion until it slams into a dumpster.

I crowned the third one—who was totally distracted by the physics experiment—with the flagpole. He dropped to the ground with his pistol undrawn.

Granger got off his bike and started throwing Russians into the dumpster.

An amplified voice reached my ears. "Tom, are you ready for me?"

I turned as Cube pulled into the alley in his tan Hummer H-1. Huge and boxy with heavy bars across the front and the biggest light bar ever. He only had about two feet of clearance between the dumpster and the wall of the Beer-R-Us building. He was ready for war.

He put down the mike and spoke through the window. "Where are the girls?"

"Upstairs. I'm going up now. Granger has my back."

I looked at the other end of the alley. Nick, Scorpion, and the Russians were gone but the coyotes were still there.

"Cube, I have a problem. There are a half dozen armed coyotes ahead and about the same number on the other side of this building. They're here to recapture the girls."

He straightened up in his seat. "Like hell."

"After you're done with the coyotes, work your way to the parking lot and take Desiree out of here."

He gave me a thumbs up.

Music came softly through the speakers mounted on his light bar. An instrumental rendition of *The Battle Hymn of the Republic*. He squeezed past the dumpster and accelerated. The volume steadily increased to a deafening level.

The coyotes got squirrely. Four of them drew their guns.

The light bar flared on and flooded them with blinding light. They shielded their eyes. A couple of them fired unseeing. One of the lights went out.

The music from the speakers was replaced with a recording of machine gun fire.

The coyotes panicked and ran. But not fast enough.

A vocal chorus of the *Battle Hymn* blasted over the speakers. *Glory, glory, hallelujah. Glory, glory, hallelujah.*

Bodies flew.

Glory, glory, hallelujah. His truth is marching on.

Cube turned to the right—toward the coyotes stationed by the dojo.

I gave Granger a hand sign to cover me.

My flagpole led as I charged up the stairs two at a time.

CHAPTER EIGHTY-FIVE

The Great Escape

HER

After Tom smacked my butt, Jamie and I hurried the girls up the stairs and down the hall as fast as they could go. Some of them still had mobility problems.

We passed two doors. On the right, the one to Nick's office, ajar far enough to reveal the splattered wall. On the left, a fire exit for the restaurant, probably the kitchen.

Ahead of us near the end of the hall were two more doors. On the left, another fire exit for the restaurant, probably the dining room. On the right, the one I wanted. The back entrance to the dojo.

We walked the girls past the dojo door to the end of the hall and huddled them against the wall.

I turned and stepped over to the dojo door. Locked.

No Russians or coyotes coming down the hall. Good work on Tom's part.

I pounded on the door with the handle of my umbrella and yelled, "Help! Help! Emergency!"

No response but still no Russians or coyotes.

Back into my pounding and yelling mode.

The door swung open. A tall Asian man did a martial arts bow from the waist. "My apology for the slow response. I just got Gino's message. We finished our sparring for the night and were meditating to achieve a state of peace and tranquility—"

"Please, I have the girls Gino contacted you about."

He smiled and nodded with peace and tranquility all over his face. "My name is Siwoo. We would be delighted to assist you."

The door behind me blew open. Nick, Scorpion, and eight Russians boiled out of the restaurant. The girls screamed.

Siwoo yelled into the dojo, "Meditation's over. We're gonna kick some ass."

He stepped into the hall toward a Russian trying to draw a gun and nailed him in the head with a lightning-fast spin kick.

One of the Russians clobbered Jamie to the floor as he struggled to get his gun out of his shoulder holster.

Five of Siwoo's black-belted buddies raced out of the dojo and started on the Russians. Teeth, blood, and guns flew everywhere.

Oh no! I was in the middle of a Bruce Lee—or Bruce Li—movie.

Out of the corner of my eye, I saw Nick rushing toward me. I spun and let his stomach run into the point of my umbrella. His breath blew out but he stayed upright and tried to yank the umbrella from my hand. I zapped him in the neck, holding my stun gun against him until he was on the floor and then a few seconds more to be sure he'd be screwed up for a while.

Most of the Russians were triple-D—down, disarmed, and disabled. The two who weren't staggered back into the restaurant.

The multi-weaponed Scorpion seemed too shocked to move. Finally he helped Nick get off the floor and propped him up as they hobbled to the restaurant.

I zapped Scorpion in the back of the neck. He pushed Nick through the door and knocked my hand from his neck before I could juice him enough to take him to the floor.

He spit at me—and missed—before he slammed the door.

Very immature.

Like flipping someone the bird.

Siwoo stepped around me and tried the door without success. "Locked as I suspected. Ours can always be opened from the inside in case of emergency but is locked to prevent outside entry.

He gave me a slight bow from the waist. "Very good technique with the umbrella. I will add it to our kendo training."

I bowed also. "You saved these girls from harm. But I must ask more. Can you secure the traffickers and escort the girls to the police when they arrive?"

"Our pleasure. Duct tape for the traffickers." He nodded to a nearby black belt who went into the dojo. "We'll duct tape them until they look like they were discovered in an Egyptian tomb. If you can't fix it with duct tape, you have a serious problem. The girls will have access to our locker room facilities and hot tea while we wait for the police. You haven't told me your name."

"Call me Sabrina."

"A beautiful appellation. Do not concern yourself with the safety of the young ladies. I have a federal firearms license that allows me to possess fully automatic weapons. Sometimes the way of the open hand must be supplemented by the way of the fifty-round magazine. Any criminal who attempts to ascend our stairs will find himself—to put it in the vernacular—in a world of hurt."

CHAPTER EIGHTY-SIX

Dumpster Diving

HIM

My flagpole and I were three-fourths of the way up the stairs when the two coyotes from the U Move truck came around the corner above me. I went up two more steps and stopped, hoping the high ground would give them false—even fatal—confidence.

They swaggered to the top of the stairwell. Ratty jeans, untucked stained T-shirts, straw cowboy hats, five-day stubble, and a stink that made the girls smell like fresh-baked bread. Almost twins except the coyote on the right had a feather in his hatband like Yankee Doodle. Pinned to the crown on the hat on the left was a small girl's ring that I didn't want to think about.

Ring Hat smiled without humor. "*Mira*, Juan. *El hijo de puta.*" He switched to broken English. "You and *amigo* think funny kill *camión*, how you say, truck. Now we kill you."

I bounced the flag up and down. I said with panic in my voice, "No, no, not me. I was at the dance. Please, please, not me, not me."

They looked at each other and laughed. Yankee Doodle went for a gun in his belt under the tail of his T-shirt. I flopped the flag over his head, went up a step, and slammed the bottom end of the eight-foot flagpole into the crotch of Ring Hat hard enough to lift him off the floor. He doubled over with his knife in hand. Before he could flick it open, I had my hand on the back of his neck pulling him forward. He tumbled down the stairs.

Yankee Doodle jerked the flag off his head and almost freed his revolver. The hammer caught in his shirt and he got off two wild shots. I swung the flagpole around and caught him under the chin. His eyes rolled back in his head then—with an assist from me—his body rolled down the stairs.

"Hey, Tom."

I turned around. Granger kicked the coyotes in the head then grabbed both of them by the necks of their T-shirts with one hand. He said, "If you're going to keep sending these down, I'm going to have to find another dumpster."

"This should be the last of them. You don't have to stand guard any longer. Might be smart to move out before the police get here."

"I still owe you. Tonight doesn't count. This was for Desiree and these girls. I'm gone. I'll see if Cube needs help."

I climbed the remaining steps and peeked down the hallway.

Freddi was living up to her moniker of Zapper by zapping Scorpion by the fire exit, but he fended her off and ran into the restaurant.

A gaggle of black belts tended to the girls and checked bodies lying on the floor. Chaos but under control.

I ran down the hall toward Freddi, flag held high.

CHAPTER EIGHTY-SEVEN

Chef's Special

HER

I spotted Tom at the far end of the hall while I helped a groggy Jamie to his feet.

"Siwoo," I said, "you and your compatriots are heroes."

He bowed again, smiled, and strode into the dojo.

Jamie groaned and pointed. "Is that Tom?"

He was almost upon us, jogging with his Nights Bavarian flagpole held high. When he got to me I threw my arms around him. "Thank God you're alright. I heard shots."

He hugged me back with his non-flagpole arm. "I saw Scorpion escape into the restaurant. How about Nick?"

"I gave him a good zap. He was on the ground. Scorpion helped him into the restaurant. Two beat-up Russians made it into the restaurant also. We can't get in. These are fire doors locked to outside entry."

"We don't need to get in. They're all armed and desperate. We'll watch the doors and wait for Gino and the task force or SWAT or TPD, whoever gets here first."

At that moment, the kitchen fire door moved. An Asian teenager opened it all the way, jammed a door stop under it, and came out with an odd-looking canvas-sided cart made for stair use and heaped with filled garbage bags. He paid no attention to us and eased the cart down the stairs.

"Not good news for the guys in the dumpster," Tom said.

"What guys in the dumpster?"

Tom gave me a half-smile. "Tell you later."

Jamie crept to the open fire door and put his face against the edge of it to see in with one eye.

"Jamie," Tom said in an urgent whisper. "Get away from there."

Jamie turned. A hand grabbed his collar and he was propelled into the kitchen.

An unseen person with a Russian accent said, "Who the hell is this?"

Tom rushed through the door, Nights Bavarian flagpole forward. I followed. He drove the flagpole into the gut of the Russian who fell backward and banged the back of his head on a mobile stainless steel prep table.

I stepped farther inside. I had assumed that with Scorpion being the owner and in this part of town, this would be a Mexican-Cuban restaurant. I overlooked that he was half Asian. All the kitchen workers were Chinese.

Oh no! I was in a Jackie Chan movie.

The prep table rolled into a worker cleaning a giant pot and knocked him over. The soapy water dumped and covered the floor. The worker got up and grabbed a carving knife off a nearby counter and lunged toward Tom.

I knew from Jackie Chan movies that restaurant workers could be on the testy side. My umbrella wasn't going to do it. I grabbed a cast-iron skillet from a hanging hook and slammed it on his head. He'd be in style when flattops came back.

The chef screamed, "My kitchen, my kitchen!"

Tom was leaning on the flagpole for stability when from the other side of the kitchen Scorpion charged with his switchblade ready for action.

When he hit the slippery water, his feet went in circles like Fred Flintstone. Tom held out the Nights Bavarian flag and said, "Toro, toro."

Jamie raised his hand and shouted, "Olé!"

Scorpion slid through the flag and smacked into the already rabid chef, knocking a tray of potstickers to the floor.

The chef glared at Tom and pulled a cleaver from a butcher block.

Scorpion dropped his knife and pulled a pistol from his belt. He tsk-tsked. "You are too clever, gringo, so I shoot your ass."

He ignored little old me standing beside him—a mere woman, one who zapped him before and was about to do it again. I jammed my stun gun into his throat and kept pressing. The gun fell from his hand.

Tom pinned Scorpion's arms behind his back and spun him around as the chef was swinging.

The chef cleaved but not the right noggin. Tom let Scorpion—with his new decorative hardware—fall to the floor. He looked down at the body.

Oh no, please don't say it, Tom. Please, please, please don't say it.

"I believe he has a splitting headache."

He said it.

The chef tore off his apron and threw it on the splitting headache. "This is the last straw. I quit. I have three better offers in Vegas anyway."

He stomped off—with a slip and a skid here and there—his chef's tall hat held high.

Jamie—looking like a first-time ice skater—worked his way to us.

"Are you okay, Jamie?" Tom said.

"I'm fine," he said as he struggled to keep his balance. "But where's Nick?"

CHAPTER EIGHTY-EIGHT

Horse Play

HIM

Freddi stopped Jamie's slide. I had the same question as Jamie. Where the hell was Nick? We couldn't let him get away. He'd go back to Russia and be untouchable. He had to pay for what he did.

Maybe he and Scorpion had decided the best way to escape would be in the chaos on the street. Scorpion was here until the chef cleaved him through the gates of hell. That meant their way to get out of the building was limited to one person at a time.

The trash cart!

Nick was in the trash cart that went by us.

"Sabrina and Jamie, wait here. Nick slipped by us in the trash cart."

I ran to the stairway and went down two steps at a time. I heard a lot of clomping behind me. As usual I had wasted my breath.

When I reached the alley, the teenager with the cart was throwing garbage bags in the dumpster. I said, "Which way did he go?"

The kid hesitated like he was thinking about lying. I lifted him off the ground by his collar. He pointed north where bier drinkers still cluttered the sidewalk and traffic was a disaster. The Clydesdale was clopping toward us in the carriage lane, unfazed by the commotion and the load he was pulling.

Not far ahead of me a guy about Nick's size, wearing a chef's coat and tall hat, was on the sidewalk pushing his way through. I got in his wake and moved up on him. As he neared the carriage—with me about six feet behind—he angled toward the curb like he was going to cross the street before the horse reached us.

I tapped his arm with the flagpole. "Nick, give it up. It's over."

He looked over his shoulder. "You! I knew you were a problem."

Nick drew a gun from under his coat. Yep, a Desert Eagle. I couldn't let him shoot that thing in a crowd so I pulled the flop-the-flag-over-his-face trick.

It worked once. Twice—not so much.

He slapped it away and tried to draw a bead on me but stumbled.

I yanked the flagpole back and stuck it between his feet. He fired a deafening shot into the concrete curb as he continued to stumble.

The Clydesdale reared up.

Nick fell into the street.

A huge Clydesdale hoof came down on his head. The horse reared again. His hoof mashed Nick's head for a second time before he continued clopping up the street.

The carriage—loaded with two bier-drinking couples who didn't appear to be concerned with anything except their bier—bumped over Nick's head. Over the froth of a sloshing cup one said, "Can a carriage get a flat wheel?"

It wasn't pretty.

You could slide Nick's head under a door.

I kicked his Desert Eagle into a storm drain.

Freddi and Jamie came up behind me. I said, "Don't look down. That's not a pizza."

Of course they did.

Freddi did okay but Jamie turned green and held his hand to his mouth. I handed my key fob to Freddi. "I'll meet you and Jamie at my car. Go now before the police arrive and tag you as witnesses."

I heard a slurred voice. "Hey, there's my flag."

Handlebar Mustache—not to my surprise—was part of the bier migration. I handed him the flag. He said, "Thanks for filling in for me. Are you going to Beer-R-Us? I'll buy you one."

"I have a late date but thanks anyway."

He continued his migration, pumping the flag like an unstable drum major.

My personal cell phone buzzed. Missy said, "Cube picked up Desiree in a big scary Army vehicle with bullet holes in it. I thought I'd been teleported to Iraq or Iran or one of those sand countries. And an even scarier motorcycle was with him."

"Wait for me in my car with Freddi and Jamie. I'll be there in a few minutes."

I wound my way across the street through the crawling traffic. I went to the Borismobile and Erik's Mustang in the parking lot and retrieved the GPS trackers. Freddi, Missy, and Jamie were sitting in my SUV when I flopped into the driver's seat, trying to decide if there was a degree of tiredness beyond exhaustion. I had to get rid of Jamie before he slobbered on the back seat upholstery sitting next to Missy.

"Jamie, go home and get some rest, then go to work tomorrow like nothing happened. If the police contact you, don't say anything. Call me. Leave via Rail Avenue. Southbound traffic is moving. There's no exit from this lot onto Rail so drive over the curb."

He bounded out of my car. "You got it, boss. I can't wait for our next case."

I was too tired to shudder.

Gino called. I said, "The woman who brought you the flash drives is with me and you're on speakerphone." No point in mentioning Missy since he didn't know she existed and I wanted to keep it that way.

"An update for you. Fifteen girls rescued at the dacha and two Russians guards arrested."

"How about the dojo?"

"Still in progress but TPD arrived with a bus to take care of the girls. As soon as they're all out of the shower and dressed, they'll be transported to Tampa General for medical checkups then turned over to Immigration. Our guys have their hands full with duct-taped arrestees, emergency room patients, and one for the morgue. Not to mention five we found in pretty bad shape in the dumpster."

"Did you get the coyotes I saw outside the building?"

"They were all gone although there was blood in the street. Do you have some kind of backup you haven't told me about? Never mind. I don't want to know. I have way too much on my plate already."

"Sorry but I'm about to add to it." I told him about the shootout in the office—omitting Misha's and my parts—and where to find Natasha. Then I gave him the highlights—or lowlights—of Nick's tragic accident and where to find his Desert Eagle. Gino sounded close to hyperventilating when I finished.

"Okay, Tom, it's going to take the rest of the night and then some to sort out the crime scenes and get everybody in for questioning. If I'm lucky I'll get a couple hours sleep. It will be tomorrow afternoon before I call to start filling in holes."

"Whatever you need. What do you think about being able to keep me out of the official investigation?"

"I'll do my best. Let's hope surprise telephone camera videos don't surface."

"One more thing, Gino. There's a bright blue Corvette inside the building. It has a GPS tracker under it that could confuse the issue."

"I'll take care of it. We can arrange for your mystery woman to get it from me later. Tom, this is the wildest case I've ever heard of, but because of you and your associates—however many you have—thirty-five girls were saved tonight and a lot of scumbags are off the street. That's something we all can be proud of. I can't thank you enough. And give my thanks to...to whoever they are." He clicked off.

"Ladies," I said, "You heard the man. It's been a hell of a night's work but we need to get out of here before we get caught up in a police canvass. Missy, are you too tired to drive?"

"That is so considerate of you to ask but my adrenaline is pumping like I just won a blue ribbon for sweet potato pie at the county fair. I might not be able to sleep until next week. Freddi, I'm beginning to admire your life as Sabrina."

She got out, waggled her fingers at us, and trotted to her car.

That left Freddi.

We kissed—and what a kiss it was. Maybe I wasn't as tired as I thought.

When we came up for air, I said, "Your place or mine?"

"Mine. Do you want to follow me?"

"I know where you live."

She looked startled then said, "From when you were investigating me? You bastard." She smiled and kissed me again then got in her car.

I watched until she left the lot safely then went out the same way. I worked my way to I-275 and phoned The Squid.

"About time you called."

Always a joy. "I've been a little busy but it's over."

"Just in time."

Not something I wanted to hear. "Just in time for what? I'm exhausted and I have follow-up to take care of."

"Sleep is overrated and this is right up your alley."

"Which is?"

"A kidnapped girl. I'm working on confirmation that it's not a hoax."

The Squid knew how to get my attention.

"So now—what's the downstroke on Boris?"

A long conversation to say the least. His snorts and grunts lasted until I was nearing Crooked Foot Key.

And Freddi's house.

And Freddi.

CHAPTER EIGHTY-NINE

Home at Last

HER

I shouldn't have kissed Rick a second time. I was ready to drop the back seats in his SUV and go at it in a car again. Or would *again* be the right word since I was with Tom before.

How long would it take for me to get used to calling him Rick?

If I were speaking aloud, I'd be blithering—as in idiot.

My hormones were out of control.

The drive to Crooked Foot Key seemed to take forever. Finally I pulled into my driveway. Rick pulled in right behind me. I didn't bother to garage my Chevy. I wanted to get inside right now.

He kissed my neck as I unlocked the door. I almost couldn't manipulate the key. Inside, he nuzzled me causing an earthquake shudder while I relocked. I turned and we kissed long and passionately. I said, "I want to shower first."

"Sounds like a good place to start."

We played in the shower until we ran out of hot water then dried with fluffy towels, rubbing and kissing and kissing and rubbing.

In my king-size bed we pleasured each other on and on and on then snuggled together as one. I marveled at the combination of our incredible attraction and Rick's natural ability as a lover.

He pressed buttons I didn't know I had. My sigh of contentment was probably heard by my neighbors.

I made my snuggle even tighter and more intimate.

This night wasn't over.

CHAPTER NINETY

Shangri-la

HIM

I looked down at the gorgeous creature tucked into my shoulder and wondered how I could be so lucky. I needed her so badly I wasn't able to let her unlock her door without ravishing her. Our passion was endless in her shower and bed.

Good things in the universe had converged. Our powerful attraction. Our physical pleasure—in sync and intense, reaching new heights. She was everything—loving, caring, intelligent, strong, sensuous, passionate...

She tucked in tighter. Her breathing grew deeper as did mine. Sleep was near. I thought I found Shangri-la that night in her car. Nothing compared to now.

My phone buzzed.

Text message.

Freddi's eyes popped open.

About the Author

BUCK BUCHANAN is the author of *The Secret Files of Hugo and Victoria*, which was a silver medalist in Humor for the 2019 Florida Authors and Publishers Association's President's Book Award. Buchanan was the winner of the inaugural short story contest at SleuthFest hosted by the Florida chapter of the Mystery Writers of America (FMWA) and received an FMWA Award for Writing Excellence. He conducted a writers' workshop for the Palm Beach County Library for many years.

His crime writing was a progression from his crime fighting. For a good chunk of his life, he conducted and supervised major criminal investigations—ranging from homicide and narcotics smuggling to official corruption and fraud—for the Florida Department of Law Enforcement.

Buchanan lives in South Florida with his wife Susan and every stray dog and cat she can drag in. (But he can't complain—she dragged him in too.)